THE COOPERS FIELD MURDERS

THE COOPERS FIELD MURDERS

Wonny Lea

Chapter One

The heavy rain that had been an almost constant feature throughout July had given way to intermittent warmish curtains of drizzle as the month drew to a close and visions of a glorious summer faded once again.

'Maybe August will be better,' suggested Detective Sergeant Matt Pryor, as he and his boss walked up the steps leading from the car park in Sophia Gardens and started to cross the bridge leading to Coopers Field. As they got to the middle of the bridge Matt looked in both directions, but what should have been a stunning view was limited to the short distance he could see through the miserable weather.

He bounced up and down and the bridge gently moved with him, making him smile. 'My nieces call this the bouncy bridge,' he told Detective Chief Inspector Martin Phelps. 'You can see why – it really does feel a bit like a trampoline.' He demonstrated further and the whole structure seemed to shake.

'Yes, I get the picture,' replied Martin. 'Unstable bridges are not really my thing – so quit making it wobble and tell me exactly what Sergeant Evans said.'

Matt got back into step with Martin and the two men fell into their well-established pattern of briefing prior to their arrival at a crime scene.

'Well, for once, he wasn't the first on the scene,' Matt began. 'This time it was the dynamic duo of PC Davies and PC Cook-Watts, but the Evans team wasn't far behind.'

'The call came through to Goleudy at ten past seven this morning, and the first pair of officers was at the scene before twenty past, as they were already in the area. Apparently it was a dog walker that called, after her dog refused to fetch ball that had been thrown for him – he chose instead to bark madly and sniff

1

around a pile of discarded clothes. After a few minutes, and when he showed no signs of coming back to her, the woman went to drag the dog away from the clothes and that was when she found the dead body.

'According to Sgt Evans, the poor woman was in a hell of a state, as the body has apparently been there for some time, with not a stitch on and with bits eaten off, presumably by rats or whatever animals lurk around here when the picnickers go home.'

'Is it a man or a woman?' asked Martin.

'Sgt Evans was in some doubt about that. It seems the genitals and the chest area are the most damaged parts, so we won't know for sure if the body is male or female until after the post-mortem. Professor Moore is already there and so is Alex Griffiths, and the message from both of them is that we are going to need our wellies – it's apparently like a mud bath – what a good start to the week. No wonder I hate Mondays!'

The rain was actually easing off, and there was even a vague sighting of sun as the detectives walked through Bute Park, making their way along a path bordered to the left by a deep bed of seasonal flowers and a variety of shrubs. Martin reflected that it would be possible to walk this route every day and always be presented with a different canvas to admire. In spite of the dreadful wind and rain of the past month, the whole area had still managed to produce wave after wave of colour that contrasted and yet complemented one patch of flowers with another to make a perfect picture.

There were a number of benches, dotted at intervals in front of the flowerbeds, but the weather was not conducive to sitting on park benches and so they were all empty. To the right of the path were large areas of grass and several plots where shrubs and flowers had been planted.

The grey railings at the back of this area marked the bank of the River Taff and, looking around, Martin, not for the first time, told himself how lucky the people of Cardiff were to have such a terrific park at the very centre of their city. The trees, the flowers, the shrubs, and just the sheer open space – it was like a beautiful living picture.

What a shame that today they would be looking at a very different sight – one nothing like as pretty as a picture and

2

certainly not living.

At the end of the path there was a choice of two paths – one going right and leading in to the city, with an offshoot to the landing platform for the Cardiff Castle waterbus, the other leading to Coopers Field. They took the left-hand option, walking away from the river. This immediately took them to a paved area, where more empty benches waited to welcome visitors to the park, and behind that a rather old-fashioned garden of five raised beds surrounded by paths. In the round central bed was what Martin thought looked like a shaped bay tree, but He was no tree expert – his guess was based on it looking like a much smaller version he had in his back garden. The four surrounding beds were shaped to form a small inner circle and a larger outer circle, with the edges framed by neatly cut low hedges and the middles full of pale pink roses.

The vast expanse of Coopers Field stretched to the right and to the left, bordered by a huge expanse of trees of variable types, shapes, and sizes. It was in this area where nature and nurture worked hand-in-hand that they sighted the cold reality of what they were looking for – the familiar white tent that signalled a crime scene.

As they got nearer they spotted another familiar sight in the form of Sgt Evans, who was patrolling the outer edge of the surrounding area that was cordoned off with blue and white scene of crime tape.

A veteran in the procedure for protecting a crime scene, Sgt Evans issued Martin and Matt with suits, masks, and boots before lifting the tape and allowing the senior officers through.

'We were worried about Mrs Pattern, the woman who found the body, as we thought she was having a heart attack – but luckily a nurse walking to work, helped us out. She used the paper bag that her lunch was wrapped in and after Mrs Pattern had taken a couple of large breaths into the bag she recovered.

'Since then we haven't been able to stop her talking and, as you can see, PC Cook-Watts is standing over there with Mrs Pattern, still having her ear bent. The nurse has gone to work as she says they're short of staff, but we have all her details and she's prepared to give a statement or whatever is necessary.'

'OK, thanks for that,' said Martin as he focused his mind on the scene that would now unfold inside the white tent.

'I won't say good morning – it's hardly that,' said Alex as Phelps and Pryor walked under the canvas. 'At least you've frightened off the rain. And is that pale yellow thing actually something called sun?'

Alex Griffiths greeted his colleagues and made a feeble attempt to lighten the atmosphere, knowing that the two detectives were about to witness an ugly, and what had struck him as a somewhat pathetic, sight.

'The body hasn't been moved yet as we knew you'd want to see it as it was found – but we have photographed extensively and taken samples of everything and anything that surrounds it. The professor is, as always, keen to get the body back to the laboratory and look for clues that will help us with identification and cause of death – we can't even be sure at this stage, if we have the remains of a man or a woman.'

'It's a woman.'

The words came from the mouth of Professor Dafydd Moore, who was kneeling at the side of the body and who continued examining the head without saying another word.

No one was surprised at that as when it came to conversation at a crime scene the professor was best known for his silence. He had acknowledged the presence of the CID officers with just a nod of the head while continuing to be completely absorbed with the left hand side of the partly revealed skull.

Alex looked at Martin. 'Well I'm not sure how he can tell the sex considering the state of the body, but if he says it's a woman then I'll put my next month's salary on it being a woman – never known him say anything he isn't able to substantiate.'

Being able to substantiate theories had seemingly always been a way of life for the professor. He was first and foremost an academic with a brilliant mind but unlike most of his university colleagues he was immensely practical and the combination of these two qualities made him a brilliant criminal pathologist.

It was the latter that for most people allowed them to excuse his personality, but did not prevent Matt from frequently referring to him as a 'miserable old git'.

Martin knew better than to ask Prof. Moore a load of questions at this time. A man who was often silent, morose, and some would

4

say downright rude, the professor would become more animated during the post-mortem and become a complete show off during his presentation of findings to the assembled murder enquiry team.

Although he believed he already knew the answer, there was one question Martin had to ask. 'Do you think she died of natural causes?'

'She was murdered! Her skull was hit hard on one side but I won't know if that was the cause of death until I have done a full PM examination.'

Prof. Moore picked up his Gladstone bag, lifted the flap of the tent, and started to walk out when Martin risked another question. 'How long has she been here?'

The prof. turned back and viewed Martin over the top of his half rimmed glasses. 'I am not a clairvoyant, DCI Phelps,' was his reply. 'I can't tell you when she arrived at this exact spot but I can say she has been dead for some time – unlikely to be just days, could even be weeks – but the absence of flesh on the face and other parts is not just down to tissue decay, it has been eaten away by small animals. However, if you will let me get away, I'll be able to offer you some scientific evidence rather than attempting to gaze into a non-existent crystal ball.'

On that note of sarcasm the professor left, and Alex shrugged his shoulders. 'There is no denying the brilliance of that man, but an occasional smile or kind word wouldn't go amiss. You should have been here when he first arrived – anyone would have thought I had personally and deliberately set out to ruin the start of his week.'

Martin turned his attention to the pile of clothes that had been partially scattered by the dog that had found them earlier. In spite of the fact that the shoes and one of the garments were strewn around, the majority of the clothes were in a peculiarly neat pile and looked to have been deliberately placed at the lower end of the body, close to the feet.

'Was this how you found the clothes?' asked Martin.

'It's exactly as we found them,' replied Alex. 'I would think that all the clothes including the shoes were originally placed together, and I guess the dog took the shoes off the top first and then pulled that jacket along by the sleeve. All the rest are precisely folded and we should be able to get quite a bit of

5

information from them.'

Matt had been looking over the body and pointed out the area of the skull where the woman was likely to have been bludgeoned. 'It's not a very big area,' he remarked. 'But then she isn't very big, is she?' He continued looking around and making random observations. 'She definitely wasn't very tall, and look at her shoes – they look quite new and what I would call very sensible. Certainly not the height of fashion.'

'Could even be school shoes,' suggested Alex. 'So perhaps we aren't looking at a short woman but a tall child, or maybe a teenager.'

'We do have one child still unaccounted for, missing since April,' Matt told them. 'But he's just six years old, and as the father has also disappeared it's likely to be a family thing and we have no reason to suspect external foul play.'

'Well, this is definitely not a six-year-old, and we aren't likely to find out anything else by just looking here, so let's get everything back to Goleudy and start unravelling the mystery.'

Martin referred to Goleudy with his usual due reverence, as he believed beyond doubt that it was one of the best places in the world for solving crime. To the public at large it was their local police station, but behind that front the enormous, modernised Victorian building were floor after floor of the very latest crime-busting technology.

The thing Martin liked best about the place was that it brought all the facets of modern day policing together in a building that was solidly constructed with tall ceilings and a general feeling of space. It was not unusual for police forces from other parts of the country, and even foreign constabularies, to visit the set-up and be highly impressed with the opportunity it gave for experts in the various fields of criminal detection to work so closely together.

The body they had found this morning would be taken to the fourth floor, where Professor Moore headed up a team of brilliant technicians and forensic scientists, each one with a particular skill and all eager to be part of discovering facts crucial to the solving of cases. Even as Martin thought of the PM rooms and their proximity to the laboratories he could mentally smell the pungent odour that signalled entry to Prof. Moore's domain.

As if reading his boss's thoughts, Matt declared. 'The only

good thing about finding a body in the open air is that you aren't knocked over by the smell. Do you remember when we were called to that place on Newport Road where the couple had been dead since the day after their daughter went for a ten-day holiday to Egypt?'

Alex interjected. 'I really don't want to be reminded about that case. It wasn't just that the couple had decided on a suicide pact for themselves, but overdosing their cat, dog, and tropical fish meant we had the stench of decomposing pets as well – and after a week of warm weather. I could still easily throw up at just the memory of it.'

Alex indicated to members of the SOC team that the body could be removed and the clothing put into four separate bags in line with the four positions in which it had been found. Each shoe was bagged separately, as was the jacket that had been partly pulled from the main pile, and finally the remaining items were lifted – ready to be put into one of the larger evidence bags.

'Hold it there!' shouted Matt as he spotted something white near the bottom of the neatly folded clothes. 'Is that a letter or something – is it too much to hope it's a suicide note?'

Alex carefully folded back two-thirds of the clothes, all of which were soaking wet, and looked at the single sheet of A5-size white paper which had been revealed, without touching it. 'It looks to be a blank sheet of paper,' he said and he sounded somewhat disappointed. 'I won't touch it here as it'll probably fall to pieces, and there's nothing written on it as far as I can see. If there ever was anything written on it our best bet will be to get it back to the lab and look at it there.'

With the body now moved all three men could take a closer look at the site where it had lain, but there was nothing of any obvious significance to be seen. Alex called to his team to work quickly, because murky water from the saturated surroundings would soon seep into the recently vacated space and dilute any existing evidence.

The team were ahead of him and had thrown a large plastic sheet over the whole area. The newly positioned cover was already capturing the incoming fluid and protecting the crime scene.

'We have taken samples of the mud and grass surrounding the body and if, as the professor suggests, she was murdered by a blow to the skull we would probably expect to see more evidence of blood. However, we all know what the weather has been like over the past few weeks, and much of it could have been washed away. That may not be the case for any evidence underneath the body, so we need to make sure that nothing stops us from looking more closely at that area.'

Martin nodded in agreement. 'Of course, the other reason for lack of blood here could simply be that she was killed somewhere else and her body dumped here – although I have to say that never before have I come across a murderer who dumps a body and puts the victim's clothing in a neat pile at her feet – that is weird.'

'The other thing is that there was no real attempt to hide the body. She was just put under the trees not far from the edge of the field. There is some growth around the base of this tree and it did provide a bit of cover for the body, but not that much. If there had been less rain in July more people would have been walking around the area and she would almost certainly have been discovered earlier.'

'Yes, this field's also used for festivals and the like,' said Matt. 'I got two of my sisters tickets to the Florence and the Machine gig in June, and we bring all the nieces here for the Sparks in the Park firework display every November – it's brilliant. Don't know the last event that was held here but I'll check it out when we get back.'

Alex had finished giving instructions to his team and pulled down the hood of his scene of crime suit to reveal his perfectly smooth, hairless head. There was no fear of contaminating the crime scene from him, but that was not the reason for his shiny scalp and Martin recalled that Alex had shaved his head even before joining the force.

Matt couldn't resist a comment. 'Thought the new Mrs Griffiths would have persuaded you to grow your hair,' he teased the recently married SOC expert.

Matt had been unable to attend the wedding as he had been recovering from a near-fatal knife wound at the time, inflicted when he and Martin had apprehended a serial killer. Alex's marriage, to Charlie Walsh, who headed up the IT arm of the Goleudy setup, had been organised by Charlie in less time than it took most people to do their weekly shop – that was Charlie!

Although confined to a wheelchair following a serious car accident when she was a teenager, Charlie managed to live life to the full – more so on two wheels than most people did on two legs.

The wedding in Charlie's hometown of Balbriggan had been a harmonious meeting of the Celts, with the family and friends of Charlie providing the warmest of Irish welcomes to Alex and his family and friends from South Wales. No one would have guessed that the wedding had taken so little time to organise, and from start to finish the whole affair had been a perfect match of solemn commitment and lots of fun.

Martin had his own good reasons for remembering the occasion. He had been Alex's best man, and contrary to his expectations he had thoroughly enjoyed the experience, but the main reason for his terrific memories was the time he had spent in the company of Shelley Edwards.

Shelley worked as a civilian member of the Police Force and was the health and safety expert of the Goleudy Training Department. She was responsible for training officers at a local level and for providing quarterly seminars for the whole police force in Wales. Not being a technical expert, Shelley had looked for help in setting up the IT arrangements for these sessions. Charlie, a whizz at anything involved with pushing buttons, had willingly obliged and the two of them had soon become really good friends.

In true Irish fashion the wedding celebrations had gone on through the night, with a magical mixture of Welsh singing and Irish dancing – helped along by a constant flow of the local brew. It was at half-past five in the morning, when the sky was getting light, that Martin and Shelley had wandered off to the beach some twenty minutes' walk away, and then on to the small harbour to watch the early morning activities of the local fishermen. Just prior to the wedding Shelley and Martin had begun a relationship, but that had been a secret shared by just the two of them, and they had attended the wedding as individual friends of the bride and groom. They had left as a couple, and Martin remembered that morning as one of the best mornings of his life – worlds apart from the one he was facing today. This was cold reality. A Monday morning, with a sky signalling rain and a field full of mud, and the discovery of a naked body the order of the day – one that had to be faced.

9

Alex indicated that he and his team would be about another hour at the scene and would then be taking everything back to base. He agreed with Martin that it should be possible to get the first meeting of the investigation team together by early afternoon.

As Matt lifted the tent flap for himself and Martin to leave, he was momentarily blinded by a flash of light and quickly realised they were no longer alone under the trees, as they had been joined by a number of onlookers and what looked like just a single member of the press.

The one reporter, who was holding a flash camera, wasted no time and immediately bombarded the officers with questions. After all, he was the first of his colleagues to arrive at the scene, and he knew from past experience that when the rest of the news reporters arrived he would be unlikely to get a look-in. Very soon the whole area would be swarming with people from every section of the media, and he had to make the most of this unique opportunity.

'Morning, DCI Phelps,' he began. 'The woman talking to your officer over there has a very loud voice and we have all gathered that she discovered a body here, within the last hour or so. Is that right?'

'Good morning, Mike,' returned Martin as he recognised the reporter as Mike Hiscock, a journalist from one of the smaller local papers and was more than happy to give out the known facts of the case to him – it would make his day to get information ahead of the big boys.

'Yes, the woman you refer to did find a body when she was exercising her dog this morning.'

'Is it the body of a man or a woman?' Hiscock quickly interrupted and was keen to know more.

'I'm afraid I can't give you that information at present,' replied Martin.

'Is that can't or won't? How did he or she die? Was it of natural causes or was she murdered?' The reporter persisted, obviously trying to get as many questions as possible answered.

Martin and Matt had now passed the barrier of the blue and white tape and were making their way back to the car park but their footsteps continued to be dogged by this young hound from the press.

'OK,' said Martin. 'As you appear to have beaten your

10

colleagues to this story I will give you an official statement. At ten minutes past seven this morning the police received a call from a member of the public who had been exercising her dog in Coopers Field. It would seem that the dog failed to retrieve a ball and when the woman went in search of it she discovered a body. You can see for yourself where the body was found and I can confirm that we are treating the death as suspicious.'

'That's it?' questioned Mike.

'Don't push it,' retorted Matt. 'DCI Phelps has already given you more than you could have hoped for at this stage, so just hop it.'

Although enough was never enough for Mike and his colleagues, he did hop it, and in fact raced ahead and was over the bouncy bridge well before the detectives had reached it – no doubt running at the behest of that ever-looming deadline.

The journey back to Goleudy should only have taken fifteen minutes but they encountered the delights of the morning rush hour in the city and that, coupled with the aftermath of a minor accident, meant having to tolerate a journey lasting almost an hour.

Not that the time was wasted as it was an opportunity to reflect on the detail, albeit scanty, of this new case and to construct a plan for solving what was most definitely a murder – but what sort of murder?

The two men tossed around every possibility they could think of. At the one end of the spectrum they considered a brutal murder, possibly premeditated, having happened at some other location and the body dumped in the field later. At the other end there was the possibility of a simple accident. An accident that had resulted in the death of the victim could easily have caused the perpetrator to panic and move the body away from where he or she, the killer, could be identified.

Who was the victim? They needed an answer to that question as quickly as possible and there were a few ways in which that answer could be provided. When Prof. Moore had completed the post-mortem examination they would have a much better picture of the deceased and then trawling through the missing persons files would be easier. But the deceased may not have been reported missing.

The scientists would be able to provide them with the all-important DNA profile but that would only be helpful if it matched records on existing databases. As on many other similar occasions, Martin considered the pros and cons of there being a compulsory national DNA database.

A closer examination would also throw more light on the cause of death – was it just a single blow to the head or had the victim been subjected to a more sustained attack? Would they discover sexual abuse or other evidence of pre-death torture? Toxicology reports would also be interesting – and was there any underlying pathology? Would they discover that drugs were involved, either prescription or otherwise?

When did she die? The level of tissue decay, together with factoring in the effects of the elements, should put a reasonably accurate date to that. Martin had his usual feeling of frustration, a feeling very familiar to this stage of any investigation – it was the questions with no answers stage. If he could choose the answer to just one question at this moment, he would be provided with the name of the dead female. It didn't even occur to him that the professor could be wrong about the sex.

As he thought about her identity it raised even more questions in his mind. Did she have a family, and if so, where were they? If the body was indeed that of a child or teenager surely someone would have missed her but he was unaware of any recent investigations in the area. However if the death had occurred elsewhere they would have to link up with records of existing cases throughout the UK, and Charlie and her team would have their work cut out. What if? Why? When? How? More and more questions flooded Martin's mind as he turned the corner of a particularly familiar stretch of road and pulled into the car park at the rear entrance of Goleudy.

Although Martin had been engrossed with his thoughts, he had not been unaware of the grumblings of his sergeant's stomach – especially as they had mirrored his own. Matt opened his mouth to speak as the car came to a halt but Martin second-guessed him.

'Yes, we should be in time for breakfast, but in any event Iris will rustle us up an omelette, so let's head straight for the staff café and put these stomach gremlins to rest.'

Matt grinned. 'No wonder you're such a great detective,' he teased his boss. 'Linking my intestinal protestations to the absence of food, now that's really profound!'

Iris did indeed cook them each a cheese omelette of enormous proportions, which she brought to the table with an equivalent mountain of toast.

The grapevine had already been working and she knew that the two men had just returned from the site of a murder. She couldn't imagine what that must be like but held the view that any situation could be improved with the TLC of good home-from-home cooking and she could certainly provide that.

For the next ten minutes neither Martin nor his sergeant said a word as they both devoured everything that had been put in front of them and then picked up a second cup of coffee to take back to their offices.

'If you can set the ball rolling regarding missing females that would be something,' said Martin. 'We haven't got much else to go on until after the PM, but I noticed Mrs Williams was called away from her coffee back there so I assume it's already underway.'

Mrs Williams was the post-mortem room technician, without whom the professor would not start an examination. The two had worked together for more than twenty years and no one knew more about the professor's idiosyncrasies than she did.

It was rumoured that the professor even changed his holidays to coincide with hers, as he was very much a creature of habit and Mrs Williams knew his habits and preferred ways of working, if anything, better than he did. Whatever their relationship, it worked and Mrs Williams was regarded as something of a saint by those who thought that working with Prof. Moore would be a living nightmare.

Matt went off to do whatever he could to kick-start the investigation and clear some of the existing paperwork that seemed to grow in his in-tray every weekend. Martin closed the door of his office before opening his desk drawer and taking out a sheet of paper on which he wrote the three headings he always used to brainstorm his way into an investigation.

He let his mind wander back over the crime scene and wrote down anything that he thought would help to discover who the victim was and how she had been killed. For some reason he tried to remember the victim's hair, and the only thing that came to mind was the lack of it. The skull was certainly not exposed, other than where a blow had been struck, but he couldn't recall much hair and the colour had not struck a chord in his memory. For the moment he just noted it as something to be checked out later, not something of particular significance.

An hour later, and with no more than twenty words written on his paper, he headed for Incident Room One. The usual selection of crime scene photographs were already on display and Martin knew that the clothes and soil samples, were being worked on in the laboratories. Everyone had specific jobs to do at the start of this murder investigation and the work was well underway.

Over the next few days the room would be a hive of activity as the individual experts and their teams brought forward more information and supported Martin's efforts to discover the identity of the body found in Coopers Field and to bring her killer to justice.

Chapter Two

'I got here as quickly as I could,' Sarah told the uptight night nurse who had changed out of her uniform and was pacing between the reception desk and the main entrance to the Parkland Nursing Home.

'It was quite exciting really,' continued Sarah, ignoring her colleague's moans about her lateness. 'Some woman was out with her wire-haired terrier and the dog was messing around with some soaking wet clothes. When Mrs Pattern, that's the lady's name, went to get her dog from under the trees she found a dead body.'

The night nurse, who called herself Sister Grey although she had only been qualified for just over six months and had so far failed to get a job in the NHS, stopped moaning and stared at Sarah. 'Seriously?' she said. You found a dead body on your way to work?'

'No, I didn't say that. I said that someone called Mrs Pattern found a dead body – or rather her dog did – and I only got involved because as I walked past I saw that she was hyperventilating,' Sarah continued. 'I think one of the police officers thought he was about to have a second body on his hands so I suggested the old paper bag routine, and within a couple of minutes she was fine.'

'I'm surprised the police let you go,' chipped in one of the care assistants who had been listening to the conversation.

Sarah raised her eyebrows. 'What do you mean? I'm not a murder suspect or anything, and anyway they have my details, and they'll probably turn up here later on as I've agreed to give a statement.'

'You said a murder suspect!' said Sr Grey. 'When you said that the woman had found a dead body I assumed it was someone who had just had a heart attack, or perhaps a tramp – anyone could have died of exposure if they had been sleeping rough in the weather we've had for our so-called summer. But you said a murder suspect – so the police think the person was killed?'

Eva Grey had forgotten all about her apparent need to get away early that morning, and continued to question her colleague, but Sarah cut her short. 'I know nothing,' she said. 'I certainly didn't see the body, and I left as soon as I was sure that Mrs Pattern was OK. The police seemed to understand the issue of us being short of staff and so I was free to go.

'The only other thing I heard was Mrs Pattern telling a woman police officer that the experience had been terrible and asking why anyone would want to take all their clothes off as it was hardly the weather for it.'

'So the body was naked,' suggested Jayne Foster, the care assistant. 'I wouldn't have been able to come to work. I would have had to take a look.'

'I don't think the police are opening up a viewing gallery,' retorted Sarah, and she silently remembered how little it took for Jayne not to be able to come to work. Her level of absenteeism was horrendous, and the only reason Parkland still employed her was that when she was there she was one of the best care assistants Sarah had ever worked with.

'Anyway,' said Sarah, turning her attention back to Eva Grey. 'I thought you wanted to get away – so just give me a quick handover of anything I particularly need to know and I'll catch up with the rest from the Kardex. It's my first day back after what should have been a long weekend but I couldn't have Friday off because there was no one to cover – and I'm back this morning for the same reason.'

'We had a bloody awful night,' reported Eva. 'The day staff must have willed old Mr James to hang on until after we came on duty last night, or maybe he had already gone. He was certainly dead before I got to his room and it's only the third one along the corridor.'

'His relatives didn't want to come in to see him but I suspect his daughter will arrive this morning and you can expect her husband to demand Colin's watch and his wallet – they make me sick! The undertakers have been to collect the body and we've cleared his room, but I dare say Mr Cooper will have it filled with the next name on his list before I get back here tonight.'

Sr Grey was less than courteous about the man who owned the nursing home and little wonder as none of the staff had any illusions about him. He was a hard-nosed businessman who had no time whatsoever for the people in the beds, but who promised the earth to their relatives in order to secure a placement.

'It was Colin James who died?' asked Sarah. 'I spoke to him on Friday evening and I thought he was getting better.'

'Well, apparently after his relatives had visited him on Friday evening Dr Shaw was sent for and that must have been after you'd left,' Eva responded.

'It must have been,' replied Sarah. 'Anyway Colin's relatives didn't visit him, they were here to see Mr Cooper.'

'I don't know anything about that,' said Eva. 'As you know, I didn't work Friday night, but it was obvious when I got here on Saturday night that he wasn't going to be with us much longer – I was amazed he lasted all day Sunday.'

'That just goes to show how unpredictable the vulnerable elderly can be, but I am just really surprised at how quickly Mr James deteriorated,' said Sarah. 'It hardly seems possible that only a few weeks ago he was one of the residents able to go out to the pub – but I guess he never really recovered from that chest infection. I can see from the notes that Dr Shaw saw him again yesterday evening so there'll be no problem with the relatives getting a death certificate. It's probably already written and sitting on Anthony Cooper's desk.'

'See you tonight,' said Eva as she walked towards the door. 'I guess you'll be doing the twelve-hour shift again.'

'You guess right,' called back Sarah as she headed for the office. 'Whatever happened to the Working Times Regulations? Their rules seem to have escaped the notice of our illustrious leader Mr Cooper, but that doesn't surprise me. We were supposed to be interviewing some new staff last Thursday, but not one of them turned up and I doubt they were ever going to. It's cheaper for him to work us around the clock than to pay the extra employment costs of additional staff.'

Sarah was talking to herself as Eva had already left, probably to take a different route home, one that would take her past the place where she knew a body had been found.

Sarah looked from the office window into the lounge where the elderly sat in the same chairs as they had sat in yesterday – with the exception of Mr James, of course. She was constantly asking the care assistants to move the residents around, but it never seemed to happen, and so when one of them died the empty chair was obviously where the deceased had sat the previous day and all eyes seemed to focus on it.

For some reason she couldn't explain, this annoyed Sarah more than usual today and she walked into the lounge calling out a cheery good morning to the forlorn faces as she moved the offending chair to the edge of the room. Jim Knott acknowledged her actions but not in the way she would have wanted.

'Bet you wish it was that easy to move the rest of us on, don't you? I can't believe Colin went just like that. Until a few weeks ago he was the only one I could have a pint with, so God help the rest of us. Who'll be the next, I wonder?'

Out-of-character Sarah rose to the bait. 'At least he died in the comfort of his own room, and wasn't found dead in some wet and muddy field like the poor sod the police found this morning.'

Sarah had broken the cardinal rule. She had spoken the words 'died' and 'dead' in front of the residents who spent most of their time thinking about death and she immediately regretted her words. The incident of the body in the field this morning had obviously had more of an impact on her than she had realised.

She needn't have worried, as her news seemed to have had the opposite effect to the one she had anticipated and immediately caused a ripple of interest and even excitement amongst those who were even vaguely compos mentis.

'Where did the police find a dead body?' asked Jim. 'In a field you say – what field was that?'

Sarah realised that most of the eyes in the room were on her, and the only thing she could do was to repeat the story of her journey to work – but that was obviously not enough to satisfy her audience.

'How many policemen were there?' enquired Margaret, a ninety-four-year-old woman who was usually slumped in her chair but who now sat forward eager to hear more.

'Four officers, I think,' replied Sarah. 'Yes, there were three policemen and one policewoman, why do you ask?'

'Was there an ambulance?' Margaret continued without

answering Sarah's question.

'No, obviously if there had been an ambulance I wouldn't have been needed to help with the woman who found the body.'

Barely had Sarah finished her sentence when Margaret put forward her opinion. 'A-ha!' she exclaimed. 'Four police officers and no ambulance can only mean the body was well and truly dead – probably murdered.'

Sarah laughed. 'OK, Miss Marple, but you're probably letting your imagination run away with you. It's more likely to be some poor tramp who's been sleeping rough and died of pneumonia. Now may we change the subject, please – it's not the most pleasant of topics to start off the week.'

But as Sarah returned to the office she heard the somewhat animated conversation and guessed that a million causes of death would be considered by lunchtime. Maybe that's what it was. Maybe they were all stimulated by being able to discuss someone else's death instead of pondering about their own.

It was curious that they never discussed the death of a fellow resident. Jim had briefly mentioned Colin but Sarah knew, from past experience, it was unlikely he would be spoken of again. Perhaps it was just too close to home – the death of a stranger, even if it turned out to be a murder, was sufficiently remote to create macabre interest but not personal panic.

A few weeks ago Sarah had asked the proprietor, Mr Cooper, for an electric kettle and a mini fridge for the office, as it was on the opposite side of the building to the kitchen and the residents couldn't be observed from the kitchen anyway. He knew that due to the low staffing levels he just managed to get away with it was almost impossible for the staff to get their breaks, and so he had agreed to the request.

However, Sarah hadn't been surprised when a second-hand kettle and a cool-box had turned up. It was unlikely that he had bought either of them and more likely he had ferreted amongst the unclaimed property of past residents.

The man was a complete cheapskate when it came to the staff. What a different picture he presented to potential clients who, when they first visited his office, were offered anything from cappuccino to green tea presented in cream-coloured china cups. If they looked really promising they could even be seen sipping sherry or joining Mr Cooper in a 'wee dram'.

Although he still referred to the partaking of a 'wee dram' he had in fact transferred his allegiance from Scottish to Welsh whisky when a friend of his became involved with its production at the local Penderyn distillery. Sarah had heard him boasting to potential clients about the excellence of the product, but she suspected that his enthusiasm would be more likely something to do with the discount his friend offered him.

There seemed to be no shortage of money for his side of the business, and that included the fancy glossy brochures that were handed out.

The staff found themselves doing a reality check when they read about the individual meal selection on offer to residents and saw the photographs of happy clients and smartly dressed staff. The uniforms that were actually provided were basic, and if staff wanted more than two they had to buy them from Mr Cooper. Sarah could only assume the advertising company had searched the net for 'images of contentment in one's twilight years' – they certainly hadn't shot the pictures at Parkland!

She concentrated her mind on reading the Nursing Kardex, a transportable card filing system, where the nurses made their notes. She was able to get a quick update on what had happened to each of the residents since she had left them at eight o'clock the previous Friday night.

Her colleague Eva had mentioned having an awful night, but as far as Sarah could actually see from the nursing notes there had been very little activity. Everyone had slept soundly with the exception of Mr James, who it could be said had slept more soundly than was normal.

She thought about Mr James and had to agree with Jim Knott regarding the rate of his demise. He had been almost exactly the same age as Jim, and only a few weeks ago they had both celebrated their eighty-third birthdays. They were youngsters in comparison with the majority of the residents and had wound up their birthday celebrations by drinking at a local pub and returning to Parkland rather the worse for wear.

Sarah smiled as she remembered the two of them helping one another up the drive and to the side door, probably hoping no one would see them. It had not been late as her shift that day had

20

finished at eight p.m., and she had made it her business to see that both men were toileted and tucked-up in bed before the night staff came on duty.

That shift had been the last of a ten-day stretch for Sarah, and she had then had four days off followed by two days' annual leave. So six days off, before returning to work and finding a much-changed Colin James.

Apparently Dr Shaw had been called the day after the birthday spree as Colin had been complaining of a headache. Sarah knew she would have put this down to a hangover and given him a couple of paracetamol tablets and plenty of fluids – but she hadn't been there.

The qualified nurse who was on duty was one of the many who came and left after a couple of weeks and she didn't know Colin, so rather than take any chances she simply referred him to the doctor.

Colin had not been the brightest of men, and according to his medical notes he had had some learning difficulties. His inability to cope at home on his own had been the main reason for his admission to Parkland.

Sarah had met his daughter Patricia once, together with her overbearing husband, and the meeting had left her feeling profoundly sorry for Colin. With the right family support he could easily have remained in his own home, but his daughter was spineless and she bowed to her husband's opinion that her job was to look after him and not to pander to her father's needs.

Colin's parents must have been quite well-off, and it was clear from the way he had spoken about them that they had loved and cared for him. They had even supported him when he married someone who was obviously more interested in his money than in him, and they had been more than happy to take on Patricia when his wife met someone else and left Colin with the child.

But Colin's parents had been dead for many years, and his daughter had married a pompous maths teacher whose values in relation to women's rights were well and truly rooted in the Victorian age. He probably considered Emmeline Pankhurst to have been evil personified and wished to see women back in their 'rightful place' at the kitchen sink.

Colin's bedside cupboard had always been full of photographs

21

of his family, and lots of his daughter when she was growing up – but none of her husband, not even one of their wedding.

All the staff had seen photographs of Colin's house and it was rumoured that since his admission to Parkland the daughter and her husband had moved into the large detached property overlooking Roath Park Lake. Well, there was nothing to stop them now, and according to the nursing home administrator Colin had been an obsessive saver so consequently died a wealthy man. Sarah thought it unlikely that Colin would have made a will, so his daughter would inherit and her husband probably had the flags flying this morning.

Sarah read Colin's nursing and medical notes looking back to those six days she had been off work. Following Dr Shaw's visit Colin had been prescribed a cocktail of medication including sleeping tablets, although Sarah had never been made aware he had any sort of insomnia problems. Yes, he had type 2 diabetes and a low-grade heart murmur, and was possibly in the early stages of dementia, but none of these things had been causing him any real distress. Sarah belonged to the 'if it ain't broke, don't fix it' camp, but she had learned during her fifteen years of nursing that the majority of doctors had their feet firmly in the 'fix it at all costs' camp.

On the face of it the medication that had been prescribed was totally appropriate for each condition but for someone to go from only taking vitamin pills to swallowing daily doses of more than twenty pills – well, that was something else. Sarah had questioned the level of medication on her return to work but could see how it could be justified. Gradually Colin became more and more withdrawn, and then he contracted pneumonia.

That, of course, had had nothing to do with the medication he was receiving, and four other residents also developed the same condition all around the same time. Unfortunately for Colin this infection meant even more medication and there was talk of transferring him to the University Hospital of Wales. It was then that some of the medication she had queried was stopped and he seemed to improve, so he had stayed at the nursing home.

He had obviously deteriorated rapidly since last Friday night and Sarah referred to his nursing notes to see the exact series of events. She had been talking to Colin in his room last Friday evening and remembered feeling pleased at the progress he was making. He still looked frail but had become more chatty and had returned to teasing her about what he called her 'love life'.

'Got some handsome young man waiting for you at home?' he had joked. 'Only to be expected with a beautiful girl like you – no wonder you can't wait for your shift to finish.'

Sarah had picked up on two elements of his description and suggested a visit to Specsavers if he could see anything resembling any sort of girl, especially a beautiful one.

'Don't put yourself down,' he had told her. 'By my standards you're very young, and beauty has got little to do with what you look like and everything to do with what you are.'

As Sarah had pondered on whether or not there was a backhanded compliment in there somewhere, they had been interrupted by one of the care assistants. She had told Sarah that Mr Cooper was looking for her and wanted her to go to his office before she went home.

Sarah remembered being surprised that the home owner was still on the premises so late on a Friday night and had immediately expressed these thoughts to Annie, one of the care assistants.

'Well he's had some visitors in his office for the past few hours,' Annie had replied. 'I didn't see who they were, just that it was a man and a woman, and they've gone now. Perhaps it's another lot wanting to get a relative in here ahead of the queue.'

There was a lot of in-house gossip about how and why some people got a place in Parkland almost immediately while others whose relatives had expressed an interest, often went elsewhere when they got tired of waiting. Sarah had kept her own counsel as to why this should be; after all, she had left the NHS because she had got fed up with the politics of management, and she was determined she was not going to be sucked into it here.

When Sarah had gone to Mr Cooper's office her first thought had been that the place smelled like a brewery, and three empty glasses and an almost-empty whisky bottle told her why.

She had been summoned to hear that it had been Mr James's daughter and her husband who had been the visitors, and apparently they had expressed concerns about Colin's care.

'What concerns?' Sarah had demanded. 'What do they even know about Colin's care? When did they last see him, and why didn't they visit him tonight? I've just been talking to him and he is still a sick man but he is well up to receiving visitors.'

Anthony Cooper had bristled, and although he had smiled at Sarah there was no sign of a smile in his eyes, and his voice was unusually harsh, even for him. 'We are not here to tell clients what they should or should not do, just to comply with their wishes wherever possible.'

'And just what are the wishes of Colin's absentee relatives? More importantly, what about Colin's wishes? Which set of wishes takes precedence?'

Sarah remembered realising that she was virtually shouting at Anthony Cooper and he had responded in a similar manner. 'Don't ask so many questions. The relatives have every right to question issues of care, and it would appear that Mr James has told them that on no account does he want to be admitted to hospital. So we need to get Dr Shaw involved and ensure the request is properly documented.'

As Sarah boiled the second-hand kettle and made herself a cup of coffee, she remembered that that conversation with her employer had gone from bad to worse. She had been outraged by the suggestion that Colin had given instructions to his daughter and had said she didn't believe it. However, Anthony Cooper had been adamant that the request had been made, and had said that Dr Shaw was expected later, to give his written professional support to the family's wishes.

The last thing Sarah remembered about her visit to Mr Cooper's office was the significant pile of twenty-pound notes on the table alongside the empty crystal whisky glasses. The money hadn't really registered at the time but now she found herself wondering why it had been there and where it had come from. After all, it had been a Friday night and there was always a last-minute flurry on a Friday afternoon to ensure that any cash or money was banked.

A pathetic cash float of twenty pounds made up of small change was all that was ever left for the weekend. It was never enough and Sarah had often used her own money to buy things like bread and milk when the kitchen ran short. True, she could claim it back with the presentation of receipts to the home administrator, but she resented having to do it in the first place.

The home administrator, Peter Doster, was an old school friend of Mr Cooper's, and they must certainly have taken the same interest in lessons on getting blood out stones. Mr Doster was the master of recycling anything that could be reused in the nursing home and when it came to reducing waste he was the king.

The cook's food waste bins were regularly inspected and the thickness of the potato peelings was the cause of many a kitchen dispute. No wonder there had been so many cooks – not one of them had stayed more than a few months.

Sarah became aware that her mind was wandering and she was having difficulty in concentrating on any one thing. The office door suddenly burst open and William Morris, Colin James's son-in-law, barged in, leaving the door open for his wife, Patricia, who was still halfway down the corridor.

'I've come for his things and to pick up the death certificate,' he announced.

Sarah turned to face him and, trying desperately to keep her temper under control, she replied, 'Good morning, Mr and Mrs Morris, and may I say how sorry I am at your loss.'

Turning to Patricia, who had now entered the office, Sarah continued. 'Your father, was well thought of here, he was a real gentleman. We all loved him and will miss him greatly.'

'Yes, well, you didn't actually have to live with him, did you?' said William Morris. 'You get paid for looking after these old fogies, it's not something you do out of the goodness of your heart, so don't come the Florence Nightingale with me.'

Sarah couldn't remember when she had met a more objectionable man but she bit her lip and said nothing. She had some sympathy for Patricia Morris, but couldn't understand how the woman could be such a pathetic wimp. Even now she couldn't find the words to defend her father.

'Mr James's belongings are in the home administrator's office and that's also where you will get the death certificate,' Sarah told them. 'I am afraid he doesn't start work until nine o'clock, and in any event the death certificate won't be available until after Dr Shaw has signed it.'

'That's been sorted,' retorted Mr Morris. 'We were told to come over now to collect everything.'

'Who told you that?' asked Sarah.

'Who do you think?' was his reply. 'I deal with the organ grinder, not the monkey, and Mr Cooper himself rang us this morning. He's not here himself but assures us that the death certificate is signed and that Mr Doster will be in his office early so that we can collect it from him.'

'In that case I suggest you go to Mr Doster's office, as you seem to know more about the management arrangements of this establishment than I do.'

Sarah turned to the paperwork she had on her desk in a manner that dismissed her visitors, when there was a knock on the office door and one of the care assistants shuffled outside.

'Come in, Maria,' said Sarah. 'Mr and Mrs Morris were just leaving. What is it you want?'

'It's not what I want, it's what the police want. There are two policemen in reception and they say they want to speak to you about the body.'

Mr Morris had already pushed his wife halfway down the corridor but he had overheard the conversation and with his colour draining he turned back to face Sarah. 'What does she mean, the police are here to see you about the body? Why are the police involved?'

Sarah could now see no reason to contain her anger and turned sharply towards William Morris. 'Maria has just brought me a message that is none of your concern. Why should you care that the police are here to see me about a body? Unless of course you murdered the person they found dead in Coopers Field this morning!'

Chapter Three

Martin Phelps had barely had enough time to take a good look at the photographs on the first of the display panels in Incident Room One when Matt Pryor came looking for him.

'I've been with Charlie and we've trawled through the local and national databases looking for any females who have been reported missing over the past two months. Locally, there are only three reports, but nationally there are hundreds – makes you think doesn't it? All those people unaccounted for.

'Some of the reports link the person's disappearance to a family row, but in a large number of cases the person reported missing appears to have just vanished without any plausible explanation. The other thing that has amazed me is the age span. There are missing children aged from three up, an old man who was aged ninety-one when he was reported missing eighteen months ago, and all ages, sexes, and ethnic groups in between. Where are they all?'

Martin knew his DS was not expecting him to answer this, but Matt was anticipating the next question from his boss and Martin obliged. 'What do we know about the three locals on that list?' he asked.

'I have the computer printouts on all three of them and from the little information we have so far regarding our body she could be any one of them. The information provided for these missing people is really excellent and I must confess I didn't realise we kept so much on file about them. We have photographs, of course, but also details of height, weight, build, shoe size, blood group, and medical history – some have dental records, and even DNA profiles.'

Martin laughed. 'If you had come up through the ranks like me you would be aware of the time and effort taken to put together these files – not something they make graduates do, is it?'

It was not unusual for Martin to tease his sergeant in this way, but there was no malicious undertone and both men recognised the way in which they complemented one another in their approaches to detection. Martin had indeed come up through the ranks and, by any standard, he had not been tardy. The position he had held the longest was that of a constable, and on reflection he realised that he had been blocked at that stage because a cantankerous old sergeant probably thought that Martin was after his stripes.

The first-hand experience he had gained as a constable and sergeant was something he valued, and was a key factor in his ongoing positive relationship with uniformed staff. After passing his sergeants' exams he had moved for a short time to Swansea in order to get a position at that rank, but was there for barely a year. As soon as the opportunity had presented itself he was back in Cardiff, transferred to CID as the DS sidekick to DCI Austin. His DCI was everything Martin was not, and for almost two years Martin endured working for one of the rudest, most brash, and generally objectionable men he could imagine. The time was only made tolerable by the fact that DCI Austin was an exceptionally good detective, and Martin had learned to ignore the man while soaking up his mind and methods.

It was now nearly four years since he himself had become a DCI and Matt was only the second DS he had worked with. DS Pryor, unlike Martin, was a graduate entrant into the force, and working with Martin had given him his first experience of real-life detection. Most of it was quite different from the theory he had been taught.

The two men had hit it off from the beginning and had an excellent working relationship that allowed for a bit of banter but respected rank.

Until recently Martin had sometimes teased his DS that his acceptance by the constabulary had only been because they needed a prop forward for the South Wales Police Rugby Squad. This was now a jibe that very much needed to be avoided as Matt had recently been forced to give up playing.

He had been with Martin when a particularly dangerous killer had been tracked down and Matt had been injured when he kicked a knife from the man's hand. The incredibly sharp knife had pierced Matt's femoral artery and he had needed immediate, arterial surgery.

The surgery had been very successful and Matt, being a fit young man, had recovered quickly, but had then been devastated to learn that for the foreseeable future any contact sports were out of the question.

Although Matt joked that not playing rugby meant he could go out on a Saturday night looking handsome and not sporting the swollen eyes and bruises of the rugby maul, he wasn't fooling anyone because they all knew how much he missed it.

'Look at this.' Matt interrupted Martin's thoughts and would probably have been surprised to know he had been the subject of them. 'As I said, our body could be any one of our local missing persons, but only inasmuch as all three of them are women. But here's a weird thing. One's a blonde, one's a brunette, and one is a redhead – don't you think that's strange?'

'Only if they are all very young women and they all disappeared at the same time only to turn up later as members of a well-known girl band,' suggested Martin.

'No chance, guv,' laughed Matt. 'They are all well past that possibility, and of course we don't know that the colour of their hair is for real – they could all be natural blondes for all we know.'

'Is there anything that really links anyone of them to the body that was found this morning?' enquired Martin.

'Nothing that I can see,' said Matt. 'However it's likely that we will be able to rule two of them out, as they are around the average height for a woman, and from what I could see at the crime scene I would say our victim was short, wouldn't you?'

'It certainly looked that way,' said Martin. 'I wonder how long it will be before the Prof is able to give us more specific information? Matt, do you think you could contact Mrs Williams and see where they've got to? Don't hassle the man himself, just ask Mrs Williams.'

'Don't worry! I'll ask Mrs Williams. She's such a nice lady, I really don't know how she's put up with him for as long as she has.'

Matt disappeared and Martin moved away from the photographs and drew his usual three vertical columns on the large whiteboard. Above the columns he put a name to the crime –

calling it the Coopers Field Murder. For the time being he merely wrote a heading for the first column, entitling it 'Absolute Facts'.

There was little to put under this heading and actually all he could do was write the date and time the body was discovered, the location, the name of the person who made the call to the police, and the time the police had arrived at the scene. It was a bit depressing to see so little in this column and in order to move his thinking forward he headed the other two columns 'Facts to be Checked' and 'What If?' At least he could have some fun and let his imagination run riot in that last column.

The setting out of data under these headings was a ritual Martin used to focus his mind at the beginning of any investigation. He was aware that some of his fellow DCIs had been known to joke about 'Martin's three columns' but it was Martin, not they, who had the best clean-up record of allocated cases.

He was about to list some possible reasons for the neatly folded clothes and the body being naked when Matt came back into the room and said that Prof. Moore was well under way with the post-mortem. 'He must be in a better mood than he was earlier because Mrs Williams has checked with him and it's apparently OK for me to attend the post-mortem with you, if you're happy with that.'

'I've got no problem with that,' said Martin. 'I'm always struck by the approach we take when a body is discovered but the murder isn't recent: we're much more laid back about it, aren't we? I guess it's because we don't have to contemplate the fact that the killer could still be at large and possibly terrorising others. Of course the murderer in this case may well be still a threat to someone else, we just don't know.'

'At the moment we just don't know much about anything,' suggested Matt. 'Alex and his lot are working on the clothes and the piece of paper, and analysing samples from the area surrounding the body. When I spoke to him a few minutes ago he suggested they would be in a position to give us some answers early this afternoon.'

'There is one other thing I'd like you to do, Matt,' said Martin. 'It's to interview the nurse who gave some assistance with Mrs Pattern, the woman who found the body. Two officers have already been to the Parkland Nursing Home and one of them was Sgt Evans.'

'I saw him in the corridor when he got back and John Evans told me that the nurse had very little to add to what we already know about her involvement. Our sergeant was, however, surprised when the relative of a resident who died last night, had really freaked out when he heard there were policemen at the door of the nursing home.'

'I can't see how it has got anything whatsoever to do with the case, but I'm reluctant to ignore Sgt Evans' nose – he has been known to have just cause for concern more often than not.'

'Yes, the Evans nose is legendary,' said Matt. 'The man he mentioned is probably one of those people with a phobia about anyone in uniform, but I'm happy to check it out. I know where the nursing home is, it's no more than five minutes' walk from where the body was found, but like you I can't see there being any connection. I'll come to the post-mortem with you now and then pay a visit to Parkland before lunch. When will we be having our first briefing, about two o'clock?'

'Yes, I think we should have enough to talk about by then and I can't see any reason to hold a press conference – it would be over in five minutes. I'll get our PR people to release a simple press statement as soon as Prof. Moore is able to confirm the sex of the victim, give us an approximate age, and come up with some idea of how long she's been dead.'

Martin was as much thinking aloud as he was talking to DS Pryor, and the two men lapsed into their own thoughts as they walked up the steps to the fourth floor. Martin was pleased his cheese omelette was well and truly settled in his stomach, as walking down the corridor he sensed that peculiar churning that inevitably came with being in this part of the building.

Matt obviously shared Martin's feelings, and as they walked past one of the laboratories he said, almost in a whisper, 'There's something about this place, isn't there? It makes me feel a bit queasy, not in a way where I would actually be sick, but more like massive butterflies in the stomach. It's a strange feeling.'

Martin nodded in agreement and they both walked into the anteroom for PM Room Two, where they took off their jackets and put on the protective clothing that Mrs Williams had put out ready for them. Matt turned to Martin and made a confession. 'I don't mind going to post-mortem examinations, provided the first incision has been made. I just hate seeing the bit where the pathologist cuts into the flesh at the beginning. How can they do that?'

Martin said nothing and moved towards the door of the PM room, where he could see Mrs Williams beckoning them in.

Matt was pleased to see that the professor was well past the first incision phase and with his new-found bravery he moved nearer to the table and caught the Prof's eye.

'If only dead bodies could talk ...'

Before Matt had finished his sentence, Prof. Moore interrupted him. 'Oh, but they can, Sergeant. The bodies I get in here tell me the truth about themselves, not like the villains you get out there who tell you lie after lie. Watch and learn, DS Pryor. Watch and learn.'

For the next hour and ten minutes that was exactly what they did. Martin and Matt were treated to a master-class in the art of making the dead talk, and as they watched they did indeed learn more than they would have thought possible about their unknown victim.

Her height was pretty much as predicted and recorded as five feet exactly. Working from head to toe, they learned that the victim was certainly not young and that she had cataracts in both eyes. The professor suggested that in order to cope with just everyday living she would have needed really strong glasses and asked if they had been found with her things.

Martin's mask covered most of his face but he raised an eyebrow in Matt's direction and Matt took the cue. 'There were no glasses that I have been made aware of,' he said. 'The only possibility could be that they were tucked into a pocket of the jacket. I know for certain there was no handbag, and that would have been the obvious place for glasses and such like.'

The victim's nose had been almost completely eaten away, as had most of the skin on the face, but as they all looked it was becoming more obvious that she was quite an old lady. Her gums could be seen as her predators had gnawed through some of the flesh on her cheek. There was no evidence of teeth – perhaps she had worn dentures, but like her spectacles they had, so far, not been found.

Like a well-oiled machine the professor, supported by Mrs

Williams, worked his way through all the major organs, taking samples of tissue and stomach content. All the while Prof. Moore called out his findings to be caught by an invisible recording machine and he moved to one side at intervals for his assistant to photograph his findings.

The 'extras' at the PM examination were not expected to ask questions, just watch in somewhat grisly fascination and occasionally respond to questions that were thrown at them. 'Did you find a walking stick or any kind of walking frame, like a Zimmer, anywhere near the body?' The Professor asked this question as he was examining the lower half of the body.

'No, why do you ask?' Martin responded with a quick question of his own.

'Because this woman would not have walked far on her own. In fact this woman would have had difficulty in walking anywhere without help. She has advanced osteoarthritis in her knee joints, they are virtually bare bone with hardly a sign of cartilage left. Walking, if it had been possible at all, would have been unbearably painful. There's a similar picture with her hip joints and I believe that for many years she would have been virtually chair-bound.

'This level of osteoarthritis could suggest a very old lady and one who has carried an excess of weight around, but there is barely an ounce of fat on this body. The other cause of such an advanced state of OA could be congenital – so if she has any siblings or children they could be sufferers.'

As he spoke, the professor dissected pieces of tissue from the right hip and popped them into the specimen pots that Mrs Williams held out and then duly labelled.

'There is no doubt that she had children, and I do mean more than one, as this uterus has definitely supported a number of pregnancies and shows signs of scarring commensurate with Caesarean section incisions. It's not surprising that she needed to be delivered by CS as her pelvis is of an irregular shape – let's hope any possible female offspring didn't inherit her bone structure.'

'Apart from her cataracts and the skeletal problems I have identified, there is nothing else that would have bothered this woman health-wise. Her heart, liver, and kidneys are in reasonably good shape for her age and apart from the osteoarthritis there is no

33

underlying disease. All things taken into account, I am going to put the age at around eighty – certainly not less than that.'

The professor had moved towards the top of the table and turned his attention on the area of the skull that had been injured. 'This blow wouldn't have killed you,' he said to Matt who stood behind him and nearly a foot above him. 'It's not a massive injury, but her bones, including the bones of her skull, are more brittle than yours and I can confirm without doubt that this wound would have killed her.'

All three men peered closely at the lesion that was almost perfectly round and measured just a few inches in all directions. All three were wondering the same thing and it was Martin who voiced their thoughts. 'What kind of weapon are we looking for? Obviously not a house-brick, but perhaps a pebble of some sort, or even the rounded end of her non-existent walking stick.'

'I'll leave that for you to determine,' the Professor replied, as he picked up an oscillating saw and leaned over the skull.

Matt averted his eyes as he knew what was coming next. Had the professor noticed the action and was he getting soft in his old age? Surely not! He probably just wanted to finish the examination without further interruption and turned his head slightly towards Martin. 'I need to open up the skull and take a look at the brain, but I think you've got everything you're going to get for now and you'll want to get on with whatever it is detectives do.'

'Toxicology reports will tell us if she was on any prescribed medication, or if she was poisoned by anything, and things like DNA results will be with you as quickly as the lab is able to process them. Just let me know when you need me to address the team and I will be there.'

Martin offered his thanks to the professor but they fell on deaf ears, as he was already passing Mrs Williams more samples to be labelled and the two of them continued working – both at ease with the established routine of their strange world.

On the way back down the stairs Matt checked that Martin still wanted him to follow up whatever it was that Sgt Evans was concerned about at Parkland Nursing Home.

'Yes I do,' was Martin's reply. 'It's obviously nothing to do with this case, but according to Sgt Evans the visitor he saw at the nursing home this morning was more than just rattled at hearing about a police presence – he was visibly shaken and took a few minutes to compose himself. As you said earlier it will probably just turn out to be someone who has a phobia about anyone in uniform but we are all aware of the renowned Evans' nose and there could be something going on there that we should make it our business to find out about. Take Sgt Evans with you.'

Matt was about to leave Martin when his boss asked him to pick up the details of the three missing local women they had talked about earlier. 'Drop them off at my office on your way past,' he suggested. 'I'll see if any information we have on them ties up with what we now know about our lady. From what you said previously there is only one to be considered but I'll take a look at them all anyway.'

'Try not to be too long at Parkland, I was thinking of getting some lunch about one-ish and then starting the first session for this case at two o'clock prompt. Let everyone know will you?'

Matt nodded and walked down the corridor towards the office he shared with two other detective sergeants. Although Matt hadn't liked the arrangement initially, he had to admit that it worked quite well. Each of the other DSs were allocated to their own DI, in his case a DCI, and because they were all involved with different cases they were hardly ever in the office at the same time.

In spite of that the three had formed a pretty good working relationship and they often used one another as sounding boards before making suggestions to their relative bosses.

The office wasn't empty now and as Matt entered, DS Janice Dilworth got up from her chair, pushed past Matt, and made her way to the door. She had been crying, but even as Matt called out to ask her what was wrong she was already out of sight. Matt picked up the file he had come in for and dropped it off at Martin's office as requested.

On his way to pick up Sgt Evans he wondered about Janice Dilworth. She had replaced one of the other detective sergeants just six months ago when she was newly promoted, and Matt found her input into office discussions really stimulating.

At first the thought of working closely with a young woman had worried Matt. He had a bit of a reputation with regards to women, but had never yet broken the golden rule of not mixing work with pleasure. He had been perversely pleased to meet a short, round-faced woman, who was pretty by anyone's standard, but was certainly not his type.

Janice was, like Matt, a graduate entrant and had achieved a first-class honours degree in Criminal Justice from the University of Essex. She was judged by most people to be 'going places', and she was one of the last people he would have expected to see in tears.

He hoped it wasn't anything too serious – he would make sure of catching up with her later. He would have to tread carefully as he guessed she would most likely be embarrassed by the incident.

Martin had a single sheet of paper on his desk and was filling in the three columns under his crime-busting headings – the same ones he had written on the whiteboard. It always amazed him how quickly information was gathered at this stage of any investigation and how each piece of data was like a magnet pulling in other facts and figures from the most unlikely places.

The purpose of his headings was to focus his mind and to ensure that the smallest of details were not overlooked. It always worked for him and now that he had written down everything that was so far known about the body he was in a position to cross-reference his findings with the information Matt had left him.

As Matt had indicated, it was easy to rule out two of the locally reported missing women. One was five feet six and looked from her photograph to weigh in excess of twenty stone. Her file indicated that she was a spinster and had no children, but did have a full set of teeth.

The other woman was reported as being just five feet and one inch and of slight build. A possible match until Martin caught sight of her age. Her relatives had given her age as just thirty-seven and her hobbies were listed as bungee jumping and social networking – he had little problem in ruling her out.

Martin sat up straight in his chair and his hopes went up too as he ticked off the features of the third missing woman against those of the body found in Coopers Field.

Mrs Daphne Mansfield, the woman on the missing persons file, had been reported missing by her sister less than two weeks ago.

Her physical description was practically a perfect match, apart from the fact that the height was five feet two. Martin wasn't too concerned about that, knowing that people are often wrong when estimating heights – even for someone they know very well. He also knew it to be a fact that women especially could lose up to a couple of inches off their adult height as they got older.

Mrs Mansfield was eighty-two at the time she was reported missing and Martin read the statement given by her sister at the time.

The statement was headed with the date and time it was given and recorded as being taken by PC Helen Cook-Watts. It read:

'I wish to report my sister, Mrs Daphne Mansfield, as missing. She came to stay with me a few weeks ago because she wanted to come back to Wales before she died. I don't think she was dying but that's what she said.

'She normally lives, if living is the word, in Doulon Bottiere, that's not far from Nantes in the Pays de la Loire area of France. Her daughter Charlotte actually lives in a smart suburb of Nantes but didn't want Daphne living with her and her husband – so they shipped my sister off to some converted chateau with dozens of other over-the-hill women to end her days.'

'She has very poor eyesight, you know, and can only get about with help on account of her being crippled with arthritis – it's a family thing, we all suffer from it and the only thing that makes my life bearable is that one day her precious Charlotte will be suffering the same pain.'

Martin looked up from the statement and grinned to himself. He could only assume that PC Cook-Watts had transcribed this statement from a taped interview, and he wondered how long it had taken. There was evidence from time to time of attempts to keep the statement relevant to the missing person although Martin suspected that Helen had been forced to hear most of the family history.

The sister making the report was named as one Miss Elsie Forrester, aged eighty-one, and her address was a street Martin recognised as being just off City Road in Cardiff.

He read, with some amusement, the rest of the statement that took up almost four pages, and then turned his attention to the fact sheet that was attached. This really grabbed his attention. Mrs Mansfield was probably the same age and height as the woman whose death they were investigating. She had severe visual and mobility problems, wore dentures, and had been reported missing just two weeks ago – it was all fitting very nicely.

What didn't fit were the last couple of paragraphs. It would appear that prior to the reported disappearance Mrs Mansfield's daughter and her husband had come to Cardiff and had tried to persuade Daphne Mansfield to return to France with them. According to Elsie they had argued and the couple had been very angry when she last saw them.

Elsie's statement went on to explain that she had rung her niece's home when she discovered Daphne's room to be almost empty the following day. The French housekeeper had answered the phone and told Elsie that M. et Mme Lefevre had called in that morning to collect some papers needed for taking Mme's mother back to Maison de Retraite. The maid apparently said that Mme Mansfield was sitting in the back of the car but did not get out as her legs were too stiff and in any event M. Lefevre was in a hurry.

The last part of the statement was in the format of a question and answer session with PC Cook-Watts asking the questions and Elsie Forrester responding.

Martin concluded that although Elsie had been told by the housekeeper that her sister had returned to France, she was unhappy with not being able to speak to Daphne and so reported her missing anyway. However, on the face of it, there was the likelihood that the woman had returned to France with her daughter and so could not be the body that was found this morning.

Martin walked around his office and stared up at the beautifully ornate Victorian ceiling. He willed the sunburst motif with its swirling bunches of grapes and flowers to provide him with inspiration, as he was sure it had done in the past.

It was possible that Mr and Mrs Lefevre had murdered Mrs Mansfield and dumped her body in Coopers Field before returning to France themselves. But the maid had seen Daphne in the back of the car, so it was hardly likely that they would have taken her back to France and then killed her and returned the body to Coopers Field. However, it was two weeks since they returned to France and anything could have happened in that time.

He told himself that there was still a chance that the woman found in Coopers Field was going to be identified as Daphne Mansfield, the sister reported missing just two weeks ago.

Her identification would make it easier for the team to find out what had happened to her since her disappearance. With any luck and a great deal of work that would lead to discovering how she had been killed, and if the Lefevres had indeed done the killing.

Martin was not happy with the number of variables and knew that his only option was to await forensic results and in particular DNA profiles. Daphne Mansfield's DNA was available to them because when she was reported missing by her sister PC Cook-Watts had taken a sample of hair from the brush that had been left in Daphne's room. If the murdered woman's DNA matched, then he and DS Pryor would be flying to France in an attempt to discover how anyone could be in two places at one time – not to mention being dead in Coopers Field and alive in France.

Some things added up, but lots of things didn't, and Martin found himself somewhat aimlessly pondering the mysteries of families. Surely the Lefevres had not committed murder – and if they had, what was the nudity and the strategically placed pile of clothes all about? It was most likely that Daphne Mansfield was safely settled back in the French equivalent of a nursing home, wasn't it?

Chapter Four

Matt caught up with Sgt Evans in the car park and they deliberately chose to drive to the Parkland Nursing Home in a marked police car. 'It's probably nothing,' explained Sgt Evans, who was in the driving seat. 'Lots of people expect the worst when a policeman in uniform knocks at their door, but this man's reaction was exceptional and we hadn't even gone there to see him.'

'Start at the beginning,' suggested Matt, who was getting a bit confused regarding who the man in question was and what he was doing at the nursing home.

'Well as you know, Mrs Linda Pattern, the woman who found the body this morning, was distraught, and at one time I thought she was going to collapse completely. Luckily for us a young woman noticed Mrs Pattern's condition and recognised it for what it was. She was in a state brought on through hyperventilation following a shock and not, as we thought, in a near-death condition as a result of a heart attack.'

'The young woman turned out to be Sarah Thomas, a nurse on her way to work, and within a few minutes she had the situation under control. She used a paper bag from her lunchbox and made Mrs Pattern breathe into it. We've been shown that trick at some of our first aid sessions.'

Matt nodded, as he too had attended the first aid training.

'The cheek of it was when Mrs Pattern complained to her Good Samaritan that the bag smelled of onions and she particularly dislikes onions, especially raw onions; how was that for gratitude!'

Matt grinned and shook his head. He knew better than to make any comment, as it didn't take much to get Sgt Evans wandering off on a tangent, and so Matt attempted to move the conversation on. 'I presume Sarah Thomas told you she worked at the Parkland Nursing Home and you went there to interview her.'

'Yes. I took PC Cook-Watts with me and we were met by a young care assistant called Maria. She wasn't in no way fazed at all by our presence, and went off in search of Sister Thomas, who she said was in the office. Maria went off quickly but I didn't see any point in waiting in the reception area so we followed her down the corridor and noticed her pass a man and a woman just before she got to the office.'

'I heard Maria telling Sr Thomas something about a body and that the police were there and obviously the man in the corridor had also heard these words. We saw him turn back towards the office and then he sort of staggered as if he was going to faint and when we got to him he really was as white as a ghost – not that I've ever seen a ghost.'

Evans stopped his account at that point and turned the police car into the small parking area just inside the gates of the nursing home. There was room for about ten cars at a push but one of the four cars already there was taking up enough space for two cars to park. This car immediately caught their attention but for Matt it was more than that and he positively drooled over the gleaming alloy wheels that effortlessly supported the silver metallic body. He was unable to resist looking through the windows and the pale grey leather interior did not disappoint.

'It's a Mercedes-Benz E500 Sport, and virtually brand new,' he told the sergeant. 'This car is a seriously expensive piece of motor. What wouldn't I give to get behind that wheel?'

Sgt Evans laughed out loud. 'I'd give anything to see the wife's face if I arrived home behind the wheel of that little beauty. She knows I've always had a longing for a sports car and would probably think I'd finally flipped and helped myself from the car showroom. As she controls all the money in our household she would most certainly know that even the wheels of that thing would break the bank.'

Matt took a sideways glance at Sgt Evans and adjusted his image of the Evans family. Everyone viewed the sergeant as a father figure and valued his work and life experience. Until now Matt had imagined that at home there would be a cuddly Mrs Evans, up to her elbows in flour and rolling out pastry for homemade pies. This didn't fit the picture he was now getting of a lean, mean accounting machine and he grinned as he thought that the truth was probably somewhere in the middle.

'Remind me of why we're here,' he suggested to Sgt Evans as they crunched over the gravel in the car park and made their way to the front door.

'Well, I've already taken a statement from Sr Thomas regarding her involvement in Coopers Field this morning so there's nothing more on that count. When I mentioned the incident with the gentleman in the corridor to DCI Phelps he suggested we speak to her about that. As I said before, it's probably nothing, but the man's behaviour was odd and the DCI probably just wants to put my mind at rest.'

The cheeky young face of Maria answered the doorbell and she beamed at Sgt Evans, remembering him from his earlier visit. Matt looked at her and thought that it could almost be worth being a resident here just to have such a ray of sunshine in attendance. He returned her smile, albeit somewhat less widely, and after introducing himself formally he asked if it was possible to speak to Sr Thomas.

'She's doing some dressings at the moment but if I tell her you're here I'm sure she will see you as soon as she can.'

'No rush,' said Matt. 'Tell her we just want to speak to her for a few minutes, but only when she has finished what she's doing.'

Maria led the visitors from the reception area down a corridor to a small room that was obviously used for visitors and asked them if they would like some tea or coffee. Realising they may have to wait a while Matt accepted her offer on behalf of both of them.

Maria all but skipped off, leaving the two men who were simultaneously aware that they were both grinning. It was Sgt Evans who fell into spontaneous laughter.

'She's a real tonic. It's almost impossible to look at her face without smiling. How old do you think she is?'

'Barely seventeen, I would have thought, and I would put her as even younger, but there's an age limit to working as a carer so she must be seventeen at least. You don't see many girls of her age with their hair tied back in bunches and no vestige of makeup.' Matt's thoughts moved to his twelve nieces, and in particular to the oldest ones aged between twelve and fifteen. They were well into make-up and fashion and often scared Uncle Matt with their level of sophistication. They seemed to be growing up far too quickly.

Sgt Evans was thumbing his way through some of the nursing home brochures that were on the central coffee table. 'Looks like a fair amount of poetic licence within these pages, but nothing actually libellous. I bet the owner paid well for these glossy photographs, but he missed a trick. Just one picture of the smiling Maria on the front cover would have seen potential clients beating a path to the door.'

Matt nodded in agreement and they both turned as the door opened and a tray of coffee was brought in, but not by Maria. Sr Thomas pushed aside some of the advertising material, deposited three cups of coffee on the table, and turned towards Sgt Evans.

'I didn't realise you intended making a return visit,' she said. 'I hope you haven't wasted your time because I really don't think I can tell you any more than I did this morning.'

Before Sgt Evans could respond DS Pryor did her the courtesy of showing her his official identification and explaining that their visit was not directly related to the body found in Coopers Field.

'So what is it?' asked Sr Thomas. 'Maria said it was me you wanted to see, so I naturally assumed it was in relation to this morning's episode. I'm not in any kind of trouble, am I?'

Matt rushed to reassure her. 'No, Sr Thomas, of course not, and in a way it's not something that directly involves you but something you may have witnessed.'

'Sounds intriguing, but as this is the last time today I am likely to get a break let's all sit down and drink our coffee – and will you please call me Sarah.'

'Happy on all counts, Sarah,' replied Matt. 'We shouldn't need to take up too much of your time, but I will let Sgt Evans explain why we are here.'

'You will remember that I came here this morning with PC Cook-Watts and we were let in, as now, by one of the care assistants, Maria. We told her that we wanted to speak to you and she was obviously expecting us and hurried off to find you. Rather than hang around in the reception area we followed her along the corridor towards your office.' Sgt Evans swallowed a mouthful of what just about passed for coffee and continued. 'She was way ahead of us and within view, but not quite within hearing distance. Almost as soon as she reached your office, a man and a woman

44

came out, and we held back as you seemed to be still carrying on a conversation with them. We don't know what was said but the man came out of your office followed by the woman and they walked down the corridor towards us.

'I heard Maria telling you that the police had arrived to speak to you about the body. I'm not sure if it was what she said or the sight of two police officers, but the man's face suddenly changed from a very angry red to a greyish-white, and his knees buckled. The woman held him up with the help of our PC, and then he seemed to gain some inner strength and shrugged himself free of both of them and made his way to the front door. As he passed me there was a very particular look on his face – a look I have seen many times before, a look that betrays a person when they have been caught out, a look that is a mixture of fear and guilt. Anyway that look left a lasting impression on me and when I got back to the station I mentioned the episode to DCI Phelps and he suggested a return visit to check out my concerns.'

Matt took up the conversation. 'You see, Sarah, Sgt Evans here is well-known to be able to smell trouble from fifty paces and we have in the past unearthed criminal activity not through the marvels of modern science but via the twitching of the cilia in his famous nose!'

They all laughed, and Sarah went on to say that she had not witnessed any of the activity in the corridor but remembered well the conversation leading up to it.

'Just to put you in the picture, the man and the woman you saw are Mr and Mrs Morris, the son-in-law and daughter of Colin James, one of our residents who sadly died last night. They were here to collect his belongings and a death certificate and I was getting wound up by Mr Morris, who never showed anything but contempt for Colin while he was alive but had come like a bat out of hell to benefit from his death.'

'I couldn't bear to look at either of them and so I turned my back on them and was about to get on with some reports when Maria knocked the door just as they were leaving. She had come to tell me the police were here to talk to me about the body and Mr Morris who was walking away from my office obviously overheard her and turned back to ask me what she was talking about.'

Sarah blushed slightly. 'To be honest I think I basically told him to mind his own business, and shut the office door – and that's when you must have come across him in the corridor.'

'That fits in,' Sgt Evans nodded. 'He'd heard Maria say that the police were here to talk to you about the body and then he saw us walking towards him – but why did he react the way he did? Is he a particularly sensitive man?'

Sarah, who was at that moment drinking the last of her coffee, almost choked on the sergeant's words. 'He's a maths teacher besotted with money and would probably have to ask the English teacher at his school if he even wanted to spell the word sensitive.'

'Look, it's been interesting talking to you, but I need to get back to work – and anyway, what has Mr Morris got to do with the body found in Coopers Field this morning?'

'Absolutely nothing, I'm certain,' replied Matt. 'However you would be surprised at the number of times the routine investigation of one crime leads to the uncovering of other wrongdoings. We won't keep you much longer but if you could tell us a bit more about Colin James that would be helpful.'

Sarah gave her visitors a potted history and surprised herself with the depth of her knowledge. It made her feel good to realise that she must have really talked to Colin during his time at Parkland, and she hoped he had enjoyed their chats as much as she had. She ended with the comments that she had already made to others about being concerned by his untimely end and DS Pryor picked up on this.

Sarah was quick to justify her comment. 'Oh, I'm not saying there was anything untoward about his death, Sgt Pryor – you must realise that many people come here at the end of their lives, when they are alone or their relatives can no longer cope. It's not unheard of for them to die within hours of getting here, and a number of our residents are only with us a few weeks.'

'On the other hand we have two ladies and one man who have each been here for more than ten years. They have no relatives that we know of and are people with sound financial backing, but they would probably have died years ago if they had been left to cope on their own.'

Matt interrupted gently. 'But from what you told us a few minutes ago you were surprised at the rate Mr James changed from being reasonably independent to passing away last night.'

'Yes, and I have had similar feelings when a few other residents have died, but there has never been anything that has really made me overly concerned.' Sr Thomas looked thoughtful as her mind had immediately jumped back to the death of Nancy Coleman. Now there was a lady whose death was unexpected – but treated by everyone as sad, not sinister.

'Look, Sarah, we are probably boxing at shadows here, but I don't want to leave things only half investigated so if you could cast your mind back to any deaths that on reflection took you by surprise we would like to know about them.'

Sarah looked at Matt and liked what she saw – he seemed like a decent bloke. He was not short in the looks department, and she found herself wishing she had at least straightened her unruly curls before coming to work that morning. Shaking her head to rid herself of these thoughts, she questioned Matt. 'So what are you asking exactly? Have there been residents who, in my view, have died unexpectedly – is that it?'

'Well I guess so,' replied Matt. 'We have no absolute reason for asking you to consider this it's just the remote possibility that things may not be exactly as they seem.'

It was obvious that Sarah was already raking through her memory and was realising its limitations. 'Right,' she said. 'If it's OK I'll ask Maria to help me, it's unlikely we'll ever get time to look at things here and if I ask for old records Mr Doster will have a fit.'

'Luckily Maria is coming to my place tonight as I'm helping her with her NVQs, and as she's been here for almost a year she'll be able to jog my memory.'

'Thank you for your help,' said Matt. 'As I said, it's probably nothing, but the boss, DCI Phelps, values the nose of Sgt Evans here and thinks it merits a look!'

As the three of them got to their feet the door actually burst open and a red-faced, angry-looking man glared at Sr Thomas.

'You are aware that I have asked to be informed immediately when anyone in an official capacity arrives at Parkland. Imagine my horror to hear from the cook that this is the second time today that we have been visited by the police. When exactly were you going to put me in the picture?'

Matt interrupted before the man, he guessed was the home's owner, could say anything else. 'Our presence has nothing whatsoever to do with the nursing home, and we are here simply because Sr Thomas was extremely helpful this morning. Please allow me to introduce myself, I am DS Pryor and this is Sgt Evans.'

Mr Cooper attempted to dominate the conversation but Matt was having none of it. He had taken an instant dislike to the man, and judging by the intimidating way her boss was glaring at Sr Thomas it was Matt's view that the man was a bully.

'On her way to work this morning Sr Thomas helped the police deal with a member of the public who had just had the unpleasant misfortune of finding a dead body in an area near Coopers Field. Her help was much appreciated and the only reason we are here is to talk to her about her involvement.'

By now almost purple with rage Mr Cooper managed to get a word in. 'Yes but that doesn't explain why you have been here twice in one day, not if it's just to gather a routine statement. It comes to something when I have to learn that the police are on my premises from a distraught man, just recently upset by the death of his dear father-in-law.'

It was as much as Sarah could do not to laugh out loud. Colin's son-in-law distraught and distressed by the passing of his wife's father – she didn't think so! What Sarah did think about was the fact that Mr William Morris had found it necessary to ring Mr Cooper about the earlier police visit. It really had freaked him out.

But that being the case, it was likely that the phone call would have been made straight away, so why had Mr Cooper taken several hours to track her down and interrogate her?

The owner of the nursing home answered her silent question as he blundered on. 'I should have been on the ferry by now, but the phone call I received persuaded me to turn around and make my way back to see what the hell was going on.'

'There was no need for you to go to such lengths,' suggested Matt. 'Surely a quick phone call to Sr Thomas would have put you in the picture and set your mind at rest.'

Sarah interjected. 'If you didn't want to speak to me there was always Mr Doster. According to Mr Morris, you had made arrangements for him to come in early to hand over Colin's death certificate – so you knew he was here.'

Now practically purple with frustration, Mr Cooper almost spat out a response to Sarah's suggestion. 'Doster is losing his marbles. I wouldn't trust him to tell me the time, his head is so full of rubbish.'

Sarah pricked up her ears at these comments and wondered if there had been a breakdown in the relationship between Parkland's owner and its administrator. Surely the jungle drums would have beat out that message if there was even a whisper of discord …

She was not a spiteful person, but Sarah was enjoying seeing this level of angst in someone who so frequently caused it in others.

'You do seem to have put yourself out considerably for what was after all just a routine visit from our officers earlier.' Matt smiled and appeared to make a joke but watched closely for the reaction. 'Unless of course you thought they had come to take you away for some unspeakable crime.'

Anthony Cooper desperately tried to mirror Matt's smile and join in with the joke, and in doing so came up with what he believed would be a reasonable response. 'Sorry, DS Pryor, the only thing I am guilty of is concern for my staff and the reason for my spontaneous return is to ensure them of my support.'

'Quite so,' replied Matt looking out of the corner of his eye at the look of absolute disgust and disbelief that had settled on Sarah's face. 'Anyway, you're here now, and our business is complete, so we'll be off – but only after thanking Sr Thomas once again for her help.'

Matt turned to Sarah and shook her hand and she was aware of what felt like a conspiratorial squeeze, but she couldn't be sure.

Mr Cooper opened the office door and ushered his unwelcome guests to the front door. 'Fabulous car in the car park,' remarked Matt as they were being let out. 'It's a Merc E500 isn't it – probably the car of my dreams. We thought it must belong to the owner of the home but as you weren't here when we arrived then you must have a very rich or very lucky employee.'

'You were right first time, Sergeant, it is my car. I left it here for the mechanic to pick it up for a brakes check but he obviously hasn't got around to it yet. Typical! The car that is now parked alongside it is my wife's car and that's the one I was driving this

49

morning. No crime in that, is there?'

Matt couldn't be bothered to answer and made his way towards the official car but couldn't help notice the one that was now parked alongside the Mercedes – another example from Matt's dream collection.

'I'm clearly in the wrong business,' said Matt as the heavy, functional wheels of the distinctively marked police car passed the 20-inch senta alloy wheels of the zircon blue Jaguar XK. He wondered what the P and the R stood for on the personalised number plate, guessing the C would be for Cooper. It wasn't possible to determine the year the car was manufactured without the original plates, but Matt thought it was about four years old.

So the Coopers had known quite serious money for some time – the sleek two-door convertible was still worth well over £25,000, and the value of the numberplates possibly exceeded that of the car. In all a pretty expensive package.

'Never seen the attraction of personalised numberplates,' muttered Sgt Evans. 'The wife considered getting a set as a birthday present for our daughter last year and we went on the internet to look for one that incorporated her name. When the prices came up on the screen we thought there had been a mistake and the decimal point was in the wrong place, but no, they were asking for thousands, even tens of thousands of pounds for some of them.'

Matt laughed and went on to say that he remembered hearing a couple of years ago about a single letter-zero-one set of plates being sold for £440,000. 'The only thing to say is that the value of the plates is likely to appreciate, while the car will be worth less from the minute it's driven from the showroom.'

Evans expressed his own views on what Matt had just told him. 'It's a topsy-turvy world and totally unfair that some men can, without having to think about it, toss away that sort of money for some fancy pieces of metal while others struggle to make ends meet. I can't bear to think about it, really, it's not good for my blood pressure and for sure there is nothing I can do about it, more's the pity.'

Matt looked at the man sitting in the driver's seat who suddenly seemed to have taken the cares of the world on his shoulders. The car joined the traffic moving along Cathedral Road and nothing more was said until they had passed through the city and were heading for Cardiff Bay.

The two men had seen a lot of the evil of the world during the past couple of years since Matt had joined Martin's team. Sgt Evans was able to add almost thirty years to Matt's total and must have witnessed more than anyone's fair share of human depravity. Somehow he had managed to keep a sense of decency and was one of the few officers who was respected by his seniors and actually liked by his subordinates. When asked how he managed to cope with whatever the job threw at him his answer was always the same.

He insisted that a life outside the force was the only way to survive, and that in his experience the officers who burn out are always the ones who live for the job and have no outside interest. For him it was Mrs Evans and his daughter, but they were only slightly above his passion for playing darts. John Evans could possibly have been a champion, but the unsociable hours of his job and those of a professional darts player often clashed and made his availability for set matches impossible.

But after a particularly horrendous day he was able to pick up his darts and imagine that in the space between the wires he needed to hit for a double-ten finish was the face of the evil he had been confronted with, and the point of his arrow flew at the target.

They passed Cardiff Castle, and Matt noticed that a large international coach was unloading its cargo: what looked like Japanese visitors seemingly all armed with cameras and capturing the images of the Victorian animal wall. Matt smiled as he realised that a few months ago he wouldn't have really noticed the subject of their interest, but his niece, Tia, had been involved with a school project looking at the building and restoration of Cardiff Castle. He now knew that there had originally been nine stone animals sculptured by Thomas Nicholls, and he could remember Tia telling him that there were two carvings of lions, a lioness, a wolf, and a hyena but for the moment he couldn't remember the other four.

There were now fifteen animal sculptures on the famous wall – the other six being the work of Alexander Carrick who added a pelican, an ant-eater, a pair of racoons, a leopard, a beaver, and a vulture to the wall when it was moved a few decades later – Matt couldn't quite recall the date. When he had brought his niece to the castle to take some photographs they had noticed quite a lot of damage to some of the animals and they had both agreed that it was sad to see them looking so neglected.

However just a week later a delighted Tia had skipped into Matt's kitchen and announced that the animals were going to be saved! No, she hadn't joined an animal liberation movement – she went on to tell Matt that a man from the castle had been at their school to listen to the presentation of their project. At the end he had told them that a lot of money was going to be spent this year in Bute Park and they were going to restore the animals to their former glory.

The castle was now well out of sight, as was the impressive collection of buildings around City Hall, and with the traffic being unusually light they were making good progress back to base.

'Hope that visit wasn't too much of a waste of your time,' Sgt Evans said to Matt. 'It was just that when I saw DCI Phelps on my return from the first visit to Parkland I had that Morris man locked into my head. I still think his reaction in the corridor was way out of the ordinary but I should have realised that the DCI was at the start of a murder investigation and could really do without this distraction.'

'We've only been gone just over an hour and who knows if that will turn out to be time well-spent. I think I will suggest to the DCI that an interview with Mr Morris is merited although I am not sure what peg we'll hang that interview on. Maybe just the benevolent Police Force checking on a good citizen they may have inadvertently distressed. Anyway, it will be interesting to see the outcome of Sr Thomas's deliberations.'

Sgt Evans gave Matt a wicked grin and couldn't resist a different interpretation of Matt's interest. 'It certainly gives you a good reason for a return visit to look into the dark green eyes of a very attractive young woman.'

'What!' retorted Matt. 'I can't say I noticed she was about five feet nine inches tall, weighed around a shapely ten stone, had naturally curly light brown hair, a lovely smile revealing perfectly even white teeth and, as you say, dark green eyes a man could get lost in. As I said, I hardly noticed.' Matt returned a grin of equally wicked proportions.

Chapter Five

Matt's initial thoughts were to make his way straight to Incident Room One, but as he got out of the squad car he checked the time and was surprised to see it was already twenty past one. The cheese omelette and mountain of toast he had eaten earlier had sustained him well, but now just the thought of it possibly being a mealtime led him in search of food.

Others had beat him to it and in one corner of the staff dining room, on a table set out for four people, were essentially two couples and he felt strangely reluctant to intrude. However as soon as Martin saw his sergeant walk through the door he waved and indicated to Matt that he should join them.

Matt decided on a slice of corned beef pie and got a generous helping from Iris, who also added an extra scoop of mashed potato alongside the vegetables. He didn't argue with her generosity, but he did make a mental note to himself that he would have to consider some new form of exercise now that he was no longer playing rugby. The waistbands of his trousers were definitely getting tighter, but as he loved his food he would have to think of a way of burning off the calories rather than restricting them.

Charlie was one of the four at the table but as she was in her wheelchair there was a vacant seat for Matt and he joined the group. 'Hope I'm not interrupting ...' Matt started to say when Charlie butted in.

'Happy to have anyone interrupt this bizarre conversation. We're sitting here considering why someone would be left in a field, obviously dead, stark naked, but with her clothes, including her shoes, strategically placed in a neat pile at her feet.'

Alex and Shelley laughed at the way Charlie not only set out the scenario verbally but also mimed it with her eyes and her arms. 'Sorry if I don't sound very respectful, but we have wandered far into the realms of fantasy trying to come up with an explanation and nothing makes any sense.'

Martin took up the conversation. 'I thought it would be useful to get some independent ideas on the naked body and the set of clothes but Charlie and Shelley have made no more sense of it than I have.'

They continued knocking ideas around while Matt made short work of his lunch, and then the group broke up.

Charlie whizzed her wheelchair around and pointed it in the direction of the door and at the same time Shelley got to her feet. 'If we think of anything more realistic than aliens who may or may not be being pursued by Captain Jack Harkness from *Torchwood*, we'll let you know,' she said as she followed Charlie towards the door and left the three men considering whether to grab a coffee or get back to work.

They compromised and Martin and Matt made their way to Incident Room One, leaving Alex to pick up three cardboard cups of coffee from the vending machine and follow them.

The various teams had been hard at work and the large room was now looking exactly as it always did at the start of a murder investigation. A whole display panel had now been taken up with images of the body and the setting in which it had been found. Normally this would have been labelled the crime scene but as yet it was not clear whether the woman had been killed there or the crime committed elsewhere and the body dumped at a later stage. Saying the body was dumped was strangely inappropriate given that the woman's body had been left very neatly lying on her back with her arms at her side and her legs out straight.

The images went from the top to the bottom of the panel with the final pictures showing the area where the body had been. This must have been taken after Alex and his team had caught the water from the surrounding area in the plastic sheets. It now showed an area beneath the tree with nothing more than a light impression on the grassy patch – no sign of blood and looking at it no one would guess that a murdered body had just vacated the spot.

Relevant post mortem photographs were attached to the second board and Martin skipped over these – not just because he actually attended the PM but because he knew that Prof. Moore would cover the findings in his part of the briefing session.

Matt had, as promised, notified the relevant people of the 2 p.m. briefing session and the room was now filling up.

Although in general there was a good working relationship between CID and uniformed officers, Martin noticed that, as always, individuals sat within their own disciplines. The only exception today was PC Cook-Watts who had joined a table with two of the detective constables. This was no surprise as Martin was aware that on Friday, she had an interview that if successful would see her transferred to CID. He obviously knew about the interview as he was to be one of the panel members with the chairman being Superintendent Bryant. Martin would be totally supporting Helen's transfer but he would need to be careful, as he and the Superintendent had not always seen eye to eye in the past and his superior officer could be difficult, just for the sheer hell of it. Still, that worry was for Friday and for now it was back to the business in hand.

As Martin called the briefing to order, PC Cook-Watts slid across to join her current colleagues knowing that Sgt Evans was likely to ask for her input at the start of the session.

'As you will all be aware, the extended team in this room has been charged with the responsibility of investigating the circumstances surrounding the discovery of a body on the edge of Coopers Field this morning. I'm not going to say any more at this point as I would prefer to let the various factions here tell it as it happened. I normally encourage everyone to ask questions as and when they come to you but this time I think we should leave questions and discussions until the end. Let's start with Sgt Evans.'

Sgt Evans got to his feet and confirmed the date and time the initial report of the finding of a body had been logged. Martin moved to his whiteboard and checked the information he had written under the column headed 'Absolute Facts'.

'PC Cook-Watts and PC Davies were the first on the scene, and when I arrived with PC Francis they were having a hell of a time trying to calm down Mrs Pattern, the woman whose dog had found the body and who had made the call to us. As luck would have it, a nurse was on her way to work and helped with Mrs Pattern. I have since interviewed the nurse, one Sarah Thomas, who is unable to add anything to what we already know about this part of the investigation.'

Sgt Evans looked towards Martin and the DCI nodded his head. They had spoken briefly before the meeting and agreed that any concerns regarding possible untoward behaviour at the nursing home should not be brought up in this session. It was unlikely that their concerns in that direction would be well founded and Martin was anxious to keep minds focused on the actual case. He would talk to Matt and Sgt Evans about their visit to Parkland in more detail later.

'PC Cook-Watts got the story of the finding of the body from Mrs Pattern so I will let her relate it to you.'

Helen Cook-Watts got to her feet, and as she did so it crossed her mind that her existing work team, one member of her forthcoming interview panel, and what she hoped would be her new set of colleagues were all looking in her direction. Her stomach did a bit of a wobble.

She would keep it simple and avoid the unrelated outpourings of Mrs Pattern, who once she had recovered from the initial shock, had gone on and on about every experience she had ever had when exercising her dog.

'It would appear that Mrs Pattern is a regular to this part of Bute Park and leaves her home just off Westgate Street around 7 a.m. each day to walk the dog. She almost always takes the same route and the dog enjoys a good run in the field. For the past few weeks she had avoided the grassy areas because they had been waterlogged and she has thrown the dog's ball near to the pathways. However, this morning a couple of young lads took an interest in the dog and she was happy to let them play the usual game of throw and fetch the ball.'

'Happy that was, until one of the boys mischievously threw the ball, hurling it with all his might, so that it went well over the area of soaking wet grass and into the undergrowth surrounding the trees.'

'The dog took off but instead of bringing the ball back, Mrs Pattern says she could see him going in and out of the area at the base of one of the larger trees. She says he was barking madly, and that although she called repeatedly the dog was paying no attention to her. Finally she had to wade through inches of mud and water to get to him.'

'The first thing she noticed was what she thought was a pile of old clothes, and the dog dropped a shoe at her feet before dragging a garment from the pile and pulling it by the sleeve. The next thing she remembers is taking hold of the dog's collar and pulling him away, and it was when she bent down to do this that she saw the body.'

'She told me she was almost sick on the spot, and that's not surprising, but she managed to drag the dog away and dialled 999 on her mobile phone – and we were on the scene less than ten minutes later.'

Sgt Evans took up the story, and described the exact location of the body and the manner in which the crime scene had been secured prior to the arrival of SOCO and Professor Moore.

'Seems like an appropriate place for you to tell us what you found and what, if anything, you have been able to discover since your return.' Martin addressed Alex who had already got to his feet and signalled to Charlie to get the technology operating.

The first images that flashed across the screen showed the tranquil setting of a lush green field with, to one side, a border of well-established trees. The lens scanned towards the trees and zoomed in on the largest one, tracing the features of the branches, leaves, and bark and panning down towards the area of bracken and shrubbery at the base.

Here the wonders of nature came to an abrupt end, and what was likely to be the ugly handiwork of mankind came into sharp focus.

While guiding everyone through the pictures of the scene, Alex described what he and his team had done and the order in which the tasks had been carried out. From time to time he deferred to Prof. Moore, especially when it came to the issue of whether or not the body was that of a man or a woman.

'We were unable to decide on the sex of the victim but the Professor thought it was a woman, and I am sure he will tell us why in a moment.'

'Not thought, Mr Griffiths,' interrupted the professor. 'I didn't think it was a woman. I knew it was a woman. Thinking and knowing are two different things.'

Alex shrugged his shoulders and turned his attention to the images that had now appeared and knew that the next twelve pictures were all related to the clothes that had been found. First of all there was a clear image of the whole scene with the clothes in the position the police had found them.

Martin interrupted at this point. 'It is important to remember that although this is the position in which we found the clothes it is not how they were before the dog found them. I believe they were in a neat pile with the shoes possibly on the top. Heaven only knows if there is any significance in that, but it is critical that we read the crime scene correctly.'

Alex continued. 'As you can see, a single sheet of paper was found amongst the folded clothes and I will now go on to tell you what we have discovered about the paper and the clothes following our initial examination.'

An image of one brown shoe appeared, and Alex explained that this was the one the dog had dropped at Mrs Pattern's feet. 'There are traces of the dog's saliva on this shoe and on the other one that will be shown next, and also on one of the sleeves of the jacket. Apart from that the only thing on any of the clothes is what you would expect to discover, given where they were found. So we have rainwater and pieces of the local vegetation – nothing else.'

'We have analysed the fabrics and there is not a trace of washing powder or fabric softener in any of the fibres and the tread on the shoes is as one would expect on a brand new pair. Consequently we have come to the conclusion that all these clothes, including the shoes, have never been worn!'

Martin pricked up his ears and his mind started whirling in yet a different direction, and he had to confess that he would never have considered such a possibility. He had assumed that the clothes would have for some reason been taken off the dead woman either before or after she was killed.

'The shoes, as you can see, are plain brown sensible shoes with a very low heel and Velcro front lap-over fastening. Apart from being brand new, they have one other thing in common with the rest of the clothes: they were all bought in the same shop. Well at least that is a strong possibility, as they all bear the M&S label. Of course they could have been bought in different branches of Marks and Spencer but given that they are all new and seem to come as a package the one-store purchase seems most likely.'

Martin had positioned himself at the side of the whiteboard and was pleased to be adding a few snippets to his 'Absolute Facts'

58

column, even though at this stage they were random words with very little meaning.

'Let's take a closer look at the items of clothing,' urged Alex. 'The shoes are a size four and the clothes are all bought to fit a women's size ten, and as I understand it that is a petite size.'

There were nods at this from most of the women in the room and a few comments such as 'I wish!' and 'Three sizes down from me'.

For the second time Martin interrupted. 'So although this set of clothes has never been worn by the victim, or anyone else for that matter, she could have bought them or they could have been bought specifically for her.'

'I guess so,' replied Alex. 'As you have just mentioned a set of clothes, it leads me on to something that is missing from a complete set. We have brown sensible shoes, heavy fawn-coloured tights, plain cream cotton knickers, a wool mix black and brown checked skirt, a high-neck lightweight sweater, and the jacket that was pulled off the pile by the dog. The jacket is of the same design as the skirt so may well have been bought as a suit.'

'What about the bra?' Charlie asked. 'Is that the missing item?'

Alex smiled at his wife and took in a picture that he was grateful that no one else in the room would be imagining. Charlie was well-endowed and it amused Alex that the first garment she reached for in the morning was always a bra – laughingly suggesting that her boobs had a will of their own without one! He kept his own thoughts as well in control as her bra kept her when he replied. 'Yes, that appears to be the missing item, at least it is in terms of completing the normal range of clothing for a woman.'

Some general discussion ran around the room and Martin let it continue for a few moments before asking Alex to continue.

'We thought we had struck gold when DS Pryor spotted a piece of paper amongst the folded garments but we didn't remove it at the site and it appeared to be just a blank sheet of A5. Unfortunately it didn't turn out to be a note explaining the circumstances surrounding the demise of the victim. However when we got things back to the laboratory it did turn out to be a very useful piece of evidence.'

Pointing to the screen, he demonstrated how at the crime scene the clothes had been carefully lifted back to photograph the paper in-situ but not far enough to get the whole of the paper in the frame. He continued. 'We were able to painstakingly remove the paper when we got everything back to the laboratory.' Behind it and attached to the top right hand corner by a now slightly rusty staple was a till receipt.

'At some point there had been writing on the piece of paper we had first noticed, but the ink from that had seeped through onto the till receipt making that item difficult, but not impossible, to read. It has also been possible by extreme enhancement to make out some of the words that were originally on what we thought was a blank piece of paper. The DCI joined us earlier to consider these findings and may have some conclusions to share with us all.'

'Well,' said Martin. 'My part in this piece of the jigsaw was made easy thanks to Alex and his team, and I believe what we have here is a list that someone has made out for the purchase of these items of clothing. It is possible the list was taken to the shop and the items purchased, but in that event I suspect the purchaser would have kept the original list. The only scenario I can think of where a customer's list is attached to the till receipt is one where a member of the store's staff has been asked to aid the shopper. In which case, it could have been the victim who made the purchases, because as we will hear from Professor Moore she probably had very limited mobility.'

'Off you go, Alex. I am standing here marker-pen in hand to write down the details of that till receipt – facts I believe will be crucial to solving this mystery.'

Alex grinned. It was typical of Martin to allow him to be the bearer of vital information, and without hesitation he launched into a commentary of his team's findings.

'Thanks to modern technology the amount of information we get on our receipts is phenomenal, as you can see from the computer-enhanced version of our original find. We have the date and the time of the purchases, and of course an itemised cost of each thing bought and the total cost. Although the actual cost is probably not significant, what is relevant is the fact that the bill totalled £268.98 and was paid for using a Mastercard.

'We'll be able to get full details of the owner of that credit card and I have already put in a request for that information. As I just said we know the time and date of the purchases and we can also see that the transaction took place at the Culverhouse Cross branch of M&S.

'That's all I have for the moment, but needless to say we have taken all sorts of samples from the area surrounding the discovery and I know the professor has things to add, so I will hand over to him.'

There was nothing Professor Moore liked better than enthralling an audience with the wonders of pathology, but he had just taken a phone call and appeared somewhat distracted as he got to his feet. 'So sorry, ladies and gentlemen,' he began. 'That was a call that requires an urgent response and so I am going to have to give you just the bare facts with none of the usual elaboration.'

'The woman was around eighty years of age, had very poor eyesight, and due to advanced osteoarthritis would have found movement difficult. She has borne children, at least one with the aid of a Caesarean section, and taking account of her height and her weight I would say that if you put the clothes described by Mr Griffiths on this body, they would be a perfect fit.'

'Her bones were brittle and on the left hand side of her skull is an almost perfectly round injury that in my view caused her death – there is nothing else in the PM finding that would have been directly responsible. She ...' The professor's sentence was cut short by the flashing and vibrating of his phone on the table in front of him. He looked at the incoming caller identification and then across at Martin. 'My apologies, DCI Phelps – I really do need to be somewhere else, but the full report of the PM is being completed by Mrs Williams and is probably even now ready to be picked up.'

Martin simply nodded as Moore left the room, but was left with the question of what could have called him away, with no apparent warning. It was quite out of character and Martin found himself hoping that it was just the Prof's profession that was calling him to more macabre business, and not a personal problem.

Having settled themselves down to a lengthy session surrounding the findings of the post-mortem the room was now at odds with the proceedings and Martin struggled to get everyone's attention back on track.

'DS Pryor and I were there for most of the PM examination and so will probably be able to answer any questions. The task now is to follow up on the information we have uncovered and ensure that nothing is missed.

'During the PM the Prof talked about the difficulty this lady would have had with walking and asked whether or not some sort of walking aid had been found. He also asked if there had been any glasses found in the clothes or near the body, as she would have been almost blind without them. It's extremely likely that the woman wore dentures but they haven't been found either. Up to now we have found nothing other than the clothes.'

Martin turned towards Sgt Evans and asked if anything else had come to light.

'Nothing at all so far,' was the reply. 'We have extended the area we are searching but have absolutely nothing to report. Is there anything else uniform can help with?'

'Reluctantly I have to say that there's nothing I can think of at the moment, so if you all have other things to do it just leaves me to thank you for your help. I will let you know of any progress.' Martin looked around for Matt as the room almost cleared, leaving just Alex who was also preparing to leave.

'If you're looking for Matt, he's just nipped out to get you both some coffee,' said Alex. 'Unless there's anything in particular you require I want to get back to see how things are going with some of the tests we've set up.'

'That's fine with me,' replied Martin. 'I'm just going to stay here and take in all the information we've accrued so far and hopefully I will be able to prioritise the things that need to be done next.'

By the time Matt returned with the coffee, Martin had made a list of the things he wanted tackled by himself and his team, and had posed three questions that needed to be answered. Top of his to do list was an interview with Mrs Pattern. He had no reason to think she would be able to tell them anything other what she had already said to Helen Cook-Watts, but she was to a certain extent yet another victim in this crime.

She was just an ordinary member of the public, doing ordinary things, when she had witnessed a sight quite likely to give her nightmares for the foreseeable future. Martin believed it was his duty to personally call on her and thank her for her assistance and ensure she was being well supported. It wouldn't take long, and he would ask Helen to go with him, as she would be a face already known to Mrs Pattern.

The next thing wouldn't even require his moving from the building, as it concerned the urgent chasing up of the details of that Mastercard. Martin knew, and quite rightly, that even the Police Force had to jump through a number of hoops before information could be released. He would be surprised if Alex had been able to get the information they needed and the card company would be totally within their rights under the Data Protection Act to protect the details of their client – even if he or she was part of a murder enquiry. But with the right checks and balances the information would be made available.

The third thing he had committed himself to was a re-check of that local missing persons list, or specifically a more detailed look at Mrs Daphne Mansfield. There were lots of things about her that fitted the dead woman, but there was of course the slightly tricky probability that she was alive and living in France. If he visited Miss Forrester, it would demonstrate, if nothing more, that public concerns about missing persons were treated seriously and by such a senior officer.

Here again he would have liked to take Helen Cook-Watts along, as she had seen Elsie Forrester when she reported her sister missing. However, it occurred to him that using her too much may not look good this near to her interview – one in which he could have a deciding vote if more than one candidate was in the running. He juggled things around in his mind and decided it would be Matt to go with him to see Mrs Pattern, and Helen to pick up where she had left off with Miss Forrester.

Martin looked at the questions he had written on the whiteboard and then turned his head as Matt came in with two cups of coffee and an explanation as to why he had taken so long to get them.

'I got cornered by Superintendent Bryant, who has obviously heard about the body in Coopers Field and wanted an update. He's keen that we hold a press conference later today and didn't seem too impressed when I said that we were thinking a simple press statement would be more appropriate until more information is known.'

'What he actually said was, "Surely, Sergeant, you are aware that the public have a right to be given timely and accurate information when something like this happens on their doorstep. We ignore the public at our peril, and any good detective will tell you that information received from the public has solved many a complex crime. Please pass on my concerns." I think that was it.'

Matt was a first-class mimic and had the voice and facial expressions of the Super off to a T. Martin wondered how close Matt came to accurately impersonating him when he was out of earshot!

'Just what I didn't want to hear,' Martin sighed. 'I think I will still duck out of it for today and get the statement out with a view to meeting the press head on – say tomorrow lunchtime. With any luck by then we will be that much nearer to at least having the body identified, and that should take us one step nearer to the murderer.'

Looking back at the questions he had set out Martin fired the first one at his sergeant. 'How did the body get into Bute Park – how many entrances are there?'

Matt rubbed the side of his face and ran his mind over what he has made it his business to find out about the area. 'Well, there's the entrance from Sophia Gardens, over the bridge – the way we went this morning. I believe there are other entrances, but I can only visualise the one that comes from somewhere on or near North Road and the one shoppers usually take when parking in Sophia Gardens and heading for town.'

'We could benefit from taking a good walk around the area,' suggested Martin. 'As well as there being entrances for vehicles and pedestrians there is also access by water. I can't say I've ever paid much attention to the set-up but I know there is a waterbus stop somewhere along the Taff, and I'd like to look at where it is in relation to where the body was found.'

'My precise knowledge of the area is no better than yours,' Matt added, 'and I don't think I have the answer to your question on access, but we have requested an up-to-date map from Cardiff Council.'

Both men looked at the whiteboard where Martin had written his second question. Was she dead or alive when she arrived at Bute Park?

Suddenly realising his mistake, Martin picked up a marker pen and drew an arrow from the second question, placing its point just above the first. 'I've put the cart before the horse there,' he explained to Matt. 'Our first priority is to find out if she arrived in the park dead or alive, as that could make the world of difference regarding how she got there.'

Matt nodded. 'Judging from what we have heard from Alex, my money is on her being killed somewhere else and her body being taken to where it was found by Mrs Pattern. Whoever the dead woman is, she would have been easy enough for most men to lift single-handed, so it would have been possible for her to be carried quite a distance – but surely someone would have seen a body being carried through a public park!'

'I'm calling it a day,' concluded Martin. 'There's a café just over the bridge we crossed this morning, and I noticed they sell breakfast baguettes, so meet me there at half eight tomorrow.'

Chapter Six

Sarah was expecting her intercom buzzer to sound but nevertheless it made her jump, as always. She was pottering around her kitchen, putting the finishing touches to the evening meal she had prepared for herself and Maria, and needed to wash her hands, before picking up her end of the speaker. Before she got to it the buzzer struck again and Sarah snatched it out of its cradle, pressed the door release button, and shouted into the mouthpiece. 'Have patience, Maria, I was on my way! The front door's open now, and my door is on the latch, so come straight through.'

Having heard the sound of the front door being unlocked and Maria closing it behind her, Sarah returned to the kitchen to tackle the cheese sauce. She was a reasonably good cook – perhaps not up to the standard of *Masterchef*, but she prided herself in the fact that, for the majority of the time, she cooked from scratch rather than resorting to ready meals.

For the past nine months she had been helping Maria get some National Vocational Qualifications and found it hard to decide who had been the most delighted when Maria had flown through Level 1 and was now well along the road to obtaining NVQ Level 2. She remembered the first session that they had organised in Sarah's home, and how it had ended in tears, but not because they had fallen out – in fact, quite the opposite.

During their time together at Parkland, Sarah had learned very little about Maria, and now as she thought back she realised that the sum total of everything she had known then was that Maria was the oldest child and had two brothers and a sister. She recognised Maria as one of those people who manage to learn a lot about everyone else but who gave away very little about herself, and smiled as she realised that the recognition was a bit like looking in the mirror.

What had first impressed Sarah was the way Maria interacted with the residents. She had a way of anticipating their requirements, often before they did themselves. They had only been working together for a couple of weeks when Sarah asked Maria if she had ever considered applying to do a nursing degree.

The reaction from Maria had been totally unexpected, and it was the one and only time that Sarah had ever seen Maria angry. She had thrown down the shoes she was about to put on one of the elderly gentlemen and rushed out of his room, slamming that door and every other door that she passed through on her way to the front entrance.

Half an hour later, after searching the nursing home, Sarah found Maria sitting on the bench outside the front door with her head in her hands. That was when, within a matter of ten minutes and between bursts of sobbing, Sarah had got to know more about Maria's life, and in particular her dreams, than probably any other living soul had done before.

Maria had gone to Sarah's flat that same evening and from then on the sessions had become a weekly occurrence. It transpired that Sarah had touched a raw nerve when she had asked about nurse training because it was the one thing that Maria wanted. She had not seen her mother since she was nine years old and her memories were not good. Maria could recall the time when her mother stayed in bed most of the day and constantly smelled of alcohol and tobacco. Her own father had long since gone and her mother was with a more often than not out-of-work labourer. They had produced a half-sister for Maria, followed by twin boys, and even before Maria had reached her tenth birthday it was she who was the mother figure to the youngsters.

Needless to say, her education was greatly affected, and Maria spent more time at home tending to the needs of her family than she did in school – and the situation got even worse when her mother finally left, apparently to move to London with someone she had met in the local off-license.

Although Maria described the time when her mother left as horrendous, she admitted that in some ways it was the best thing that could have happened, maybe not for her but at least for the rest of the family. Tony, her stepfather, with the threat of Social Services taking his family into care, managed to pull himself together and miraculously, given the general job shortage, got himself some steady employment. The hours were long and the pay not brilliant, but it was work, and he stuck at it as never before.

Maria was most of the time late for school as she had to take her brothers and sisters to their school first and if one of them was ill then she had to stay at home with them. The education officials wrote several letters and paid a few visits to see Tony, and always after these visits there was a short period when Maria's school attendance improved – but the improvement, because of the underlying situation, could never be maintained.

Even when Maria did turn up for her lessons she was far too tired to absorb any pearls of wisdom, which was not surprising given that before getting there she would have done what many people would consider to be a day's work. Consequently she had left school at the earliest opportunity, and with nothing to show that she had ever been a pupil. As the twins had come down with chickenpox at the time her classmates were sitting their GCSE examinations, Maria hadn't been sitting pen poised to answer the questions on the maths paper – she had been at home dabbing on the calamine lotion.

Sarah thought it was truly amazing that Maria had turned out the way she had, and told her so on that first visit. It was those kind words that had reduced Maria to tears. Quite unused to anyone praising her, Maria had dissolved into tears for the second time that day and in the evening it was as if a dam had burst. Sarah thought the emotions had never dared to escape before, and she had not seen Maria cry before or since that day. She believed that in just those few sessions of release Maria had washed away years of pain and resentment and had then started, for the first time, to put herself and her own hopes and aspirations just that little bit ahead of the family her mother had left her to nurture.

'Something smells good,' said Maria, as she hung her shoulder bag on one of the four wooden chairs grouped around the matching dining table. 'I love coming here, it's so quiet – do you need any help? What are you cooking? Do you want me to get my books out or are we eating first?'

'Why ask one question when you can ask three?' laughed Sarah. 'You can set the table as food is just about ready. I've just fried some mushrooms, bacon, and garlic in a knob of butter, cooked some penne pasta, and I'm mixing everything into the cheese sauce – it's simple but tasty, and I've got a bowl of chopped peppers and tomatoes to go with it and help lift our levels of antioxidants. I haven't stocked up the wine cellar recently but there are a few cans of Strongbow in the fridge if you want.'

Within minutes they had sorted out the preliminaries and were tucking in to what turned out to be a very tasty meal, and it was not until she had almost finished eating that Maria picked up her glass of cider.

'He was quite dishy, wasn't he?' she smiled. 'It's a pity Mr Cooper had to come back and spoil your cosy chat.'

Sarah realised immediately that Maria was talking about DS Pryor, and returned Maria's smile. 'I won't disagree with you on your first point but we were hardly having an intimate tête-à-tête: don't forget, there were three of us in the room.'

'Oh yes, the lovely Sgt Evans,' giggled Maria. 'He's my idea of a perfect dad. I bet he comes over all strict to his children, if he has any, but is like a big marshmallow inside.'

They both laughed at the thought of Sgt Evans turning into marshmallow-man, but then Sarah pushed her plate to one side and went into the bedroom she used as a sort of study, coming back a minute or so later with a small notebook.

'I know you're here so that we can go through the last set of questions you need to complete your coursework, but contrary to what everyone thinks the police didn't return to Parkland in relation to the body in the field and they've asked me to help them look into any recent and unexpected deaths in the home.'

Maria sat bolt upright in her seat and Sarah could see her mind and her imagination not just going into overdrive but shooting off the scale. 'Why?' Maria asked and then added. 'Do they think the body came from Parkland? How long had the person been dead? Was it a man or a woman? Were they murdered or what?'

Sarah shook her head. 'The police didn't brief me in any detail, but in answer to your last question I heard on the news just before you arrived that the body found in Coopers Field was that of a woman aged about eighty, and that the police are treating the death as suspicious.'

'But I still don't get the link with Parkland –' Maria started, but Sarah interrupted.

'They were keen to tell me that they didn't believe there was a connection and that their second visit was only because during his initial visit to Parkland, to get my statement, your Sgt Evans had been puzzled by what he called an "overreaction" to their presence. Do you remember you let the sergeant and a PC in, and came ahead of them to my office?'

Maria nodded and said, 'Yes, I got there just as Mr and Mrs Morris were leaving, and I told you the police were there to see you about the body.'

'That's it exactly,' replied Sarah. 'As you know, Mr Morris turned back to ask what you meant, but I didn't see his behaviour in the corridor. Apparently Sgt Evans had a gut feeling that the reaction of Mr Morris, to you relaying the message that the police wanted to speak to me about the body, was out of all proportion to the situation. He couldn't really explain why, but Sgt Evans was convinced that there was something more behind the reaction than just a possible phobia of policemen, and mentioned it to one of the CID Officers. So we had the pleasure of a return visit from Sgt Evans and the second time he was accompanied by DS Pryor.'

'What sort of things did they ask you?' prompted Maria.

'Well, I explained to them why Mr and Mrs Morris were at Parkland, and probably showed my disgust at the fact that the couple were never around when Colin was alive but had arrived post-haste for his belongings and the death certificate. Then they asked me about Colin, and I found myself voicing the concerns I have had regarding how quickly he went downhill, but explaining that there was nothing I could put my finger on and that I was definitely not suggesting anything untoward.'

'So that was it?' said Maria, sounding a bit disappointed.

'Well, I thought so,' Sarah said. 'Then Matt, that's the detective, asked if there had been any other occasions when I'd experienced similar and possibly equally unsubstantiated concerns. I tried to explain that by the very fact that most of our residents are elderly and often infirm, there is a likelihood of us having frequent deaths and the worst day I could remember was when we had three within six hours. However as we spoke, the person who jumped into my mind was Nancy Coleman. Do you remember her, Maria? I'm not even familiar with the fashion designers of today, so when Nancy spoke about people she had worked with in Paris and Milan in the 1950s I was at a complete loss.'

'Do I remember her?' replied Maria. 'I loved her, and the stories she told about her life in the fashion world were fantastic. She obviously made a heap of money, and some of the rings she wore were apparently very valuable. I remember her telling me that one in particular – it was a ruby set in a plain gold setting – had been given to her by a male member of the Royal Family.'

'That doesn't surprise me,' said Sarah. 'The photographs she had of herself at the height of her success showed a beautiful woman always surrounded by friends, and most of them men friends. I'm trying to remember how she came to be placed in Parkland.'

Maria remembered. 'Her sister was her only living relative and she was many years younger than Nancy and totally unprepared to look after her sister when she became ill – but I can't remember exactly what was wrong with Nancy.' Maria got to her feet and started to clear the table as Sarah was thumbing through the notebook she had brought from the other room.

'Leave that,' said Sarah. 'I can do it later, but as you're on your feet you can get the last can of cider from the fridge and we'll share it.'

'Here, I've found her,' shouted Sarah to Maria who was returning from the kitchen with not one but two cans of cider, having found a second can hiding behind a large carton of orange juice.

'It's six months since Nancy died – I would have thought it was longer than that but no, I've actually written down the date and time of her death. You're right to remember that she only had one sister, but the sister had a husband and they had two daughters.

'Apparently, when Nancy was diagnosed with dementia, the daughters wanted her moved into a home as quickly as possible because she embarrassed them in front of their friends whenever she was around, and none of the family ever visited her. It's all coming back to me now. The only time I ever saw Nancy's sister was when she and her husband came to see Mr Cooper and that was one evening when I was on a late shift.

'I remember the date because I should have been doing a short early shift as it was the day before my holidays, but Joanne called in sick and I had to stay because there was no one else to replace her. When I came back from my holidays Nancy was already dead, apparently from pneumonia.'

'I was there when she died,' said Maria. 'Dr Shaw was around at the time and had also seen her the day before, so everything was done that could be done, but she got worse overnight and died just after my shift started in the morning.'

'I remember looking for her case notes when I got back from my holidays,' said Sarah. 'I certainly hadn't expected her to die, and out of curiosity I just wanted to see exactly what had happened. However, I couldn't find them – and then other things took over and I haven't really thought any more about it until now.'

'I told the police that I would think back to see if there are any deaths that to me weren't really expected, and as I said Nancy was the first one I thought of – are there any that you can bring to mind?'

Seeing Sarah leafing through her notebook prompted Maria to delve into her handbag and retrieve a similar book, one used for almost the same purpose. Sarah's book contained more about medical conditions and treatments, while Maria's had notes about the personal care needed for the residents but both women had recorded their own comments on things like new admissions and deaths.

'Does your notebook take you back as far as Nancy's death?' asked Sarah, and Maria replied that she had started the current book about ten days before that date and was almost ready to start a new book.

'OK,' said Sarah. 'Well, I suggest that we independently look through our books and write down the names of anyone whose death, on reflection, was either earlier than expected or completely unexpected.'

For almost an hour both the women flicked backwards and forwards through the pages of their books and scribbled some details on the paper in front of them. On Maria's page there were simply the names of a number of people and a couple of comments and question marks but Sarah wrote copious notes alongside each of the names she had written. As she did so her face became more and more troubled and it was Maria who broke the silence and suggested they compare notes.

'I wish those policemen, even the gorgeous one, hadn't decided on a return visit to Parkland,' was Sarah's first response. 'We wouldn't be sitting here looking for probably non-existent skeletons in the cupboard, and I wouldn't be wondering if there have been occasions when I should have asked more questions. Still we are here and we are considering possible problems, so what names do you have?'

'I didn't realise how many deaths we've had over the past six months, but in most of the cases the resident who died had been very ill and the relatives and staff had all been expecting the death. In fact, in a number of cases the person took much longer to die than anyone would have guessed – but that's not the issue we are looking at. I have seven names on my list but it looks as if you have a lot more.' As she spoke Maria looked over at the couple of pages that Sarah had in front of her and attempted to compare the simple list of seven names she had with what Sarah had written.

'On the contrary,' replied Sarah. 'That's actually one more name than I've got – it's just that I've scribbled a lot more facts and figures about each of the residents I've identified. The interesting thing now will be to compare the two lists, as in theory we could be looking at anything between seven and thirteen names.'

'Yes, I see what you mean, so let's see how many names we have the same,' said Maria. 'The next death I have after Nancy is George Perkins. That wasn't something I expected at the time.'

'Snap,' said Sarah. 'He's the next name on my list too, and I've racked my brains trying to remember anything at all about him. All I can do is mentally place him in the garden, on a particular Thursday evening, and waving to him as I left for home. It was the beginning of March and I'd booked a long weekend off to visit a friend of mine who lives in Weston-Super-Mare. Because I wanted to travel that evening, Eva Grey, who had only joined us a few weeks before, agreed to start her night shift early and so I was leaving at about seven.'

'It had been a nice day and looked set well, weather wise, for my weekend but it was getting quite dark and certainly not warm. I called over to George suggesting he call it a day but I don't think he heard me, and that's the last I saw of him.'

Maria picked up with what she remembered about George.

'When we got the report, on either the Friday or the Saturday morning – I can't properly make out my scribble,' apologised Maria, 'we were told that George had collapsed some time during the night and he was quite poorly but comfortable.'

'So what went wrong?' enquired Sarah. 'He must have died sometime during the weekend.'

'I wasn't allocated to look after George,' answered Maria. 'I don't remember exactly when he died, but I don't think it was when I was on duty. So it must have been either during the night on Saturday, or sometime on Sunday – but that was my day off.'

'I wasn't back in work until early Tuesday morning,' said Sarah. 'There was no report of anyone passing away overnight. It wasn't until the night staff gave a report on the new lady in room sixteen that I realised that George was no longer with us. And yes, I was really shocked – but I saw no reason to doubt that he had collapsed and died quite quickly following a particularly virulent attack of pneumonia. It happens in the elderly and George, although active, was nearly ninety.'

Maria nodded and asked Sarah if she remembered whether or not there had been relatives who visited George. Sarah shook her head. 'To be honest, Maria, it is, sadly, easier to remember the few residents who do have relatives that visit.'

The next three names were the same on both lists and for a while Sarah and Maria discussed the circumstances surrounding the deaths of Vera Thorne, Edward Myers, and Gladys Morgan. There was a pattern in that all three had been relatively well and then collapsed and died within a few days. Sarah was desperately trying to stop her imagination running away with her and told herself it could be argued that all the people they were looking at were well over the years of normal life expectancy and could have died at any time.

The two women talked about the common aspects of each death, and then both agreed that many of the factors could be linked to every single death at Parkland and any other nursing home.

They had now considered five deaths and Maria was about to give the sixth on her list when she looked as if she had just had one of those eureka moments. 'You weren't around when any of these residents collapsed and died,' she said almost accusingly to Sarah.

'The deaths all happened when you had a long weekend or you were on holiday.'

'What's that got to do with anything?' Sarah asked.

'Hell, I don't know,' replied Maria. 'You did say to think of any common factors with the residents that we are looking at – and that is a common factor!'

Sarah laughed and got up to make them both a cup of coffee, then called from the kitchen for Maria to put forward the next name on her list. Mavis Clegg wasn't a name Sarah recognised and as she put the two coffees on the table she asked Maria what she knew about the lady.

Maria looked at her notes. 'All I have here is that she was admitted on the 19th of April and I helped her get settled in – and to be honest I have to say she was a most objectionable old woman. Nothing I did for her was right and I remember thinking "I hope she isn't going to be here long".'

'I didn't mean that I hoped she was going to die, just that she was hopefully only going to be with us for a week to give her family some respite. I did feel guilty when I went on the late shift the following day and was told that she had collapsed and died that morning.'

'I don't remember her at all,' said Sarah and then stopped as she looked in her notebook and noticed her own jottings for the period around April 19th. 'Oh well, it's not surprising, given that from Saturday April 16th until the following Saturday, the 23rd, I was staying at the Hostal Miguel in Nerja.

'Nine of us from my university set went. We do something every three years, but this was the best thing we had done and I was really pleased because I had made all the arrangements. The hotel was typically Andalusian, and more like a guest house; and there were only nine bedrooms so we took over the whole place and had a whale of a time.'

'So once again you were conspicuous by your absence,' suggested Maria.

'It would seem that way but it's hardly of any significance – what are your last two names?'

'Terence Watts and Connie Marshall,' replied Maria.

'That's the same as I have,' said Sarah. 'I guess that we were both looking for people who were perhaps fitter and more ambulant than the majority of our residents, and who had a sudden-onset episode of one kind or another, resulting in spontaneous deterioration in their health and sooner-than-expected death.'

'I'd say that was it in a nutshell,' answered Maria.

'But if we looked at every single death over the past year, wouldn't we find more or less a similar pattern?' queried Sarah.

'That's as may be – but no, I don't think that we would,' was the reply. 'If that was the case, why or how have we come up with exactly the same set of names? There must be something about the death of these residents that caused both of us to identify them in the way we did.'

For a few moments they both finished their coffee, and then Sarah gathered together both sets of paper and they spent the last hour of their time together going through Maria's final assignments for her Level 2 NVQ.

Sarah marvelled at the way in which Maria's written work had improved over the past few months, and she seemed to be soaking up the years of missed opportunity. If she had not been forced to neglect her education who knew what she could have achieved, but at least now she was creating a future for herself.

'This is really good stuff,' commented Sarah. 'It must have taken you hours to do, how did you manage to find the time?'

'Well there's one good thing I would have told you about if we hadn't got stuck into our detective work.' Maria winked. 'My stepfather's met a woman, and although at first I thought it would be a disaster, it's worked out very well. She's not exactly living with us at the moment, but she is there quite a lot, and seems to like cooking and cleaning – even ironing! The kids have taken to her, and so far so good from my point of view.'

'That's brilliant news,' said Sarah. 'Now you can really start to think about yourself and plan that elusive nursing career. Anyway, there's nothing in particular that I would change in these assignments, so just get them in whenever you like.'

'What are you going to do about the names we've come up with?' asked Maria as she was leaving. 'Get in touch with your dishy detective, or what?'

Sarah couldn't imagine what Matt's reaction would be to Maria's description of him and she laughed. 'I think I will have to, as that's what he's asked me to do, but I'm very reluctant to stir up trouble when there's probably none. There is just one thing, Maria. I don't think we should mention any of this to anyone, as we could both be in danger of losing our jobs if we appear to be suggesting things we are completely unable to substantiate.'

'Got you!' said Maria. 'My lips are sealed. But please let me know if anything develops.'

'Of course,' replied Sarah, as she let Maria out through the front door and returned to plonk herself down on the sofa. Her mind was racing over the evening's revelations and she was now regretting that last cup of coffee, as caffeine and mental activity did not go well together in offering a good night's sleep.

If there were question marks surrounding any of these deaths shouldn't she have asked them at the time? The question itself brought her thinking around to the point that Maria had identified – she hadn't been around!

She tried to calm her thoughts and question logically why there should be anything in any way sinister about deaths at Parkland. Who could possibly benefit from the earlier than expected deaths of the residents she and Maria had identified? Relatives? Mr Cooper? Mr Doster? Dr Shaw? She didn't like any of the three men, but to suggest they were in some way responsible for, or conspiratorial in, the early demise of at least seven residents was unthinkable – wasn't it?

Chapter Seven

'Good morning, Matt,' said Martin. 'I only arrived myself a few minutes ago, and I've ordered us both a breakfast baguette, as promised, and some coffee. Before we think about what we want to look at here, perhaps you could just fill me in on the visit you made with Sgt Evans to Parkland Nursing Home. I don't expect you discovered anything of relevance to us, but I have always valued John Evans' instincts and he was convinced there was something not quite right.'

'Well, it was not without interest,' answered Matt. 'One thing for certain is that you and I could definitely do with a career change, and I suggest we become the owners of a nursing home. I thought such establishments were having a hard time, but there was no evidence of that, certainly not in the car park.' Matt went on to describe the two dream cars that were parked outside the home, belonging to the owner and his wife – he waxed lyrical about the appearance and potential performance of the Mercedes in particular.

For a moment Martin envisaged the sleek machine parked on the driveway of his end-of-terrace cottage in the quiet coastal village of Llantwit Major and decided it would look completely out of place.

Not for the first time Martin surmised that there were two types of men on the planet, and he definitely put himself into the group which saw a car as a means of getting from A to B. Matt most definitely fell into the other group, who could spend hours talking and fantasising about the latest models. Strange, therefore, that the car Matt actually drove was a robust 4x4 that permanently housed three booster seats and frequently taxied a number of his twelve nieces. He was most definitely the favourite uncle and, seemingly, always at their beck and call. With a reality like that it was little wonder he dreamed of a sports car of his very own.

During the time they had worked together Martin had seen many sides to his sergeant, and he now found himself hoping that Matt would soon find someone with whom he would settle down. Perhaps it was being in love oneself that made you want to see others in that same happy state. Martin realised that during the past week every time he thought of Shelley he knew it was with an intensity he had never before experienced. It didn't require any of his expert skills of detection to bring him to the conclusion that gradually over the past few months his feelings for her had deepened and now he knew for certain that he wanted to spend the rest of his life with her – how serious was that? It took some effort to force his mind back to the business in hand and even more effort to force his sergeant away from his own dreams, which flashed invisibly before him in the shape of a Mercedes sports car.

'Thank you,' they both said in unison as an elderly gentleman set two mugs of coffee on the table and returned a moment later with two baguettes that were hopefully going to taste as good as they smelt.

The watery sun that Alex had briefly spotted yesterday had turned into a more significant celestial object and although it was early in the day there was some definite warmth in its rays.

Matt took off his jacket and rolled up his sleeves. 'We spoke to Sr Thomas, that's the nurse who helped out yesterday with Mrs Pattern. Sgt Evans had thought she hadn't witnessed the episode in the corridor with this Mr Morris. However she was able to tell us who Mr Morris is and what he was doing at the home.

'Apparently his father-in-law, Colin James, had died the previous night, and he and his wife were there to collect Mr James' belongings and a death certificate. Maria, one of the care assistants, had just told Sarah, that's the rather gorgeous Sr Thomas, that the police had arrived to talk to her about the body – and that was when, according to Sgt Evans, this Morris character freaked out. He initially had some sort of argument with Sr Thomas, but it was when he saw the officers walking towards him that he almost fainted on the spot.'

'I asked Sarah if there was any reason that Mr Morris could have assumed that the body the police were there to talk to her about was that of his father-in-law. She said the thought hadn't occurred to her, and then I asked if there was anything untoward surrounding the death of Mr James. Her answer to that was somewhat hesitant, but she said she had certainly made comments to a number of people regarding her surprise that Colin had gone so quickly and then she quite spontaneously remembered another resident whose death had prompted her to make similar comments.'

'She quickly reined in any suggestion that her concerns were of any relevance, and gave us a bit of a tutorial regarding the situations that result in residents being admitted to the home and the huge range of reasons why they may suddenly just simply give up and die. It was obvious that her mind was thinking back so I suggested she take a look at deaths over the past six months and then let me know if there was anything she wanted to talk about – I left her my card.'

'For purely professional reasons, of course,' remarked Martin as he used the last piece of his baguette to mop up some of the mushroom and tomato juice that had escaped onto the plate. 'OK, well I'm getting the feeling that there is unlikely to be anything more for us to do regarding the Parkland Nursing Home, so let's finish our coffee and look around this area.'

The man who had brought their food was hovering ready to collect the dishes and clear the table, and looking around Martin could see why. Every other table was occupied, and there was a queue of people placing their orders at the café window. 'It's been like this since late yesterday morning,' said the waiter. 'People have been flocking here to get a glimpse of the place the body was found. Some were here even before the news broke on the radio and there was a line of people waiting for us to open this morning. You were lucky to arrive just after most of the sightseers left the café to confirm the news that television cameras had been sighted. That must have been misinformation because it looks as if they have all come back wanting to be fed and watered. They are just like animals!'

The man was shaking his head in disbelief, but it was a scene totally familiar to Martin and Matt who had witnessed many occasions when certain members of the public had flocked to stand and stare at the misery of others. Martin remembered reading a piece of research that had looked at a cross-section of what the researcher had called the 'morbid mob', only to discover that the majority of them had more than enough misery in their own lives without looking for more.

'That was a great breakfast,' said Matt and looked back over his shoulder at the setting in which they had eaten. 'It's new isn't it? That's the first time I've been there, but then we tend to come into Bute Park from the city end and so rarely come up this far. It'll definitely be a time out place for me next time I bring the girls to the park.'

'Yes,' replied Martin. 'It is new, and was only officially opened just over a week ago, but has been trading since April. I was on the internet last night knowing that we were coming here this morning. It's to be known as the Summerhouse Kiosk and was built as part of the Bute Restoration Project. Apparently it's a timber-framed building, but they used stone from the old demolished toilet block to ensure the overall look is in keeping with what was here originally.

'There actually was a Bute Summer House designed by William Burgess but that was taken down in the seventies and reconstructed in the grounds of St Fagans.'

'Yes, I've seen it there, but I hadn't realised it had been moved from here,' Matt said. 'St Fagans and Bute Park are two of my family's favourite picnic sites, and looking around today it's no wonder people flock here – it's a stunningly beautiful park.'

'It's a shame that the body was found here this week, because on Thursday there are plans in place to host an event to celebrate the fact that the park has been awarded the prestigious Green Flag Status for the fourth consecutive year, no mean achievement, apparently.'

'Yes I have been made aware of that,' said Martin. 'I got a call from the superintendent yesterday evening, to say he was being urged by the organisers to get all evidence of the crime scene, together with the media and all their ghoulish followers, out of the area as soon as possible. After his call I spoke to Alex and he said he would get down here this morning and could see no reason why the area shouldn't be restored to normality, and he planned to talk to the gardeners and enlist their help.'

'Are we going to walk the length and breadth of the park, or have you got something more specific in mind?' asked Matt.

'Definitely the latter,' came the reply. 'I learned last night that the park measures a total of fifty-six hectares, which in language we can understand is the equivalent of seventy-five football pitches. I'm only concerned with the entrances and exits in relation to how feasible it would be to bring a body in without attracting attention. Let's walk down to the water bus stop first and hopefully rule that one out.'

Martin thought of the words of the song 'What a Difference a Day Makes,' as he looked at the flowers and herbaceous borders that had shown such promise yesterday and today were responding to the warmth of the sun and unashamedly showing off their beauty for the world to admire.

The two men walked towards the city centre but then took the turning as directed by the wooden sign etched with the words *Water Bus Stop* (and for the benefit of Welsh speakers, *Arhosfan y Bws Dwr*).

They walked under the trees and as the path sloped gently down towards the River Taff the gravel changed to a more solid concrete walkway marking the start of the entrance to the water bus stop. There were metal barriers on either side of the path and ahead of them was a steeper slope that would take them down the embankment and on to the wooden boarding platform.

However, their access to this area was made impossible by a formidable metal barrier, nearly five feet high. It was locked, and all the two of them could do was look at the platform beyond and consider the feasibility of a body being transported.

'OK,' said Martin, turning back. 'I hadn't thought this entrance would be an option and now, seeing it for real, I'm ruling it out. Very few people would know the opening times for these gates, and from what I've read the main users are the public and tourists travelling from Mermaid Quay to the city centre. The scheduled boats are probably crowded and if a private boat had been used it could easily have been seen from that bridge there.'

Martin pointed towards the bridge that crossed the river just ahead of them. It was a busy road with a pavement from which there was an excellent view of the river.

'OK,' he said again. 'That was a bit of a waste of time, but it means we can cross one thing off our list. The entrance alongside the castle is one I know well, so we can skip that and take a quick look at how things are getting on at the scene.'

Within a few minutes they knew they were approaching the area where the body had been discovered because of the increase in the number of people standing around. When Martin had been educating himself about Bute Park on the web, he had read about the red minivan that stocked up at the Summerhouse Kiosk and then drove around the park offering drinks and light refreshments. It was doing a roaring trade now as the onlookers and the media filled gaps in their stomachs and their time – it was an ill wind, he thought!

The white tent that had marked the scene yesterday was no longer visible, and to Martin's delight he caught sight of Alex's shaven scalp glistening in the morning sunshine. Alex had spotted the two detectives walking in his direction and lifted his arm beckoning them to where he had parked his van.

Some members of the press had also noticed their arrival and one young journalist, still bearing the scars of adolescent acne, left his colleagues and made a beeline for Martin. Even before he had the chance to speak Martin cut him short. 'There's a press conference this afternoon, as I am sure you are aware, and until then I have absolutely no intention of making any statements or answering any questions.' Not wanting or waiting for any response Martin turned to Alex who seemed to have just a few more pieces of equipment to load into the van.

'We're just about finished here,' Alex confirmed. 'Don't remember another occasion when we had things cleared up so quickly but this area doesn't deserve to be remembered as the dumping ground for a corpse – it was developed for much better things.'

'We all agree,' said Martin. 'I know the organisers of the event planned for Thursday will be over the moon with this progress, but I just hope we haven't compromised anything by moving so quickly.'

'Absolutely not,' was the reply from Alex. 'With the photographic evidence, soil samples, and of course the body, we could now do a virtual reconstruction with all the tools we have at our disposal. Sgt Evans' team did a thorough search of the surrounding area yesterday afternoon but as you know, found nothing significant.'

'Yes,' said Martin. 'He rang me this morning to say they had been looking for a potential murder weapon, any sort of walking aid, hopefully a handbag, and the remote possibility of some dentures. Nothing was found and I think I would have been surprised if anything had been. I am convinced she was killed elsewhere and then brought here.'

The other two nodded in agreement. 'What we need to know,' Matt suggested, 'is the identity of the woman – and to unlock the mystery of the clothing, that's really bugging me.'

For the next few minutes they talked about the entrances to the park. Alex pointed out the route he had used to bring the van to the scene and suggested that that would be the entrance of choice. The road he was indicating had not been in existence long, and had been the subject of a lot of controversy, with regular park users expressing concern that the whole environment would be destroyed if vehicles were allowed such easy access.

Matt said that even large trucks drove over the field when events were being set up. Their discussion brought to Martin's mind the fact that, with the advent of the road, a car or van in that part of the park would no longer look out of place. A vehicle could have driven across the field, parked at the spot where Alex's van now stood and, within minutes, offloaded the body and been heading out of the park.

Given the level of rainfall over the past few weeks it would have taken a large lorry carrying an almighty load for the tyre prints to have remained even vaguely identifiable. No evidence of any tracks had been found, but Martin was now completely convinced that he knew how the body had got there.

They left Alex and rejoined the footpath, this time not turning off towards the river but making their way to the Cardiff Castle entrance, the route taken by most shoppers on their way for some retail therapy. There was certainly every opportunity for that as with its combination of the old arcades and the new designer shops Cardiff now had something to offer everyone.

A short walk from the park grounds and they were standing in the entrance to a block of flats and ringing the doorbell labelled Mr and Mrs A. Pattern.

The bell was immediately answered and a man with an Australian accent bluntly asked them who they were and what they wanted. Martin answered the questions and there was a loud click that only just allowed them to hear the man telling them to go straight ahead towards the one and only ground floor flat.

Even before they got to the door of the flat it opened and a larger-than-life character filled the doorframe with a considerable frame of his own, one that was well in excess of six foot and probably around sixteen stone. None of that weight was fat, and with a well-tanned face and sun-bleached blond hair he was a sight to behold and took his visitors by surprise.

The Australian accent was even more pronounced now that they were face to face, and after Martin had made the formal introductions with the aid of his warrant card Aiden explained that he was Mrs Pattern's son-in-law and that he and his wife were over on holiday with their two sons. 'Kerry, that's my wife, hasn't left her mother's side since that dreadful business in the park yesterday, but they're expecting your visit – just go through to the lounge and I'll make us all some coffee.'

Matt had brought the statement given by Mrs Pattern the previous day and suggested that the quickest course of action would be for him to read it and for Mrs Pattern to amend anything that, with the benefit of hindsight, needed adjusting. The only addition she made was to say that after one of the boys had hurled the dog's ball some incredible distance, they had both taken to their heels and run away as if the hounds of hell were chasing them.

She told the detectives that she wasn't angry with the boys, as they were only having a bit of fun and she would normally have expected Dylan, the dog, to fetch the ball back within a few minutes.

'I did feel a bit mad with the boys when I had to walk through the wet grass and it was extremely muddy underfoot – but that was nothing compared with what I felt when I saw the reason for Dylan's reluctance to return when I called him.'

At this point Mrs Pattern started to tremble and as she closed her eyes in an effort to regain her composure Martin was certain that she was once again seeing that image and he knew exactly how she felt. He leant forward in his chair and told Mrs Pattern about the services that were available to help the victims of crime get over their experience and suggested she speak to PC Cook-

Watts who could help if required.

'I never thought of myself as a victim of crime,' said Mrs Pattern, but everyone else agreed that she was and she shouldn't be ashamed of being stressed out by the experience.

The visit had taken no more than forty-five minutes but when they left Martin felt that he and Matt had helped to put things into perspective for the family and he had agreed to personally let Mrs Pattern know the outcome of the police investigations.

Back on the pavement outside the flats Martin suggested that they walk back to the car via the road and not through the park, and so they headed for Cathedral Road, knowing that from there they would get to the Sophia Garden's car park.

'The nursing home you visited yesterday is along here somewhere isn't it?' enquired Martin.

Matt pointed to one of the side streets and told Martin it was at the end of that road. 'I've got a voice message from Sr Thomas,' he added as he held his mobile to his ear to trawl through three other communications before listening to Sarah's voice.

'Hello,' she began. 'This is Sarah Thomas from Parkland Nursing Home, and as requested I went through unexpected deaths with Maria last night and surprisingly we each came up with an almost identical list. I have no idea what this means or if there is anything you want to do with this information …' she stopped at this point and holding the phone close to his ear Matt could hear someone else speaking. Then Sarah continued. 'Sorry, Sgt Pryor, but Mr Doster suggests I have other things to do than make personal calls during working hours so will you please give me a call later. I finish at four today and you can pick my number up from this call.'

Matt relayed the message to Martin who shrugged his shoulders and asked Matt what he made of what Sr Thomas had said.

'Don't know, boss,' came the reply. 'Like you, I thought there would be nothing more to do following the second visit to Parkland but now I'm not so sure – she did sound as if she wanted to talk about their findings.'

'Or maybe just talk to Detective Sergeant Matt Pryor,' chuckled Martin. 'OK, Matt, well just make that call this evening, and then we must decide if anything requires formal investigation or if Sgt Evans' nose is on the wrong scent this time. I can't afford the manpower to go on a wild goose chase – but of course if you want to take things further in your own time, that is entirely up to you.'

Matt made a face, zapped the central locking of his 4x4, and was on his way back to Goleudy well before Martin, who was sitting in his own car going through the voicemails he had received that morning. One was from Shelley and he played this over a few times. Hell, he was smitten! She was reminding him of their plans for the evening and expressing her hope that the murder she was hearing about would not scupper them. His main reason for playing the message over and over was because of her final comment, 'love you, bye for now' she had said. It was something lots of friends said at the end of their phone messages, but not something Shelley had said before and hearing it made him feel special.

His mind stayed on Shelley during his drive back to the office and he resolved that as he now knew, beyond any shadow of doubt, that he loved Shelley then it was time to tell her and to make sure that her feelings mirrored his own. Please, God, he thought, don't let anything as base as a murder investigation keep me from tonight's promise.

Martin was surprised to realise that it was almost one o'clock when he got back and the staff dining room was heaving. He decided to just have a ham salad sandwich, mainly because he didn't want to face the queue but also because he knew Shelley had organised somewhere to eat later.

Matt, Alex, and about six others were all packed around a table intended to seat four people, and as they hadn't seen Martin he was able to grab a coffee from the machine and take it, together with the sandwich, to the relative calm of his office.

Closing the door behind him, Martin's mind drifted back to Shelley, but with superhuman effort he sat down, pulled out a pen and some paper, and focused absolutely on the forthcoming press conference.

He considered possible questions and jotted down some of the facts he would need to give in response. There was so little he could provide and he knew the media would not be satisfied. He wasn't satisfied either and he knew that until they discovered who the woman was they could not even begin to think of any suspects who may have had means, motive, and opportunity. His best bet would be to use the forum as an appeal to the public for any information that could possibly lead to the identification of the body.

Matt tapped the door and told him that the vultures had gathered and were waiting to get the show on the road. 'I was going to say they're all there waiting with pens poised to take down your every word, but there's not a pen or a pencil in sight – even the local rags have gone totally electronic.'

They walked down the stairs to the front of the building and into the large room set aside for public meetings, that was now packed to the rafters with men and women from the media and their ever-more-sophisticated equipment. Wires and cables looped and swung from one end of the room to the other but as soon as the door at the front opened all eyes and lenses were focused on DCI Phelps.

'Thank you all for coming,' began Martin. 'Just to ensure we all have the initial facts correct I can confirm that yesterday morning at around 8 a.m. the dead body of a woman was found in Bute Park – in the undergrowth of one of the trees at the edge of Coopers Field. The woman's body was discovered by a member of the public, a local lady, who was in the area exercising her dog.'

'As yet we have been unable to identify the woman and on this point I would like to appeal to the public for their help. Our Chief Pathologist, Professor Dafydd Moore, has examined the body and from his findings I am able to tell you that the lady was approximately eighty years old with very poor eyesight and limited mobility. She was barely five feet tall. We are treating her death as suspicious. The PM examination revealed a blow to the left-hand side of her skull that was almost certainly the cause of her death. We obviously have no idea at this stage how she came by this injury but the fact that her body was subsequently left in this way may well indicate that she was murdered.'

Martin stopped to drink from the glass of water on the table in front of him at the same time turning his left palm towards one of the reporters who tried butting in with a question about whether or not the body was naked.

Martin didn't have to answer his question at that moment but he was pleased that it had given him forewarning about what the press already knew. He hadn't intended mentioning the fact that the body was naked but now he would do so – but unless forced to he would say nothing about the clothing.

'I'll take questions in a minute,' continued Martin. 'As I said a moment ago, we are appealing to the public – and that appeal is on two counts. The body could have been left where it was found anything up to two weeks ago, but we have good reason to believe it was either on or just after Thursday July 14th.

'So we are asking all members of the public to consider if an elderly neighbour, friend, or relative seems to have disappeared. The woman in question would certainly have needed a stick or a walking frame to get around and even then would have done so with difficulty as she was also visually compromised almost to the point of being blind.

'Please check on people you know. Maybe you think an elderly relative has been taken for a holiday with another member of the family – we are all so busy with our own lives but I urge you to check and to ask the police for help if you have any doubts about the whereabouts of anyone fitting the description I have given.'

Martin sat back and hardly took a breath before the barrage of questions began but because they were interested in the reply, the majority allowed the reporter, who had previously tried to interrupt Martin, to have first bite of the cherry. 'According to one of my sources the body was naked, are you able to confirm that? Also was the body interfered with in any sexual way?'

Martin stared hard at the journalist and remembered why he recognised him. He was the one Matt had spoken about after their last press conference, and here he was again asking questions about nudity and implied sexual interference. According to Matt they were the only questions he ever asked – and what a sad world when questions about possible sexual abuse had to be made in relation to an eighty-year-old woman.

'I am able to confirm that the body was naked and also that there was no abuse of any kind other than the injury to her head,' replied Martin.

The usual mish-mash of questions followed, with cheap points being scored between the various factions of the media, and Martin gritted his teeth waiting for it to end. His opportunity to draw things to a close came when the same question was posed for the third time. 'Given that we have all heard that question more than once before, I can only assume you have no more questions to ask and we can all go about our own business.'

Not waiting for any response Martin got to his feet and led Matt out of the room, up the stairs, and into his office.

'I always feel I need a shower when I have had a session with that lot. I know they also have their jobs to do, it's just that some of them seem to revel in learning about the worst of human nature.'

Matt nodded in agreement and then posed a question. 'Where are we going on this case? I've been racking my brains and the nearest thing we have is one missing woman who we believe has been taken by her daughter to France. I understand you're going to see her sister, Miss Forrester, with Helen Cook-Watts, as she was the one Miss Forrester spoke to at the time she reported her sister missing.'

'I did hope to do that this afternoon. Do you know if Helen's around?' asked Martin.

'Sorry guv, she isn't, and come to that Miss Forrester isn't available either. Apparently Helen knew you wanted to speak to Miss Forrester and got in touch with her earlier, but the lady has a hospital appointment this afternoon and doesn't know what time she'll be back. Helen has provisionally made arrangements for the three of you to meet tomorrow morning, and apparently you need to be prepared for a long session.'

Martin laughed as he remembered the statement Helen had put together regarding the potentially missing sister. 'Matt, I'm just going to finish off a few things here and then I'm heading home, as I've got an evening planned that, in spite of this murder, I intend to enjoy.' Before his sergeant could even raise an eyebrow Martin had set about clearing his desk, with his mind back on Shelley and already racing towards what he hoped could be a life-changing night ahead.

Chapter Eight

'Shut the bloody door!' bellowed Anthony Cooper 'Tell me what the hell is going on and don't say that nothing is going on, because two visits from the police in one day adds up to a whole fucking load of something in my book.'

'There's no need to swear at me,' said Peter Doster. 'Why don't you calm down and see the situation for what it is? You will have seen on the news that a body was found in Coopers Field yesterday morning and Sarah Thomas got involved with helping someone at the scene, that's as much as I know.'

'What do you mean that's as much as you know? Even I know more than that as the police told me *exactly* what Sarah's involvement had been. What I'm asking, because it's something I am failing to understand, is why they came here twice! Once to take a statement from Sr Thomas, yes, that makes sense, but a second time and that time with a CID sergeant interviewing her – that's the bit I don't get, what's that all about?'

The home administrator shuffled a bit and knew from past experience that it was as well for him to keep his own counsel when his boss was in this sort of mood. He knew it from when the two had been in school together and Anthony had been the class bully even then.

By nature, Peter was a hard worker, and at school had been considered to be a bit of a swot, which was probably the only reason Anthony had made any time for him. After all, why would Anthony do his own homework when he could, with a bit of persuasion, get Peter to do it for him? It was the only way Peter, who was by nature something of a loner, could be seen by the rest of the class as a member of the Cooper gang.

Thinking back now, he remembered the years when his whole school life had been dominated by the man who was standing in front of him and was causing him as much distress now as he had done when they were boys.

In their final year at secondary school, Peter had become besotted with a girl three years younger than him, and she had quickly realised that she could twist Peter around her little finger – and so in a very different way she had become the second bully in Peter's life. After all these years Peter still found it hard to get to grips with what had happened back then. He knew that Anthony was fully in the picture and that he, Peter, would have done anything to prevent his family getting to know the sad, sordid story of underage sex and DIY abortion.

The two men had gone to different universities, but possibly because there was no one to help him with his coursework Anthony had dropped out when just into his second year. Peter's university days were the best days of his life, and in his final year he met Carol, the woman who was, four years later, to become his devoted wife, and subsequently the mother of his two children.

How he wished he had summoned up the courage to tell her about the skeleton in his cupboard when they had first met. They were both young then, and lots of their friends were experimenting with drugs and 'anything goes' sexual activity, so she might well have understood. They now had two teenage daughters of their own, and the thought of any harm coming to either of them turned his blood cold.

'Well?' shouted Anthony. 'Got an answer for me? I repeat, why was the law here for the second time, and what did they want that couldn't have been dealt with by just ordinary coppers? Why involve detectives just to go over a statement from one of our staff?'

'You saw more of them than I did,' Peter mumbled. 'You went back to the office to see Sr Thomas after they went, didn't you?'

'Yes I spoke to her in the nurses' office, for all the good it did me. She said there was nothing more to say and repeated like a parrot what the police had already told me, but she was hiding something, I could tell. Dr Shaw is right about that one, she's far too inquisitive for her own good!'

Peter hesitated and then spoke. 'She was speaking to the police again this morning when I walked into her office and caught her on her mobile phone. To be fair, she's not one to break the rules, and

94

it's normally her reprimanding others for using their phones during working hours.'

The only part of Peter's sentence that registered with the home owner was 'speaking to the police again this morning' and he virtually erupted. 'Speaking to the police again this morning! Speaking to the police again this morning! What the fucking hell do you mean? When were you going to pass on this information? What was she saying?'

Peter regretted having mentioned the episode with Sr Thomas and her mobile phone, but the words were out now and the genie could not be put back in the bottle.

'You've been out all day,' he protested, as he watched Anthony Cooper wave his arms about and then pour himself a large quantity of whisky. Peter Doster was not in the least bit surprised that only one glass of whisky was poured, in fact he would have been amazed if he had been offered a drink.

'I got back here at five o'clock, so I've been back well over an hour, plenty of time for my so-called home administrator to keep me in the loop regarding something he knows is causing me great concern. Think, man, think! What exactly did you hear Sarah Thomas saying to whoever it was on her mobile phone?'

Feeling suddenly quite scared Peter tried to remember what Sarah had been saying when he entered her office. 'It was something about an almost identical list but she didn't know what to make of it and then she asked the person she was speaking to what he wanted her to do with the information – words to that effect but maybe not exactly what she said.'

'Go on, go on, you idiot! What else did she say?'

'Well that was when she realised that I had come into the office and I asked her if she didn't have better things to do than to use her phone when she was on duty.'

'For the love of God,' exploded Anthony. 'When the hell will you get your priorities right? Who cares about her using her bloody mobile phone? What happened next?'

'Well, I had obviously interrupted the message she was leaving and she just finished it off quickly ...'

'Yes, yes, but how did she end her message – did she leave her number or anything?' Anthony could barely contain himself.

'I remember almost exactly what she said,' was the reply from a man who had a pretty good idea how his next words would be received. 'She said, "Sorry, Sgt Pryor, but Mr Doster thinks I should be working and not phoning you, but I finish at four o'clock today so call me on this number" – I think that was almost exactly what she said.'

Anthony Cooper's rage reached epic proportions and he lashed out furiously, sweeping cups and glasses to the floor and even knocking over an almost full bottle of whisky. Peter watched as his boss picked up the bottle and wished he could see the funny side of how ridiculous it was that a grown man could behave like this. But there was nothing funny about the words that came out of that grown man's mouth.

'So you have known since this morning that as well as two visits from the police yesterday, one of the senior members of our nursing staff has been leaving messages for Sgt Pryor – not just any Sgt Pryor, but *DS Pryor* – the one who was here yesterday. This can only mean we are all in the shit – at least we will be if they start digging things up and making two and two make five … that's what they do, you know – you are such a fucking idiot.'

Cooper continued. 'I need to speak to Dr Shaw urgently. In the meantime I suggest you keep your mouth shut, and if you go talking to the police about anything remember there are things they may still want to learn about a certain naughty little schoolboy – and even if the police are no longer interested I know a certain Mrs Doster who would just love to be told …'

Peter practically ran from the room, and for the next half hour just sat in his car trying desperately to think how he had ever reached this position and what he should do next. There were always options but most of the ones he came up with required the resolve of a much stronger man than he was.

Sarah had already left Parkland before the two men had met, but in any event she wouldn't have seen Mr Doster in the car park because she had used the back entrance and walked through the side streets and into the centre of Cardiff. She needed a new pair of shoes for work, and with that no-nonsense purchase quickly sorted she just strolled around some of the arcades and did some people watching.

She marvelled at how shopping in Cardiff had changed over the past decade; that there was now everything from the old world charm of Edwardian and Victorian arcades to ultra-modern shopping precincts. Sarah remembered reading that the city was near the top of the list for the best shopping experiences in the UK. Scattered liberally around the shops she noted the number of coffee bars and restaurants to suit just about every taste, as well as the funky wine bars where the younger set seemed to congregate. She loved her home city and on this warm evening, one of the best in several weeks, she felt somewhat patriotic and proud to be part of the buzz that was Cardiff.

But Sarah also had other things on her mind, and throughout the day she had been looking at events with a fresh pair of eyes and asking herself questions about the people on the lists that she and Maria had made the previous evening. The more she thought, the more she was able to identify common factors in all the deaths, although she had to admit that she was not in possession of all the facts.

As she picked up some fruit and veg and treated herself to a cutlet of hake from the fish counter in Cardiff Market, Sarah found herself thinking about Matt Pryor. She guessed he was a couple of years younger than her, and he was without a doubt one of the nicest men she had met in a long time. Of course, she didn't really know him, but he had come over as being kind and considerate and she especially liked that educated Welsh accent – she thought he sounded a bit like Richard Burton and for her that was a real turn-on. She had loved the way he had dealt with Mr Cooper. While remaining polite he had made it absolutely plain that the business the police had with Sarah was no concern of anyone else.

Just after seven Sarah was at home and sitting down to the hake she had pan-fried and was now eating off a bed of rice, chopped spring onions, and tomatoes that she had cooked in a butter and lemon sauce. She looked at her watch and decided that either DS Pryor had not got her message or he had decided on no further action.

Barely had she mopped up the last of the juices on her plate when her phone rang, and as the number displayed was not one she recognised Sarah guessed it was the call she had been hoping for.

'Hello,' was all she said, and the caller responded immediately.

'Hello, it is Sarah, isn't it? – I recognise your voice.'

'And I yours, DS Pryor,' she answered.

'Oh, Matt, please!' came the quick response. 'I got your message this morning and had a quick chat with my boss about what you and Maria had come up with, although my knowledge is limited, so would you like to fill me in with the detail?'

Sarah did her best to explain how she and Maria had gone through the process of identifying residents who met the criteria they had decided on. Although she tried to be brief, she realised that she was only part-way through her explanation when she noticed that she had already been talking for almost twenty minutes.

'Look, I'm sorry about this,' she told Matt. 'I didn't realise it would take so long and I'm sure you must have other things to do.'

'Nothing apart from looking after three girls who are aged between seven and eleven, but who think they are teenagers at the very least.'

Sarah felt a bit deflated but gave a cheery response. 'Well, tell the girls I won't keep their daddy talking for much longer – I will be as quick as I can.'

Matt gave a real belly laugh. 'No, no, no, they aren't my daughters, they belong to my sister and her husband who are having a well-deserved night out, so Uncle Matt is in charge – or at least I think I am.'

Feeling strangely lifted by the response, Sarah wanted to risk a question about whether or not the girls had a Mrs Pryor for an aunt, but she decided against it and just joined in Matt's laughter, saying that she wouldn't take up too much more of his time.

When she had finished sharing the information she and Maria had gathered, she added some thoughts that had been irritating her during the day. 'Maria came up with a strange observation,' she told Matt. 'It was the fact that in all the cases we looked at I was away from the home, either at the time each of these residents collapsed and died or at a critical point leading to their sooner-than-expected deaths. At first I took it that she was joking, but in fact she was right. The only reason I mention this is that on looking back I know for sure that I would have been asking questions about some of the decisions surrounding their treatment, and in particular why none of these residents were transferred to hospital care.'

'Would that be the norm?' asked Matt.

'Yes, that's the usual thing when there is a sudden and unexpected deterioration, and strangely it's something I had words with Mr Cooper about, in relation to Colin James,' Sarah continued. 'He told me that Mrs Morris had been told by her father that on no account was he to be admitted to hospital, but I know for sure that Colin hadn't been visited by his daughter for months.

'Anthony Cooper told me that he was going to get Dr Shaw to document the family's wishes but I haven't seen the medical notes since Colin died so I don't know if he did.'

'Would you be able to look at them now?' asked Matt. 'Are they kept at the home?'

'Yes, in Mr Doster's office. He is constantly complaining that the nurses write far too many notes and he has recently had to buy an additional filing cabinet just to house dead files – pardon the pun! I could take a look at them tomorrow.'

Matt hesitated and for a moment Sarah thought he had hung up, but he had obviously been considering his response. 'Sarah, don't do anything for the time being – and at least not until I have had a chance to speak to DCI Phelps. I think deep down we all believe that we are probably looking at just a series of coincidences, but in the unlikely event that something is going on and someone has something to hide, it would not be in their best interests to have you snooping around. So do and say nothing until I come back to you.'

'When are you likely to be speaking to your DCI?' enquired Sarah.

'Well it won't be tonight,' was the reply. 'I think he has some more personal business to attend to and I would hate to be the one to interfere with that.'

'Well thanks for listening,' said Sarah, somewhat reluctant to end the conversation but aware of raucous laughter in the background. 'I'll leave you to your babysitting, although it sounds as if the babies are getting the upper hand.'

Matt looked around the room to find the youngest of his nieces strapped to one of the dining chairs by virtue of at least three crepe bandages. The two older girls were whooping around with faces covered in red streaks of lipstick almost certainly taken from his sister's dressing table.

'Girls!' he shouted pretending to be outraged. 'You'll get me shot. Can't I leave you for ten minutes to your own devices without you wreaking havoc?'

Rhian, the eldest, looked at him mockingly. 'Ten minutes, Uncle Matt? More like an hour. Have you got a new girlfriend?'

'No, it was work,' he replied, and was about to protest that it was nothing like an hour when he realised that her version of the timing was much closer than his own. He was beginning to feel a bit uncomfortable about having set Sarah off down a road that was unlikely to unearth any criminal activity, but could well result in her losing her job if her boss got even an inkling of her recent activities. Mr Cooper was a bully, of that Matt was in no doubt, but was he anything else? There was no real evidence to suspect him of anything.

Matt turned his mind and his hands towards rescuing his youngest niece, Clare, and made a mental note to speak to Martin first thing in the morning. He briefly wondered if Martin was enjoying his evening – the boss had seemed particularly elated when he left the office.

At the very moment Matt was having these thoughts Martin and Shelley were settling down to a performance of 'A Night's Tale' at the Bute Theatre, and they were both looking forward to the promise of being entertained by The Unknown Theatre Company. Before Martin and Shelley had started going out his only experience of the theatre had been watching mainstream productions, but Shelley had introduced Martin to fringe theatre and now he was hooked.

He could hardly believe they were sitting in such a beautiful setting and in such comfortable seats, and he had paid just £6 each for the tickets! When Shelley had first talked about the fringe he had thought it would be all art students, bright young things, and actors who had failed to make it through the traditional route, but he couldn't have been more wrong.

The audience was a mixture of all ages and backgrounds, but with one thing in common. They were here to witness a production that relied principally on the skills of the writers and the actors rather than special sound and visual effects. Later these dedicated fringe followers would talk about the subject matter and argue the rights and wrongs of the writer's interpretation and the actors' portrayal of it.

Martin struggled to remember some of the mainstream shows he had seen, but could easily recall the four performances Shelley had chosen for them. He had jumped at the chance when she suggested they might consider going to the Edinburgh Fringe Festival, although he had to admit he knew nothing at all about it. To him the idea of spending six days and five nights with Shelley would have swung it, whatever the location, and he had booked a five-day break in Scotland from August 15th.

Not wanting to think about murder, Martin had printed out a planner he found in the extensive Festival programme. He left it strategically placed on the kitchen table for them to look through when they got back to the cottage later. Martin hadn't asked, but he certainly hoped that Shelley had made arrangements for someone else to give her father his insulin in the morning!

He suddenly realised that Shelley was looking at him, and they would both have been highly amused to know how well their thoughts matched – Shelley was at that very moment hoping she had not been too presumptuous in arranging for the district nurse to give the pre-breakfast injection to her diabetic father in the morning.

Their eyes met, and Martin squeezed her hand so tightly she screwed up her face and they both laughed over nothing more than the fact that they were enjoying being together and then fell silent as the performance began.

Afterwards they walked out into warm evening sunshine and toyed with the idea of walking into the city centre and coming back for the car later. There was only one car as Martin had driven from home and picked Shelley up en route, and depending on the outcome of his plans for the evening he would either be dropping her back at her house or taking her back to Llantwit Major – fingers crossed for the latter.

Shelley had organised the eating arrangements, and she told Martin that she had booked a table at Gio's Italian restaurant in the Café Quarter on Mill Lane. The whole area was popular with locals and tourists for its amazing diversity in terms of cooking and for the relaxed atmosphere. 'It's so laid-back there,' explained Shelley. 'The food is great, and there is parking so we can drive there, park the car, and then maybe walk around a bit before eating.'

Decision made they drove the very short journey and were soon sitting at one of the low tables in the area outside the restaurant set aside for an al fresco dining experience. Because the whole area was busy they decided against walking around and as, thankfully, Shelley had booked they were able to skip the queue and were offered a table in a corner of the outside area. 'Perfect,' suggested Shelley, as she settled down and they were both offered menus and asked about drinks.

'I feel a bit mean,' she offered the words in the form of an apology to Martin. 'It's always me doing the drinking and you doing the driving, it doesn't seem quite fair.'

'Not to worry,' was his reply. 'Even if I wasn't driving I wouldn't be drinking much tonight – I need to make an early start tomorrow.'

'I won't ask you how the investigation is going,' said Shelley. 'It's much too nice an evening to be spoilt by that sort of thing – I'm sure we have better things we can talk about.'

Although all the tables were full and there were lots of people walking around, they seemed to be in a little world of their own and Martin was about to tell Shelley how he felt about her when the waiter arrived with Martin's J2O and Shelley's large glass of red wine – and the moment was lost. 'But just for now,' he told himself.

They had ordered the Antipasto Misto for two and were soon enjoying the sun-dried tomatoes, roast peppers, and olives, and the slices of Italian salami, Parma ham, and mozzarella cheese. They were in their own special bubble and although the food was really delicious, the chemistry between the two of them was more delicious than anything even the Italian chef could cook up.

Martin remembered the last time had eaten at an Italian restaurant and the mountain of pasta that was set before him. Not wanting that much in the way of food, he opted for fresh salmon served with a Nizzarda salad, eggs, green beans, tomato, and potatoes. Shelley must have been thinking along the same lines as she ordered Cozze Alla Crema – mussels cooked in a creamy white wine sauce with shallots and normally served a starter – for her main course.

The restaurant was excellent, the service great, and the food undoubtedly first-class, but Martin told Shelley a few months later

102

that he couldn't even remember what they had eaten because his thoughts were on other things. She had jokingly suggested that he meant the Coopers Field murder but then admitted that she knew exactly what he meant.

Deciding against coffee they made their way back to the car but on the way Martin turned to face Shelley and standing in the middle of a busy walkway he kissed her and the words he had been thinking about all day came tumbling out. 'I love you, Shelley,' he declared. 'Can you believe that? – I love you and I just want us to be together. I don't know about marriage, I've done that and I don't know if it is right for me, but whatever you want. All I know is that I love you and I'm terrified that you may not feel the same.'

Who cared that people were looking at them. Nobody looked offended. In fact the passing public seemed to want to share their experience as there were smiles on the faces of everyone around.

The biggest smile however was on Shelley's face, although she was confusing Martin because she also had floods of tears streaming down her cheeks.

'You idiot,' she whispered. 'Call yourself a detective? Everyone else in the world knows I love you. Charlie told me last week that if you didn't realise you loved me soon she was going to sort you out!'

This made Martin laugh and then with a serious face he held Shelley's face in his hands. 'Say that again,' he asked her. 'Say that bit about everyone knowing you love me – it's true then?'

'Of course it's true! I love you, Martin, and I have done since that first time we had a meal together at the Japanese restaurant in Mermaid Quay – I doubt if you even remember it.'

'I do remember it, and maybe I'm regretting all the wasted time between then and now, but if I'm perfectly honest, Shelley, I wasn't ready for anything serious at that time. But now I know for certain what my feelings are, and that I love you more than anything I ever believed possible.'

This time when Martin kissed Shelley they both blushed, as a round of applause spontaneously erupted from the groups of people standing nearby.

'Come on, let's get out of here, we're not young enough to be carrying on like this in public – you'll get me arrested, Shelley Edwards.'

Chapter Nine

Martin's years of training and dedication to his work helped get him back on track the following morning, and he spent the first hour of the day in Incident Room One reminding himself of the known facts regarding the Coopers Field body. Helen Cook-Watts wasn't expected to start her shift until 9 a.m. and he wanted a brief word with her before they made the arranged visit to Elsie Forrester.

He left a message at the front desk for her to join him upstairs and to bring a copy of the statement taken from Miss Forrester at the time she reported her sister missing.

When she joined him, Martin said, 'We'll go in my car. Even though Miss Forrester knows we are coming it can be disconcerting for someone of her age to see a police car pull up outside the front door.'

'Yes, it freaks most people out,' agreed Helen. 'The innocent anticipating bad news and the guilty assuming we've come to get them.'

As Helen sat alongside Martin in his Alfa Romeo she remembered the first time she had travelled with him. They had gone to Whitchurch on that occasion and it had been to tell an elderly couple that their gay son, Mark, had been brutally killed. She had been one of the first on the scene when his body had been discovered and could still, with ease, summon up the images of the man's torso lying on the central island of his kitchen, his severed arms and legs strewn at various angles on the floor.

Although not fully qualified for the role at that time, Helen had been allowed to act as the couple's Family Liaison Officer, and she remembered the experience particularly well because it was the time when she had decided that a career in CID was what she wanted.

That thought jerked her mind back to the present, and sitting next to Martin now it briefly entered her head that on Friday she would be sitting opposite him when he and two others interviewed her for the transfer to CID she was hoping would be granted.

This opportunity to be with him this morning could be something of a double edged sword, and she wished that it was someone other than Elsie Forrester that they were going to see. Helen would have liked the opportunity to show DCI Phelps how professional she had been in her original dealings with the woman, but Elsie was quite a character and Helen remembered nervously how difficult it had been to keep her on track.

The journey was relatively short, but the traffic was heavy and it was twenty minutes before they had turned off City Road and Helen was directing Martin down a couple of side streets. She indicated for him to stop outside the house at the end. The street they had arrived in was made up on both sides of substantial Victorian terraced houses, some of which had obviously been turned into flats, with even the split properties capable of housing a small family.

Miss Forrester's house had a decent-sized, paved front garden, with a short path to the front door and another path presumably leading to a side or back entrance.

Even before Martin had turned off his engine the front door opened and a short, small-framed woman stood at the door leaning with most of her inconsiderable weight on a metal stick that had been adapted to allow her arm to rest above it.

As they moved closer to her Martin had a bizarre thought. If she hadn't been standing before them she could easily have been the body they had found in Coopers Field. The height was right, the build was right, he could see she wore dentures, and she lived on her own so probably would not be missed for some time. Just as well that the woman who was inviting them into her home was not a mind-reader.

Behind the front door was a large hall with a wide staircase to which was attached a stairlift. The hallway was a beautiful open space and it gave Martin some pleasure to see that the floor and ceiling had not been stripped of the original tiles and mouldings. It looked as if, until fairly recently, the place had been well looked after, but was now in danger of being neglected.

'Good morning, my dear,' Miss Forrester ignored Martin and spoke directly to Helen. 'It's lovely to see you again – and this time you've brought someone with you, quite a handsome chap isn't he?'

Helen smiled warmly but refrained from answering the question directly. 'Good morning, Miss Forrester. This is DCI Phelps and we just want to go through a few things with you. We shouldn't take up too much of your time.'

'Time is something I have plenty of,' came the reply. 'Unless my maker has other ideas.'

Acting according to protocol, Martin had shown Miss Forrester his warrant card and was not surprised at her response. 'You could be showing me one of those tacky Tesco clubcards for all I can see,' she laughed. 'Why do they insist on pretending they're giving things to their customers? They should just make things cheaper in the first place – don't you think so, Chief Inspector?'

Martin could see instantly why Helen had warned him that this visit could take some time and realised that keeping Miss Forrester on track was going to take some effort. Still, this was the start of the visit, and maybe she needed time to get used to their presence so a bit of initial chit-chat was inevitable.

His concern for the probable lengthy timescale deepened as she slowly led them to a spacious sitting room and Martin could see that she had set up a small side table with china teacups, matching milk jug and sugar basin, and a large plate of assorted chocolate biscuits. She was settling them in for the rest of the morning, and he resigned himself to the fact, thinking that she probably had few visitors, and was treating their visit as more of a social occasion than it actually was.

Realising that with her limited mobility Miss Forrester would take an age to actually make the tea, Martin raised an eyebrow towards Helen who quickly caught on and suggested to Elsie that she should sit down and start talking to DCI Phelps and let her make the tea.

'You won't know where everything is,' was the reply.

'I'm practicing at being a detective, Miss Forrester, so just point me in the direction of the kitchen and then you can tell me if I measure up.'

The only thing in the kitchen that threw Helen was the absence of tea bags and the presence of a tin of loose tea and a teapot. It was the first time she had ever made tea in this way but she remembered something her grandmother said. It was something like 'a spoon each and one for the pot ... but first make sure the pot is hot'.

Interpreting that as best she could, Helen put some boiling water into the teapot, swished it around, and poured it away, hoping that those actions sufficed for the pot-warming bit. Then, using the rather ornate spoon that seemed to live in the tea caddy, she put four measured spoons of tea leaves into the pot and filled it almost to the top with freshly boiled water.

She remembered that everything else was on the table in the lounge and so she carried the teapot through to where DCI Phelps and Miss Forrester were deep in conversation, albeit largely one-sided, with Miss Forrester claiming most of the territory.

As Helen put the teapot down on the stand that had been set aside for it, Miss Forrester briefly looked in her direction and suggested that the tea should not be poured for a couple of minutes, because real tea took that time to infuse. 'It's not like the instant taste of nothing you get from those teabags,' she had added.

Without pausing for breath, Elsie Forrester turned back to DCI Phelps and completed the sentence she herself had interrupted '... but he was a gambler.'

Martin managed to get a word in edgeways, and he had to do so because Elsie's mind was jumping all over the place and he was getting no real sense of whether she was talking about recent events or things that had happened decades ago. One thing he knew for sure: this was going to be a long session. But as he was feeling totally at ease with the world this morning, he decided to resign himself to sitting back and listening.

'Tell me about your sister,' he suggested. 'Did she live here with you or was she just visiting from her home in France?'

'I'll start at the beginning. Well, not right at the beginning because I'm sure you don't want to hear about our childhood, although there are lots of stories ... no of course you don't. I think when Daphne got married would be the best place to start.

'She married a merchant banker who made a very good living in the City, but as well as that he inherited a farm that was sold as a going concern. It included some additional land that was snapped

108

up by property developers and I remember my sister saying they had paid a fortune for it.

'The only thing wrong with their lives at that time was that they both wanted a family, but my sister was having a really bad time and her first pregnancy ended with the child, a boy, being stillborn. In spite of the best medical care money could buy her second pregnancy was brought to an abrupt end when obstetricians were forced to perform an early Caesarean section. The child, another boy, was very premature and died within hours of his emergency birth.

'It was several years before Daphne told me she was pregnant again and this time she was kept wrapped in cotton wool and a planned operation at just 33 weeks into the pregnancy produced a small, premature baby girl – but she was healthy and she survived.'

Helen used this positive moment to hand around the tea, and was rewarded with praise from Miss Forrester and a puzzled look from Martin who couldn't remember when he had last held such a delicate china cup – if ever!

Elsie continued. 'From the moment Charlotte entered the world, she seemed to know instinctively that this couple who had become her parents were going to give her everything she asked for – and ask she did. Their home at that time was a beautiful house on the edge of Blackheath Common, that's South London, you know, and I was living in a two-bedroomed house in Rhoose, not far from the Cardiff Airport.'

'Initially that was quite convenient because my sister and her family were able to come to Cardiff quite regularly, but it wasn't long before Daphne was in constant pain with her osteoarthritis and it became harder for her to travel. Also, her ladyship Charlotte wanted her own room when she came to stay and so they decided to buy a house in Cardiff. It would be an investment even if only used now and then. The upshot was that they bought this house and then suggested that I move here rather than have the place empty most of the time. I was reluctant to sell my home, but there was no mortgage here and they were paying all the bills so I would have been stupid to refuse.'

'They were besotted with Charlotte and I am sorry to say that my niece returned their unconditional love by developing a lust for money and possessions. She wasn't a brilliant student, but had inherited some of her father's genes and when she was eighteen she scraped a place at the London School of Economics, and in fact did quite well.'

'In her final year at the LSE Charlotte met a Frenchman, Frederick Lefevre, and they married two years later. Fortune seemed to be staying with Charlotte as the Lefevre family were financiers and, when he was at the height of his success, and with some help from Charlotte's parents, the couple bought a truly magnificent house in a fashionable suburb of Nantes. I've only been there once with my sister, but I remember the size of the garden – and would you believe they even have a live-in maid?'

Martin added a quick comment that he didn't know anyone with a live-in maid, inwardly wishing it wouldn't be too long before the family history got to at least the twenty-first century.

With the faint hope of moving it in that direction he asked if they still lived there, and was that where her sister had been living before she went to the French nursing home.

'Yes, they are still there,' was the reply. 'However, we've skipped an important bit regarding why my sister went to live in France.'

Out of the corner of his eye Martin saw Helen lift her hand to her face to hide a grin, and he guessed she was thinking along the lines of 'Nice try, guv!' Not noticing the body language of her visitors, Elsie continued unabated. 'When I retired aged sixty my sister and her husband William handed over the deeds of this house to me. There was no mortgage and money was no object to them. They had their large London property as well as a substantial investment portfolio, but I understand it was one of the few things that they argued with Charlotte about – she clearly didn't want me to benefit by getting something that she would have expected, in the fullness of time, to be hers.'

'Disaster struck about fifteen years ago when William was involved in a head-on collision with a lorry, and he died within hours of the accident. Charlotte asked her mother to go to France and live with her and her husband, but Daphne knew it was a hollow invitation and in any event she hadn't taken to Frederick Lefevre.'

'She asked me how I would feel if she sold up in London and came to stay with me here and I told her I would be delighted. This house is large, and after they had given it to me they no longer paid the bills, council tax, and water rates. Just those outgoings put together with general upkeep and repairs had been more than my minimum state pension, and I had soon used up my little nest egg.'

'Having Daphne here was a lifesaver for me, and the time we spent together in this house was one of the happiest periods of my life. In all that time Charlotte and her husband only came here to visit Daphne on three occasions and I particularly remember one of those times – it was about three years ago. My sister was very distressed when they left and I eventually got it out of her that the couple were having business problems and needed money. I was surprised at that, and even more surprised, in fact amazed, when I learned that the sum they needed was in excess of £250,000 – more than a quarter of a million pounds, can you believe that?'

Martin's eyes widened. 'It's a lot of money. Did your sister have that much to give them?' he asked.

'Oh yes, that much and more, and she wasn't upset about giving her daughter the money because, as she said, we didn't need it and it would in time go to Charlotte anyway. Her concern was that she didn't quite believe the story of business problems. She knew a lot more about business affairs than me and said that some of the things the couple had told her didn't ring true.

'Anyway, with Daphne promising to make a cash transfer the following day they went back to France, and we didn't see them and barely heard from them for almost a year. So that takes us back to two years ago when things started to go badly wrong and within a period of two weeks we had three visits – twice with the two of them arriving unannounced on the doorstep and once when Charlotte came on her own. After each visit there was an electronic transfer of money from Daphne's account and I don't really know how much went altogether.

'The visit from Charlotte on her own was different and although money was part of the reason for her visit she was also here to persuade her mother to live with them in France. I think my sister was flattered by the fact that her daughter needed her and so she was persuaded to go. I must say, even at the time, I thought the only thing that Charlotte needed from her mother was her money – and I was right.'

Elsie got up from her chair with some difficulty and walked

111

around in a small circle before sitting down again. 'It's OK,' she said to Martin, who had held out his hand to offer her some assistance. 'It's just that I get stiff – but not to worry, I'm almost finished.'

'For the first couple of months my sister was in France she kept in touch and at least once a week we spoke on the phone. She was able to tell me what was really happening and as I think I said earlier, the problem was gambling. Apparently Frederick was addicted to just about any form of gambling – from cards to horse racing to roulette and other things I had never heard of, and most of the time he wasn't much good at it.'

'Over the years their house, which had originally been bought outright, had been mortgaged and re-mortgaged and was now at the limit of its equity value, with defaults on payments making it in danger of being repossessed.'

'Still he gambled, and Daphne told me that her own savings were slowly dwindling, although her investment portfolio remained intact and provided a good income. After a couple of months my sister told me that she was not well, and that was the last phone call I got from her while she lived with Charlotte. When I rang, I was always told she was lying down and was generally unwell. My own interpretation of the situation is that they used the deterioration in her health as an excuse to ship her off to a nursing home, but only after getting control of her finances.

'I rang the French nursing home regularly but I don't speak the language and no one there would spare the time to even try and understand what I was saying, even though I now know that some of them had a fair grasp of English. Anyway, to cut a long story short, I made up my mind to go there personally and see the situation for myself.'

Martin stared hard at her, taking in her frail figure and could see that almost any movement caused pain. 'You went to see your sister in France – on your own?' he questioned, finding it hard to believe possible.

The cheeky twinkle that came to Elsie's eyes answered Martin's question even before the words came out of her mouth. 'Yes, Chief Inspector. I got my neighbour to help me with the travel arrangements. and armed with extra painkillers I went by taxi, train, and ferry. It took eighteen hours to get there, but it was

112

worth every minute just to see my sister.'

Martin's opinion of Miss Forrester went up several notches, and he asked her how she had managed with the language. She told him that Mrs Evans next door, had insisted on writing telephone numbers and addresses on pieces of cardboard for her, and a list of useful French phrases with their English translations. 'Not that Mrs Evans speaks French, but she found a translation site on her son's computer and we had fun doing it, you just …'

Martin stopped her going into a lengthy explanation. 'Yes, I've used the translation sites myself – but I still can't get over you going off on your own like that.'

Helen shook her head and added. 'Me neither, I don't know any French and would be nervous about making myself understood.'

'Where there's a will there's a way, my dear, and I was determined not to be fobbed off any more: I had to see Daphne. I was shocked when I did see her, because she had no life in her eyes, and she was just lying on a single bed in a drab room, seemingly counting out the last days of her life. My reward for taking such an arduous and painful journey was the smile that transformed her face when she saw me.

'We talked for about an hour before an officious buxom woman ushered me out, but not before Daphne and I had hatched a plan and I left her with some hope. Needless to say I was shattered when I got back but after a few days recovering I set about putting our plans into action. Did you know that anyone can hire a private ambulance? It's not cheap but it's an excellent service.'

Miss Forrester went on to relate how, with the help of her neighbour's computer, she had found a company that was prepared to go to France and bring Daphne back to her home in Cardiff. 'They told me it would need two of their trained staff to facilitate the transfer, and of course that sent the cost up, but Daphne had already told me not to worry about that.'

'What about her passport?' Helen asked. 'Did she have it? And what about medical consent for the transfer, was that needed?'

'I had already checked the passport situation with my sister when we were scheming, and she told me that her leather clutch bag given to her by William was never out of her sight and contained her passport, her birth certificate, and her most treasured possession – their marriage certificate. I discussed the need for consent for her transfer with the private ambulance company and they assured me that my sister, as a voluntary resident, was not under medical supervision, and provided she consented to the transfer there would be no problem – and there wasn't.

'It all went like clockwork and they got back here on Friday 1st July, and Daphne told me then that nothing on God's earth would ever make her leave this house again. We were about to telephone Charlotte to tell her about the move when she phoned us and at the end of a very acrimonious conversation my sister made it clear to her daughter that she had no intention of ever going back to France.'

Elsie told Martin that in just a few days her sister's health improved, and she was able to get out of bed and potter around the house, even help with the cooking. 'She told me many times that she wasn't sure which she had hated the most, being at her daughter's house or confined to the nursing home. So you see, don't you, Inspector? When she had disappeared I could not bring myself to believe she had gone of her own free will, and that's when I reported her missing.'

'Yes,' replied Martin. 'From what you tell me I can understand perfectly that you were concerned. You don't need to tell me about the circumstances surrounding your report because all of that has been carefully documented by PC Cook-Watts, but with your permission I would like to see your sister's room before we go.'

Elsie got up and led them to a room just down a short corridor from the kitchen and adjacent to the side entrance of the house. She explained that her sister had not been up to using the stairs even with the aid of the lift, and so they had converted this room into a sort of bed-sitting room for her.

There was a bed, a wardrobe, a dressing table, and two upright chairs, apparently all moved from upstairs by the neighbour's son, and very few personal belongings. 'They must have taken her in her nightdress, dressing gown, and slippers, not even a coat, because the one I bought her is still hanging in the wardrobe and all the other clothes I got are still here too.'

'So what exactly did she take with her?' asked Martin.

'The indoor clothes I have just mentioned, her clutch-bag, as presumably she would have needed her passport, her toothbrush, and bits and pieces from the wash basin over there. We were going to convert the utility room next to the kitchen into an easy-access shower room. That's what I don't understand, we had so many plans, she wouldn't have just gone off like that – not without telling me ...'

For the first time there were signs of Elsie breaking down, and Martin suggested that Helen take her back to the sitting room while he continued to look around the room. Ironically the clothes and shoes in the wardrobe were all from Marks and Spencer and looked to Martin to be the same size as those found in Coopers Field. It was the same with the underclothes in the drawer but this time there was at least one bra!

There was an empty glass on the bedside table and two large-print books, and he noted that the bed was clean but had been slept in, so presumably Elsie had left it as she found it. The only thing on the dressing table was a hairbrush with a silver handle, and Martin remembered from the missing person report that hair from the hairbrush had been used for DNA analysis.

Martin was becoming more and more convinced that the body found in Coopers Field was that of Daphne Mansfield, but if that was the case how was it possible that the maid had seen her in France? That bit made no sense at all.

He joined the two women in the sitting room and asked Elsie if she could describe the stick her sister had been using during the time she had been there. Was still in the house?

'Oh no, Chief Inspector, it isn't here, she would have needed it to help her walk so she must have taken it with her – and as for describing it, I can go one better, as I have a photograph of it.' Elsie moved to a sideboard and opened a drawer stuffed full of photographs, but unlike most people's boxes of memories these were in an order well understood by Elsie. Within a couple of seconds she had found what she was looking for and handed a photograph to Martin.

'As I mentioned, all the women in our family suffer with their joints, and on Daphne's fiftieth birthday William bought her that stick. The wood is oak, but the top is made of silver, and as you can see is in the shape of a globe and etched with the outline of the world's continents and countries. It's unique as William had it designed and made especially for her. Over the years she has been offered thousands of pounds for it, but would never part with something that still linked her to her beloved William.'

Martin's blood ran cold as he thought through the possibility of Daphne being killed by her treasured keepsake.

'Is it alright if I ask you a question, Chief Inspector?' Elsie asked Martin.

'Yes, of course,' came the reply.

'Well, I may be old, but I still have all my faculties and it doesn't take a genius to realise that someone as important as a DCI is not sent on a routine missing person investigation. I also keep up with the news and have heard the details regarding the old woman's body that was found in Coopers Field. Are you contemplating the possibility that the body is that of my sister?'

Realising the courage it had taken to ask that question, Martin spent time explaining to Elsie exactly where his thinking was and promised to keep her totally informed of any developments. He told Helen to stay with Miss Forrester and he would get a squad car to pick her up later. Martin had two reasons for doing this, the first being just simple compassion for a woman whom he thought deserved some special care. The second was because he knew that within hours he would have the DNA results of the body found in Coopers Field and Helen would be a good person to be around if someone had to pick up the pieces of a very brave old lady …

Chapter Ten

'Are you absolutely sure?' demanded Martin, although even as he asked the question he knew that he had already been given the answer, he just didn't want to believe it.

'Beyond any reasonable doubt!' returned Alex for the second time, and with Matt nodding his head in agreement.

The three men were sitting in Martin's office ploughing through two large plates of assorted sandwiches and an enormous jug of coffee. It had been around lunchtime when Alex had gone in search of Martin with the latest news from the laboratories and met Matt who had just had a message to say Martin was on his way back. Both men agreed that the DCI would be disappointed with the test results and decided that breaking the news with coffee and sandwiches in his office would be the best course of action.

The food and drink had been well received but as expected the news was not. 'I just can't believe the DNA is not a match – I think we all expected it to be, didn't we?'

'Well we all certainly hoped it would be,' suggested Matt. 'Everything else fits perfectly and Prof. Moore and I had a discussion about the dental records. Being such a stickler for accuracy, he followed up our conversation and had another with the dentist who looked after Mrs Mansfield when she lived in Cardiff. Between the two of them they concluded that if a new set of dentures were made from the impressions kept on file they would fit the murdered woman perfectly!'

'So,' stressed Martin. 'The description of Mrs Mansfield given to us by her sister matches the height and weight of the Coopers Field body. Prof. Moore has been able to tell us that the dead woman suffered from osteoarthritis and had cataracts and so did, or does, Mrs Mansfield. I have spent most of this morning listening to Elsie Forrester telling me her sister's life story and so I know that the obstetric history of both women appears to be identical. The only thing at odds is the DNA!'

'Well of course there is also the fact that Mrs Mansfield was seen in France the morning after she left the Cardiff address,' said Matt. 'According to forensics and the evidence of the till receipt from M&S it looks as if our woman was killed the day before Daphne Mansfield was seen in France – so how does that add up?'

Alex poured out the last of the coffee, claimed the remaining solitary tuna mayo sandwich, and listened to Martin thinking aloud.

'There are two possibilities here. One is that the body is that of Mrs Mansfield but for some reason the hair taken from the brush in her room was not hers, don't ask me to enlarge on that, I can't think how or why it shouldn't be. In that scenario the maid in France was either mistaken or she deliberately lied about seeing Mrs Mansfield in the Lefevres' car.

'The other possibility is that the DNA sample from the hair is that of Mrs Mansfield, and we have found a body that does not match her DNA but in every other respect fits her to such a level of detail that it is uncanny – I simply don't believe in that level of possibility.'

'Is there anything else we can do to help with the identification of the body?' asked Alex.

'Yes,' replied Martin immediately. 'It's not an exact science but we can ask Prof. Moore if he has any colleagues in the field of forensic facial reconstruction. There are forensic artists who are able to come up with a likeness of the deceased using a three-dimensional facial reconstruction technique. I was at a seminar in Oxford last September when the technique was demonstrated and it was most impressive.'

'The other thing I thought of was the possibility of lifting fingerprints from the body ...'

'But we would have nothing to compare them with,' interrupted Matt.

Martin continued. 'I've spent hours this morning with Miss Forrester and we were shown her sister's room. It looked to me as if the bedclothes and everything else had not been touched since Mrs Mansfield left and I know for certain that there are two books and one drinking glass on the bedside table – her fingerprints could be on any or all of those.'

Alex offered to go and pick up the articles, but Martin suggested that Matt should do it and pick PC Cook-Watts up at the same time. He asked Alex to speak to the professor about fingerprints and about any contacts he may have who could help with the idea of facial reconstruction.

'There's a fair chance you'll get your head bitten off,' Martin added with a grin. 'I very much doubt if he will consider the practice to be scientific, more likely in his book to be labelled as some new-fangled nonsense – good luck!'

When Matt and Alex had left his office, Martin sat for some time at his desk with his head in his hands, trying to steer himself away from the feeling of going around in ever-decreasing circles. He hated the idea of not being able to make sense of things, and was also getting concerned that he was placing far too much emphasis on wanting the body to be Mrs Mansfield and so not pursuing other possibilities.

Martin knew his own strengths and weaknesses and was aware that top of the weakness list was his dogged determination to look at the minutiae, sometimes at the expense of the big picture. In some of his performance reviews that weakness had been identified, but no one could deny that his results were second to none.

He mentally listened again to some of the words spoken by Elsie Forrester, and he particularly remembered the numerous times she had said her sister hated being in France – so why had she gone back there? There was also her talk of the plans they had to make the house more comfortable for Daphne by changing the existing utility room to create an easy access, walk-in shower. Everything pointed to Mrs Mansfield staying with her sister and Martin had heard nothing that suggested she would ever contemplate moving back to France.

Then, the biggest thing for him was the fact that Daphne had gone without even saying goodbye to Elsie. Elsie, the sister who at over eighty years of age and with poor mobility and eyesight had made an incredible journey, on her own, to a foreign country, just to see that her sister was alright. That action would have made the strong bond that already existed between the two sisters all the more unbreakable, and Martin could not give credit to the idea that

Daphne Mansfield had just left the country without first of all speaking to Elsie.

By reporting her sister missing, Elsie had highlighted her concerns. She believed that even if her sister had gone back to France, she had been forced to go back against her wishes. Martin followed that line of thinking: at least it made sense, and would certainly explain why there were no goodbyes.

It sounded tantamount to abduction – and if Daphne Mansfield was able to tell the authorities that she had been forced into making the journey, then that was exactly what it had been. But how was he going to find out? Over the years Martin had dealt with a number of international police forces, and although their involvement had sometimes been fruitful there had been far too many occasions when language and culture differences had made for difficult working relationships. There were countless arrangements in place to enable the detection of crime to be facilitated between Britain and France, but this arm's length way of doing things didn't suit Martin and he picked up the phone to sort out travel arrangements.

While waiting for a call back from the Administration and Finance department regarding the agreed method of travel, Martin took out a blank sheet of paper and jotted down reasons for and possible outcomes of the trip to France. He knew that everything would have to be done officially with his equivalent opposite number in Nantes being made aware of the visit – but that was not his prime concern. Martin didn't want to risk Superintendent Bryant knowing that a visit to France to investigate a possible abduction was being considered when the DCI was charged with investigating the body in Coopers Field.

The Super was a stickler for protocol and if there was an abduction to investigate, and as yet Martin didn't even know if there was, it would be for Alan Bryant to allocate the investigating team – not for Martin to take it upon himself. Not for the first time Martin devised a strategy to circumvent the system. He and Matt would be on their way to France before the Super became aware of what was happening.

There was a timid knock on the door and with Martin's permission in walked a seriously overweight young man carrying a folder labelled 'DCI Phelps – Foreign Transport Arrangements'. In order to control travel costs all officers making journeys outside the South Wales Police area were required to complete a 'reason for travel' form that had to be authorised by Superintendent Bryant in advance of the journey. The form was the top document inside the folder and Martin was about to put it to one side when the young man spoke but in a voice barely above a whisper. 'I have strict orders to ensure that form RT1 is completed and on Superintendent Bryant's desk before he leaves for his North Wales meeting at 3 p.m.'

Martin looked at the youth and saw that he was red in the face and his hands were shaking – but why? Was bringing some papers to the office of a DCI such an ordeal? Was the boy under real or perceived pressure to meet the 3 p.m. deadline?

'I haven't seen you before, have I?' asked Martin looking up from the papers. 'What's your name?'

'Harry, sir,' was the reply. 'Harry Maidment.'

'Well, Harry,' continued Martin. 'Why don't you sit down, and I'll go through these papers. You can help me with the form when I know whether or not I am happy with the arrangements that have been made.'

Harry shuffled and was obviously ill at ease. 'Mrs Painter would have a fit if I sat down in your office. I have to stand at her desk and she's not even a detective.'

Martin couldn't believe that his simple suggestion of taking a seat had caused such angst, and he had the uncomfortable feeling that he was witnessing the results of bullying. He had seen more of that than he cared to remember over the years, and had vowed that if he ever got into a position of influence he would never ignore even the suggestion that someone was being bullied. Harry was an ideal target for a bully, as he was, to put it bluntly, fat, and obviously lacking in self-esteem and Martin resolved there and then to make it his business to find out if there was any substance to his concerns.

Martin thumbed through the papers and then spoke to Harry. 'How did you reach the conclusion that car and ferry is the best option?' Martin asked, trying to engage Harry in a conversation where the facts were known to him and so hopefully boosting his confidence.

It worked, and Harry eagerly explained. 'When we get a

request to arrange transport we first of all have to take account of why the officer making the request is travelling. Most of the time it's to go to a conference or a meeting so it's a simple train or plane ticket and sometimes an overnight stay at a hotel, but that requires written authorisation and is rarely given.'

'When the purpose of the journey is to follow a criminal investigation, the officers usually want to take their cars because their plans can change when they are on the move.'

Martin nodded his head in agreement. 'And in the case of my request, what did you consider?'

'Well, two major considerations are always time and cost and the first thing I looked at was a flight from Cardiff to Nantes, thinking that would be the quickest, but it wasn't. There were no direct flights, and the best I could come up with was a one-stop ticket; depending on the time of day that involved either a four- or a six-hour transfer time in Amsterdam.'

'Believe me I'm glad that you didn't choose that one,' encouraged Martin. 'Go on.'

'We have a computer programme that allows us to put in all the options with the times and any variables and basically it does the cost benefit analysis in a matter of seconds, it's brilliant. It always gives at least three options and ensures that all the discounts and special deals we have are taken into account.'

'Sounds like a really impressive piece of software, I must come down and you can demonstrate it to me,' said Martin, inwardly thinking that this would be the means of getting a better look at Harry's work situation.

Harry smiled and Martin saw, beneath the excess layers that plumped and distorted his face, a pleasant and likeable young man.

'And this is the package you came up with for me, is it?'

Harry nodded. 'It's to take your own car, as you requested, from here to Poole and then you go from Poole to Cherbourg on the high-speed ferry. There is just one thing, sir, and for some reason Mrs Painter thought this was funny. She said that as your ferry crossing leaves at 7 a.m. and with about a two and a half hour drive to Poole before that, you would need an alarm call way before 4 a.m.'

Martin said nothing but made a mental note of another reason to ensure he was instrumental in packing the delightful Mrs Painter off on as many deadly boring interpersonal skills training programmes as Shelley's department could find – preferably courses in Scotland starting at 9 a.m. and not eligible for overnight accommodation.

To Harry he just said. 'That's not a problem. DS Pryor and I will share the driving and we have two and a half hours on the ferry so we can catch some shut-eye if we need it. The longest leg of the journey will be Cherbourg to Nantes, and although we are both quite used to driving on the right it always takes a while to get back into it. Even so, we should get to Nantes early afternoon, hopefully around two o'clock, that's taking into account the hour difference between UK and French times.'

Having agreed the travel arrangements Martin turned his attention to the dreaded RT1 form and completed most of it before turning to Harry. 'Leave this with me, there are two of us making this journey so you also need a signature from DS Pryor and I know he's out of the building at the moment. As soon as he gets back I'll get him to sign and I promise the form will be on the superintendent's desk before three o'clock.'

Harry looked most unhappy with that suggestion, so Martin picked up the phone and after a quick glance at the internal directory punched in 7217 and was greeted by the 'I am a very important person' voice of Mrs Painter.

With none of his usual pleasantries Martin spoke. 'This is DCI Phelps. Harry has put together an excellent package and I am totally happy with the arrangements. Both DS Pryor and I will be travelling and so as you will know both our signatures are required on the RT1 form. At the moment my sergeant is investigating a murder and is unavailable to complete your form but it will be on the desk of Superintendent Bryant by fifteen hundred hours. Good afternoon.'

Not waiting for any response, Martin replaced the receiver, and was rewarded by the look of relief and even a slight grin on Harry's face as he left the office. At the same time Martin felt disgusted that his action was needed in the first place.

He looked at his watch and was surprised to see that it was already twenty to three. He was tossing up whether to spend an hour in the incident room or come up with some objectives for the trip to France when the door opened – Alex and Matt were back and obviously had some news.

'You first,' said Matt looking in Alex's direction. 'Give us an update on the possibility of forensic facial reconstruction.'

'More than a possibility,' returned Alex. 'We were wrong about Prof. Moore's opinion of the process – in fact he is quite taken with it. Apparently he attended the same seminar as you in Oxford last year and since then he has seen two examples of reconstruction by Professor Henrietta Van-Bruggen and apparently they were both spot on.'

'Yes, that's the woman who gave the lecture,' said Martin. 'I remember expecting her to have something of a Dutch or German accent, but she was fluent American!'

'Well, she's in Cardiff at the moment. Do you remember on Monday, when Prof. Moore made a hasty exit from the Coopers Field Murder briefing? Apparently at that time he was already ten minutes late for the start of a lecture he was supposed to be giving at the Cardiff International Arena. Prof. Van-Bruggen took his place and he filled her slot later that afternoon, and then they did a joint question and answer session that was, according to the feedback, quite outstanding.'

'I'll bet it was,' said Martin. 'I remember her session in Oxford, and as they both love an audience I could well imagine them being a superb double act – but how does that help us?'

'I spoke to Prof. Moore, and he seemed to think the visiting professor would jump at the chance of showing off her skills in a real live criminal investigation. She is doing a UK lecture tour and this would apparently boost her credibility no end. Anyway, I wouldn't mind betting she is already here, because Prof. Moore was last seen driving his Lexus towards Cardiff University on a mission to bring her back.'

Martin nodded. 'That's good. So it's possible that by tomorrow we could have an image of the dead woman worthy of circulating in the hope of getting her identified.'

Matt was keen to interrupt. 'The other thing we have to tell you is not going to make much sense but it is an absolute fact. When I went back to Miss Forrester's house she was able to confirm that she had not touched anything in her sister's room since she disappeared and that the drinking glass and the books on the bedside table did belong to Daphne Mansfield. She was more than happy for me to take them, and Alex didn't have any trouble getting prints from one of the books and the glass.'

Alex took up the thread. 'We used laser technology to scan the fingerprints of the body and we have two partial prints from the book and the glass and together they almost make a complete print. It would obviously be more conclusive if we had a total print but even with what we have I believe there is no doubt that there is a positive match.'

There was a moment's silence as Martin's brain took in the implications of this information. 'We have a body that in terms of height, weight, medical and dental history and now fingerprints match Mrs Mansfield, but DNA that we know comes from her hairbrush is not a match – you're right, it doesn't make any sense. I think I know all I should do about fingerprints, but tell me if I am wrong. People have the same fingerprints all their lives; there's no change as we get older, is there?'

'No change,' agreed Alex.

'There is a generic element to our fingerprints, but that's only a general thing, and even identical twins, who will have the same DNA, will not have the same fingerprints – similarities yes, but not the same.'

Alex nodded and Martin continued. 'When we were having our forensic lectures, I remember being very interested in the identical twin situation, because with everything else including DNA being a match you would expect fingerprints to follow the trend. It's all down to the fingerprint ridges apparently, and the differences may well be the result of early stress or movement in the womb.'

'Well remembered,' interrupted Alex. 'Family members may share a general pattern of ridges, but specific pattern or fine detail is unique. Consequently no two people have the exact same pattern, and for over a hundred years we have had the science of fingerprinting, much to the chagrin of criminals worldwide.'

'Exactly,' concluded Martin. 'Fingerprints have served us well and you're telling me that those of the body and those taken from Mrs Mansfield's room are a match.'

'Because we've taken two part prints – one from the glass and one from the book – any good defence counsel would try to rubbish our conclusions but I have seen both sets under the microscope and I am convinced they are the same,' argued Alex.

'So there are just two things standing in the way of identifying the Coopers Field body as Mrs Mansfield, and they are the DNA results and the sighting of her in France after the time of the murder. Let's take the DNA results first. If the body is Daphne Mansfield why was the DNA taken from her bedroom and provided by her sister not a match?'

'Maybe it simply wasn't her hairbrush – or maybe her sister or her daughter had used it,' Matt said.

'OK – but we know that DNA is passed down from one generation to the next and some parts remain almost unchanged, so even if the hairbrush actually belonged to her sister or her daughter we would be looking at enough of a match to be asking questions.'

'The other thing is why would the French housekeeper tell Miss Forrester she had seen Daphne in her daughter's car if she hadn't?'

'Perhaps her employers told her to say she had,' replied Matt. 'What exactly does Miss Forrester say happened when she phoned her niece's home to find out if her sister was there?'

Martin picked up the relevant part of the report he had been scanning and read aloud. 'The French housekeeper had answered the phone and told Elsie that M. et Mme Lefevre had called in that morning to collect some papers needed for taking Mme's mother back to Maison de Retraite. The maid apparently said that Mme Mansfield was sitting in the back of the car but did not get out as her legs were too stiff and in any event M. Lefevre was in a hurry.'

Matt butted in. 'So the maid may not even have seen Mrs Mansfield sitting in the back of the car, it's possible she was just told that by M. Lefevre when he rushed in to get whatever documents he seemed to need. Perhaps she was already dead and perhaps they had killed her and left her in Coopers Field. I can understand why they would strip her of any clothes that may be identifiable but I don't understand the pile of new clothes. What's that all about?'

Matt continued asking and answering his own random questions before Martin, who was looking through his office window, suddenly stopped him and handed him the folder left by Harry. 'Sign the top form and take the folder down to the Super's office, quick as you can. It's now five to three and I promised Harry it would be on Superintendent Bryant's desk by three o'clock.'

'Who's Harry and what am I signing?' asked Matt.

'I suppose you could say that Harry is our travel agent and these are our travel papers,' replied Martin. 'I spent hours this morning with a gutsy old lady who managed to convince me that her sister would never have gone to France of her own free will and without even saying goodbye. Even if she isn't our body, she is someone who may require our help, on the basis that she may have been abducted. I don't have the level of evidence to convince the Super of the need for us to follow it up so that's why I've kept the forms until now. I've just seen him get into his car at the front entrance, he's always five minutes early – would make a hopeless criminal, far too predictable. So if you get these forms onto his desk within the next couple of minutes I'll have kept my promise and we'll be able to travel in the certain knowledge that I have to some extent obeyed the rules.'

Matt didn't read the detail but signed the form and was halfway through the door when he asked the obvious question. 'When are we going?'

Martin and Alex didn't need much imagination to guess the look on Matt's face when he heard the reply.

'Pick you up at a quarter to four tomorrow morning – don't be late!'

Chapter Eleven

'I thought it would be pitch black but the sky is already getting lighter,' remarked Matt. They had been travelling just over an hour, had crossed the Severn Bridge and were well into English territory, making excellent progress. 'It's not exactly busy, but it still amazes me how many people are on the road at this hour of the morning.'

'The official sunrise time this morning is five thirty and the weather forecast for today is good, so within the next half hour or so it will really be daylight. Let me know if you want to stop at any point, because unless you do I'm happy to do this journey without a break. I feel quite surprisingly wide awake,' said Martin. 'I know this route very well as my Aunt Pat had relatives living in Parkstone. We spent at least a week with them every summer holiday, but I'm sad to say I've only visited twice since she died.

'That happens,' said Matt. 'When we were kids our parents took us to Bournemouth seven years in a row as a friend of my dad had a holiday cottage. Last year my eldest sister, Laura, took her family on a caravan holiday in the same area and they came back after two days. Laura said she kept expecting Mum and Dad to be sitting on deckchairs and looking out for them as they had done when she was last there. It spooked her and she has vowed to take her family somewhere different every year and not turn any one place into a potential shrine.'

They fell in to a companionable silence, and both men took in the beauty of the countryside as the sun woke up and the shadows of the night were lifted to reveal England's green and pleasant land. Weeks of constant rain, followed by just a few days of warm sunny weather, had transformed the landscape, and now the green of the hills and the view of animals grazing in the pastures were just like a verse by William Blake.

After less than two hours' driving, Martin turned the car onto the A350, and heading in a south-easterly direction soon had Poole well and truly in his sights. 'We should be there within the next half hour, and that will give us plenty of time to stretch our legs with a walk around the harbour, before going to the ferry port. I don't want to be among the first cars onto the ferry because that will mean we're the last off when we reach Cherbourg. We can get coffee and something to eat on board.'

The very thought of food sent Matt's stomach into a merry dance: after all, it was twelve hours since he had fed his gastric gremlins, and they were getting decidedly restless.

An hour later they were each settled on one of the reclining seats, looking out over the waves. Catering for cousins on both sides of the Channel, the on-board café had offered English- and French-style breakfasts and a good selection of coffee. Soon after eating an assortment of soft bread rolls with some ham, eggs, and cheese, Matt pushed the back of his chair into a more comfortable position and closed his eyes.

Martin looked at his relaxed sergeant and commented. 'I thought the idea of a strong black coffee with an extra shot was to wake you up – not send you to sleep!'

Matt opened one eye and grinned. 'It was, boss, but it takes some time to work on me, so if I have a doze now and then get another strong coffee when I wake, I'll be buzzing by the time we get to Cherbourg.'

They seemed to be positively gliding at high speed across the water and Martin picked up a brochure displaying details of the aluminium twin hulled catamaran that was ferrying them. It was scheduled to get them from England to France in slightly less than two and a half hours and it was the first time Martin had used the high-speed service.

Perhaps the next time he used it he would have Shelley with him. He quite fancied the idea of a short break in Paris, but they were going to the Edinburgh Festival in August, so maybe September. It made Martin feel good to be planning ahead for a future that included Shelley, and just for a moment he lay back, listening to the sounds of the ocean, and wondered where they would be a year from now.

Not just for a moment. It was almost one and a half hours later when Martin looked up to see Matt towering above him holding two large cups of coffee. 'I thought I was meant to be the sleepyhead,' he joked. 'You've been out like a light and I thought I was going to have to wake you when we arrived.'

Martin gratefully accepted the coffee and shook his head. 'Last thing I remember was looking at the waves, but they must have been more hypnotic than I imagined – certainly more effective than counting sheep.'

'We'll be docking at Cherbourg in about half an hour,' said Matt. 'I assume you would like me to drive for a bit. I'm happy with driving over here and welcome the opportunity; anyway, it's easy now that we can just follow the instructions on the sat-nav and don't even have to read the foreign road signs. Do you have any plans for when we get to the Lefevres' family home?'

Martin looked at his sergeant but was reluctant to confess the sketchy nature of his plans and just said his main objective was to interview the couple regarding the period of time they were last in Cardiff and the circumstances under which Mrs Mansfield apparently left with them. 'I'll fill you in with some extra bits of information on the journey – you know of course that their home is a bit further on than Nantes, probably about twenty minutes' extra driving time, and heading back towards the coast?'

Matt nodded and the two of them walked around the deck, stretching their legs, and making use of the toilets before heading for the car. It wasn't long before they were given the OK to roll off the ferry and Matt turned on the ignition of Martin's car. Their strategy had worked well, and within minutes they were the fifth vehicle to move onto French soil.

An hour after leaving Cherbourg they were on the E3 heading southeast and making good time, having mercifully missed the rush-hour traffic on both sides of the Channel. Two hours into the journey and with only the occasional direction needed from the sat-nav they just followed the road ahead and already Nantes was signposted. Twenty minutes later they were, according to the road signs, entering Pays de la Loire and Martin suggested they stop at the next petrol station to use the loo, get a coffee, and stretch their legs.

Matt answered. 'Well, I'll make the stop at the next manned petrol station because according to my youngest sister, the loos in the unmanned petrol stops are without exception pretty disgusting.'

He made a face as he delivered this piece of news, and Martin laughed as he imagined Matt's sister and her three young daughters making a similar face when they had told him to avoid this experience.

When they resumed the journey it was with Martin back in the driving seat and Matt relating a story about the only other time he had been to Nantes. Unsurprisingly, he had made the trip with his sisters, this time two of them and consequently six nieces. Martin assumed his sisters' husbands were also there, but the females of the group always seemed to dominate Matt's stories.

'We went to see a project called "The Machines of the Isle of Nantes",' continued Matt. 'It was very impressive. The highlight for the girls was this huge moving mechanical elephant that they could actually ride on. Apparently it's the second elephant that's been built, the first one was constructed for a play performed to mark the centenary of Jules Verne's death. This play, by all accounts, was performed in lots of locations worldwide – although I confess I had never heard of it. For some reason, the original elephant was destroyed, and then this new one was built with the capacity to carry – oh, I would think forty to fifty people. It's huge, probably more than twelve metres high. It's made of wood and steel and I particularly remember being told it weighs forty-five tons and that's the equivalent of about sixty full-grown Indian elephants. It's got loads of articulated parts and trundles along, not very quickly mind you, taking tourists on a forty-five minute circular ride.'

Martin drove as instructed by the navigation system and they headed for a bypass that took them back into a more rural setting. Matt's story had been an interesting diversion but now Martin needed to focus both their minds on what lay ahead and he briefed Matt on what he wanted to get from the visit and what he had discovered before leaving the office yesterday.

'I want to officially interview M. et Mme Lefevre but when I contacted my opposite number in Nantes, to ensure we wouldn't be treading on any toes, I was surprised to learn that they are known to the police, or at least he is. It's regarding matters of fraud and other white-collar crimes, but nothing is proven as yet, although his business is being scrutinised and they expect to be making an arrest in the not-too-distant future.

'As you know, my French is pretty good, and Lieutenant Beaumont speaks English quite well so we had no problems communicating. I got the message that although they aren't chasing Lefevre in relation to what he called "red-collar crime" there is a general feeling amongst his officers that Lefevre is a nasty piece of work.'

Matt pondered. 'Red-collar crime is not a category we generally refer to, guv, and we do tend to consider all white-collar criminals as non-violent. However I did read a paper once where the researcher found that the majority of white-collar criminals do display violent tendencies, and many do become dangerous individuals, with some turning in desperation to red-collar crime.'

'Let's hope Lefevre doesn't decide to display those tendencies during our visit,' replied Martin. 'I've got emergency numbers entered into my phone in case we run into any problems.'

'Good thinking,' Matt said.

'I intend telling Charlotte Lefevre and her husband that we're following up on a missing persons report and are anxious to know the whereabouts of Mrs Daphne Mansfield, Charlotte's mother. I very much doubt that she will be at their home and I suspect they will tell us that she's being looked after in the nursing home. Only I know she is not!

'As you know we have tried several times, without any success, to make contact with the Maison de Retraite but most of our calls have ended with the phone either being left off the hook their end or the receiver being replaced in the middle of a conversation. I don't know what sort of place it is but thankfully I already have information that means we won't need to go there to find out. I got the information as the result of one final effort to communicate by phone, and about four o'clock yesterday I actually spoke to someone who seemed to understand what I wanted.

'Her name was Annette, and she remembered Mrs Mansfield as she had been on duty when the private ambulance arrived to take her to her sister's home in Wales. She said that all hell broke loose when the owner of the home knew Daphne had gone, because he had a special arrangement with her son-in-law M. Lefevre to keep her safe and alive. She couldn't elaborate on that because she didn't know what it meant.

'I asked her if Mrs Mansfield was happy to be back and for a moment there was silence and I thought she had put the phone down. When she did speak she said if I had been given to understand that Mrs Mansfield was there, I had been misinformed. Mrs Mansfield was not there, she had never been back, and the last time Annette had seen her was the day she left in the private ambulance.'

'So the maid lied when she said that Daphne Mansfield was outside the house and that the Lefevres were taking her back to the nursing home?' queried Matt.

'Maybe lied, or maybe just believed what she had been told: we'll have to ask her,' Martin said

There were some quite stunning properties in the area they were passing through, and according to the route calculations they were nearly at their destination. The house they pulled up outside was a converted stone barn, and it was obvious that the original building had been extended and the whole renovation had been done to a very high specification.

It was not a recent project, and from the way the stone had weathered Martin guessed that it had been reconstructed about thirty years ago. The mature shrubs and trees in the garden fitted with that sort of timescale. It also fitted in with the time that the Lefevres, as a young married couple, would have moved to the area, and with the support of their respective families been able to build the house of their dreams. Whatever else they were going to find out about the family there was no doubt that they had expensive tastes.

'Great property,' said Matt. 'Worth a bomb, I bet.'

'Well, if you transported it in its entirety back to one of the suburbs of Cardiff you would be looking at well in excess of a million, and if you put it on Blackheath Common you could come close to doubling that – but it'll be worth a lot less here. That's the nature of the property market, and generally speaking house prices over here are much less than back home.'

The two detectives were standing alongside Martin's car and looking at the elaborate design of the property, but even as Martin was speaking it was becoming obvious that they were being watched from inside the house.

Matt confirmed Martin's suspicions. 'Curtain twitcher on the ground floor – third window along – shortish woman with curly brown hair – probably late fifties.'

Making certain they were not seen looking in the direction of their watcher, Matt opened the very heavy, burgundy-coloured iron-gate, and both men walked down a short path towards the front door. Martin rang the doorbell and after a moment rang it again.

'I can't hear it ringing at all,' commented Matt. 'Maybe it isn't working, but we were definitely spotted coming towards the house so why doesn't someone come to the door?'

'Well we haven't come all this way just to be left standing outside,' said Martin and this time he used the heavy brass knocker bringing it down on its striker several times and ensuring that anyone in the house would have to hear it.

A middle-aged woman with blue-black hair answered the door and in a high-pitched but very loud voice asked them what they thought they were doing. She spoke in French and Martin translated although Matt had already got a good understanding of what she had said just by her frantic gesticulation and the look of fury on her face.

Both men took out their warrant cards and Martin, speaking in French, confirmed their identities and explained that they were there to see Monsieur et Madame Lefevre.

This official action had an instant response and the woman suddenly smiled politely and asked them into the hall. She pointed to a couple of matching oak chairs on either side of a semi-circular table and then she hurried off towards the back of the house.

Neither of them sat down and Matt wandered to the edge of the spiral staircase and looked up towards the first floor. The walls in the spacious hall and all the way up the stairs were wood-panelled and hanging on each of the middle panels was an oil painting. 'It's all a bit over the top for my taste,' remarked Matt. 'I couldn't make a comment about any of the art as I'm no expert, but it looks more as if it hasn't been bought to be appreciated for itself but more as just a statement of wealth.

Martin knew exactly what Matt meant and was nodding his agreement when the woman, who they had both taken to be the housekeeper, returned. To the surprise of both men she spoke to them in English.

'My name is Madame Sheldon and I'm sorry I was angry when I opened the door, but we have had some bother recently and I thought you were here to make more trouble.'

'What sort of trouble,?' said Martin, fishing for any information he could get.

'Oh just business, just business,' came the reply. Mme Sheldon was clearly already regretting having mentioned the word trouble. 'I am sorry to inform you that there is no one at home at this moment, and I really have no idea when either Mme Lefevre or her husband is likely to return.'

Martin chose to ignore what he knew to be a lie, but he made a mental note of just how easily this woman could lie on behalf of her employers.

'That's not a problem,' he said. 'You are also on our list of people to see, so if you're able to spare us a few minutes of your time we can take a statement from you while waiting for the others to return.'

She was trapped by her lie and now looked a bit scared. 'What do you mean, take a statement from me? I know nothing about M. Lefevre's business dealings or any of the people he deals with.' She was wringing her hands now and getting more and more agitated. Martin realised that she thought they were there as part of the investigation Lieutenant Beaumont had told him about.

'Mme Sheldon,' he reassured her. 'We also know nothing about M. Lefevre's business, and for the moment it is of no interest to us, but we are very keen to talk to Mrs Daphne Mansfield and for you to tell us when you last saw her. Is she living here?'

Mme Sheldon brushed back her rather obviously dyed hair and with some difficulty got herself under control. 'No, no. Mme Mansfield has not lived here for a long time – let me think. She came here with her daughter a few years ago and wasn't here that long, possibly about three months, when her health deteriorated and as Mme Lefevre couldn't cope the old lady went to a nursing home.'

'I haven't seen her since then but I know a couple of weeks ago the nursing home rang madame to tell her that her mother had gone back to Wales.'

'How did madame react to the news?' asked Martin.

'Well, I don't think she was too bothered, but she knew her

husband would be angry and he was very …' she tailed off.

Martin was concerned that Mme Sheldon was realising she was saying more than she should, so he took another tack and tried good old-fashioned flattery. 'You speak excellent English, Mme Sheldon, although there's no doubt from your accent that you were born and raised in France. Have you spent much time in the UK? – it's definitely not American English'

'No, I've never been to the United States, and in fact only once to England. On that one occasion I met my husband, Oliver Sheldon, a tailor from Sussex, and he followed me back to France and we lived here for the next twenty years. In all that time he never learned to speak French and so it was left to me to learn English. I was grateful for that, as when he died I applied for a job as housekeeper here and only got it because Mme was keen to take on someone who spoke her own native language.'

Martin helped the conversation get back to where she had left off. 'You were saying that M. Lefevre was not pleased to hear that his mother-in-law had gone back to Wales.'

This time there was no stopping her. 'That's the understatement of the year,' she blurted out. 'He was absolutely furious, and for hours I heard him shouting and smashing china and threatening madame. He said he would go to her Aunt Elsie's house and sort things out once and for all, but then in his usual way he calmed down and poured madame a drink and asked me to join them. He can be a most charming man and it wasn't long before madame told me that they were both going to Cardiff to see if they could persuade her mother to come back to France. She even told me that her husband was going to make arrangements for Mrs Mansfield to live here and so I was really surprised when I learned they were on their way to the nursing home.'

Martin stopped her. 'Look, Mme Sheldon, this part is very important – can you remember exactly how you came to know about the nursing home?'

'Yes, it was a couple of weeks ago, on a Wednesday morning, and they had gone to Cardiff the day before. I hadn't been up long but I had eaten breakfast, so it was probably about nine thirty. That would be right because when I asked madame about it the following day she told me they had taken the overnight ferry from Portsmouth to Caen. Most people would take three hours from

Caen to here but M. Lefevre drives far too fast for my liking.'

'So did they all call in here on the way to the nursing home, at least for a comfort break, or perhaps you made breakfast for them?' suggested Martin.

'Well of course I would have made them breakfast, but I didn't get the chance. M. Lefevre came through the front door and rushed to the study, that's the room through that door,' she pointed. 'All he said was he needed the documentation for Mrs Mansfield to be readmitted to the home. Next thing I heard him starting his engine and I saw them driving off.'

'Do you actually recall seeing Mme Lefevre and Mrs Mansfield in the car?' asked Martin. 'Please think very carefully because as I said it is important.'

'Well, if I really think about it, then no, I didn't actually see them but obviously they were there because Mme told me the next day about the journey.'

'But at the time you didn't actually see them?'

'No – but why is that important?'

'I'm not sure if it is,' replied Martin. 'I'm just trying to get a true picture of things as they happened. When you spoke to Mme Lefevre the following day did she tell you why there had been a change of plans? From what you said earlier the original thinking was to bring Mrs Mansfield back here to live, so why the change of heart?'

'I asked that very question,' said Mme Sheldon. 'At first madame avoided giving me an answer but then I heard her talking to her husband and later she told me that her mother had made some very good friends at the nursing home and hadn't wanted to leave them in the first place. It was only out of loyalty to her sister that she had gone back to Wales and according to madame, all her sister, Miss Forrester, wanted her for was to pay the bills. Can you believe that? The poor woman is better off away from all the family and spending time with those nice friends she has made at Maison de Retraite, at least they don't want her for her money.'

Martin looked at the woman perched on the edge of the table and recognised that beneath the over-dyed hair and the prematurely wrinkled face was a kind and astute woman, and he wondered how she would fare when things went belly up for the Lefevres.

'What would you say if I told you that Mrs Mansfield is not in the nursing home and that in fact no one there has seen her since she left to go back to Wales?' As Martin spoke the words he watched closely for the response and when it came he was totally convinced.

'But they took her back there, M. Lefevre said they were on their way there and Mme told me how pleased her mother was to see her friends again. I don't understand what you are saying – it doesn't make a scrap of sense.'

Because she looked so shocked Matt took her arm and helped her off the edge of the table. 'Is there somewhere more comfortable you could sit?' he suggested. 'Maybe you'd like a glass of water?'

Still looking bewildered, Mme Sheldon led the men to a small lounge that she explained was the one she had prepared ready for Mrs Mansfield to use. 'So where is she? Oh, I see. For one minute I thought something terrible had happened to her, but maybe you're here because she has made her way back to Cardiff. Is that it?'

Martin shook his head. 'We can't be sure where she is,' he told her. 'She is definitely not at the nursing home and we'd hoped to find her here but clearly that isn't the case.'

'No, she is not here,' was the reply. 'But there is at least one person who must know where she is and that's Mme Lefevre.'

'So will you fetch her for us, please?' asked Martin and before waiting for a reply he added, 'We saw her partially hidden behind one of the curtains as we approached the house – her resemblance to her aunt is too strong for it not to be her. Please Mme Sheldon – I really do need to ask her some questions.'

'You and me both!' said Mme Sheldon leaving the room and also leaving the detectives in no doubt that she would return with Mme Lefevre – whether her mistress was willing or not.

Chapter Twelve

Sarah tossed and turned and then lay as still as she could in an effort to find what she desired most – sleep. It was useless. She had spent two hours before going to bed trying to make sense of what she had discovered that day and when she eventually went to bed there were still so many questions buzzing around. No wonder her brain refused to even contemplate switching off.

She had last spoken to Matt Pryor on the phone on Tuesday evening and he had told her to be careful about stirring up a can of worms in Parkland Nursing Home, just in case there was something untoward going on. He had said he would have a word with his boss and come back to her but she had waited all Wednesday morning and heard nothing.

Realistically she knew he would be deeply involved with the investigation of what the press were now calling 'The Coopers Field Murder', and the hundred-to-one possibility of wrongdoings in Parkland would be at the bottom of his agenda. But for her there were now too many small but compelling similarities between all the cases she and Maria had listed and she had an overwhelming urge to keep looking.

After lunch on Wednesday she had done a round of all the residents to ensure there were no problems and then hung around near the front of the reception area. As she expected, at exactly quarter past one, Anthony Cooper and Peter Doster made their way to the car park and a moment later she watched them drive off for their usual Wednesday afternoon meeting with the accountant.

They wouldn't be back until four thirty, and most Wednesdays wouldn't see Mr Cooper return at all, he just dropped his administrator off and went home. Sarah knew that Peter Doster would be back because he was meticulous about completing a 5 p.m. accounts summary every day.

The man was boring and Sarah didn't like him, but the nurse in her had come to the surface when she had seen him leave with Mr Cooper. Sarah guessed that Doster was in his mid-fifties but the man she had watched looked years older and he looked as if he had the weight of the world on his shoulders – or maybe something on his conscience was weighing heavy! Whatever the reason it was turning him into a wretched looking man and in spite of herself she felt a bit sorry for him. She wondered if perhaps Mr Cooper had some sort of hold over him: Sarah certainly knew that the owner could be a bully. He had got close to bullying Sarah when he barged into her office to find the police there, but there was a very good reason that he would not pick on Sarah.

Just before Sarah had decided to work at Parkland the previous home manager had left and Sarah had been asked to take over the role. It wasn't what Sarah had wanted, but it came with extra money and her flatmate had just left for London so she had all the rent to pay. There was no one else on the staff with the qualifications needed to meet the new requirements for a home manager that would be enforceable from the following January. Sarah was a first-level registered nurse with a degree in Healthcare Management, so she more than met the terms of the new regulations. For the present Mr Cooper needed her more than she needed him, but perhaps the hapless Mr Doster was in a more precarious position.

Sarah realised she was probably letting her imagination run away with her but she had reached the point of no return and now only a thorough appraisal of the records relating to her list of deceased residents would put her mind at rest – or not!

After a final quick check of the residents she made her way along the corridor and up the half flight of stairs to the administrator's office. It was on a mezzanine-type landing, situated between the residents' area and the owner's office. The door was never locked because a Care Standards Inspector had decreed that out-of-hours access to all resident information, on a need to know basis, must always be available in case of an emergency.

As she approached the door Sarah felt unusually anxious and went over in her mind the story she had invented to explain what she was doing if she was discovered in the act of reading old case notes. True to form, the office was unbelievably tidy, and she wouldn't have been surprised to see the paper clips lined up; it was uncanny.

The first thing she noticed was a full-size filing cabinet, not yet unwrapped but already placed neatly in the position it would occupy. Sarah wondered how Peter Doster had managed to get approval for its purchase knowing how long it took for anything she needed for the residents to be agreed.

Sarah had legitimately been in the office on many occasions and knew where everything was kept. All the filing cabinets were kept locked and the location of the keys known only to a few people. Much to Mr Doster's disgust it had been made clear to him that Sarah, as the appointed Home Manager, would have to know how to access anything to do with the residents and with the management of the home.

The first thing she did was to unlock the filing drawer containing the current medical records and selected a folder at random. Using a corner of Mr Doster's desk, Sarah concentrated on the front cover of the notes and copied some of the detail onto one of the sheets of paper she had brought with her.

The records she had chosen belonged to Enid Prosser, who had only been at the home for three weeks and was quite a character. The care assistants were always giggling at the stories she told them about her life before the Second World War, when she had been a young girl growing up in Tiger Bay, then a notorious dockland area of Cardiff.

In just a few minutes Sarah had filled half a sheet of paper with facts relating to Enid's weight, diet, and lifestyle, and she hoped these jottings would be sufficient to give her a reason for being in the office.

On the other sheet of paper Sarah had brought with her was the list of the deceased residents that she and Maria had agreed on. She kept that one in her hand, not wanting it to be discovered in the event of an interruption.

The files of all the residents who died had to be kept for ten years or even longer if there was any on-going legal requirement, and when Sarah unlocked the cabinet she could see why a new one had been purchased. This one was bursting at the seams. However, as she would have expected, all the records were filed in alphabetical order with each section neatly labelled. Sarah had

143

anticipated taking five minutes to scan each record and make whatever notes she needed.

Nancy Coleman was the first file she looked for and her fingers moved over several names she recognised until she came to Walter Collins, someone whose shock of ginger hair had stayed with him until he died aged eighty-something. So she had gone too far down the files and looked at the name in front of Walter Collins and remembered yet another character – Samuel Coker.

Checking all the records surrounding these two names Sarah concluded that they were all in absolute alphabetical order and that could only mean one thing – Nancy Coleman's notes were not there – they were missing!

Her heart beat a bit faster as she mentally put forward all sorts of sinister reasons why this should be the case and then checked her list to confirm the next one she wanted to check was George Perkins. His notes should have been between Albert Perkins and Thelma Peters, but they weren't there either and now Sarah's heart was really starting to race. The absence of one set of the notes she was looking for could be a coincidence but two seemed unlikely. She quickly looked for Vera Thorne and then Edward Myers, and the results were the same as before. So far none of the records on her list were in the filing cabinet.

Sarah felt compelled to complete the check and make sure that none of the names on her list had corresponding files in the cabinet. She sat on the floor and pulled out the bottom drawer to look for the records of Terence Watts and was so deeply engrossed in what she was doing that she failed to hear the office door open.

'What the hell do you think you're doing?' shouted Peter Doster, no longer the pale-faced man who had left the building just about an hour ago, but now very red in the face with rage.

If it had been Mr Cooper shouting Sarah would probably have taken it in her stride because she had heard him shout so many times, but she had never before heard Mr Doster so much as raise his voice and she virtually jumped out of her skin.

'For heaven's sake!' she replied trying to regain her composure. 'You scared me to death.'

'What are you doing in my office and why are you going through those files? They are not current, they are the files of residents who have died – what possible interest could you have with them?'

Sarah, now completely composed, rose to her feet and presented Mr Doster with her most disarming smile. 'Oh I'm really sorry, I tried to catch you before you went out with Mr Cooper but I had to attend to one of the residents. I haven't disturbed anything other than that file on the table there and I'll put it back exactly as I found it.'

'That's not the point,' retorted Peter Doster and then added sarcastically. 'I asked what you were doing going through that particular filing cabinet – none of those residents need your attention, Sr Thomas.'

Although Sarah didn't regard him as a fool she knew that Mr Doster understood very little about things like care plans and so she hoped she could baffle him with a little elaboration on the science of nursing. 'It's by looking back on old notes that we can improve the care we give now, and all I was doing was selecting random notes to check things like lifestyle and compare it with longevity.' Sarah knew she was talking rubbish but she had to continue the bluff.

'I have looked at the records of several residents who reached a ripe old age before they died and as you can see I have selected Enid Prosser as my comparison study. She came from a deprived family and paints a very colourful picture of her early years in Tiger Bay. She was probably a prostitute but she met a rich man – a bit like Julia Roberts and Richard Gere in *Pretty Woman*, don't you think?'

'I haven't got the slightest idea what you're talking about, Sr Thomas,' came back the tight-lipped reply and it was then that Sarah noticed he had lost the florid colour of anger and was now even paler than the man she had seen earlier in the car park. His gaze was firmly fixed on the notes of Enid Prosser that she had left open on his table and as she followed his gaze it became Sarah's turn to lose her colour.

She hadn't noticed it before but now she recognised Dr Shaw's handwriting and she briefly glanced at the signed and dated entry indicating that it was the wishes of Enid Prosser not to be admitted to hospital under any circumstances.

Peter Doster gathered up the case folder and replaced the loose pages in the correct order before picking up the sheet of paper on which Sarah had made her earlier notes. Fortunately for Sarah the things she had written matched the story she had spun the administrator about lifestyle and longevity, and he relaxed somewhat and then quietly asked Sarah why she had chosen this particular resident for her living comparison.

Sarah had been remembering DS Pryor's advice and was now making sure that nothing she said upset Mr Doster. 'I didn't really choose her,' she said lightly. 'I just closed my eyes and picked out a folder. On reflection it would have been better if I had waited for you so that you could have randomly chosen one male and one female resident for me. That way there could be no bias, and my findings would be more difficult to challenge.'

She continued. 'In fact, I think that's the best way forward, so would you mind just handing me the notes of two residents, chosen by you at random and I'll discard what I have done with Mrs Prosser.' To emphasise her point, Sarah tore up the notes she had written and deliberately put them in the office waste paper bin. Her ploy worked and Mr Doster gave her a feeble smile. He picked out two sets of notes at random and checked to see he had chosen one male and one female before handing them to Sarah. 'There,' he said. 'I could have done that for you in the first place if you'd just asked.'

'Thank you very much,' said Sarah. 'But I know how busy you are. We all see how much effort you put into keeping the place running smoothly and with so many nursing homes going out of business it is comforting for the nurses to know you are working so hard to keep Parkland as a thriving concern.'

Peter Doster was not used to praise of any sort and Sarah saw a vestige of colour return to his cheeks as they parted, apparently on good terms. She was even allowed to take the case notes he had selected to her office, provided she returned them before she went off duty.

Sarah walked as slowly as she could down the short flight of stairs and back to the relative sanctuary of her office. No one seeing her would have guessed the speed at which her heart was racing and how desperately she was controlling the desire of her stomach to throw up.

Why had Peter Doster come back so early? She groaned as she thought of the possibility that Mr Cooper could had come back

146

with him and wondered what would have happened if they had both come into the Administrator's Office and found her rooting through their precious files.

She didn't think she could have bluffed the two of them with her research nonsense but she honestly believed she had got away with it and had convinced Peter Doster she was just involved with a project. With the image of Dr Shaw's writing, she had seen in the notes of Enid Prosser, fixed firmly in her mind Sarah turned the corner to her office and literally bumped into Maria.

'Whoa!' shouted Maria. 'What's up with you? You look a bit peaky – not coming down with anything are you?'

Sarah shook her head and then asked Maria what she was doing in work.

'Well, as you know, it should have been my day off, but Terri rang me to say her son is ill and would I swap days with her – so here I am. I didn't think you would mind because you would need someone instead of Terri and I did try to tell you when I came on duty, but I couldn't find you.'

Sarah was barely listening to Maria as she had other things on her mind and she interrupted by asking. 'How is Mrs Prosser? – have you seen her since you started your shift?'

Maria gave a beaming smile. 'What a woman,' she said. 'She's in the lounge at the moment enthralling an audience with stories of a misspent youth and even at her age the men are surrounding her, like 'bees round a honey pot'. It's amazing how a new resident can change the whole mood of the place and this time in a very positive way.'

'So she's not complaining of anything is she – no aches and pains or symptoms of a cold?' asked Sarah.

'I've never heard her complain of anything,' replied Maria. 'True, she is typical of the residents we get with dementia and part of the time she doesn't know where she is, or what year it is, but as for complaining, it's not in her nature, so why do you ask?'

There was now no doubt in Sarah's mind that there was something going on at the Parkland Nursing Home and she believed that at least eight residents had died prematurely. Attached to each of the deaths was a set of circumstances that in her mind had too many similarities to be just coincidental. She reminded herself of the warning note struck by DS Pryor and turned to Maria with the intention of telling her she was just making a general enquiry. She wouldn't involve Maria in her thinking.

But Maria had other ideas. 'You think she's going to be the next one don't you? Oh my God! – You think Enid's name will be the next on our list.'

They had been standing in the corridor just outside the nurses, office and with Maria in mid-sentence Sarah opened the door and virtually pushed her in.

'Keep your voice down,' she urged. 'You can't go around asking questions like that, anyone could have heard you.

'Look Maria, I wasn't going to involve you any further in what is still very probably the ravings of my over-fertile imagination, but I can see you're not prepared to be excluded. I need to do a round of the residents and I'm sure you have things to do, so let's get on with the day job and if you bring your NVQ folder to the office at five o'clock I will have an apparently good professional reason for meeting with you.'

Within minutes the needs of some of the residents had taken over all the space in Sarah's mind and she went about the familiar business of arranging podiatry visits and sorting out hearing aids. Eric Walters needed his catheter changing, which took up a fair bit of time, but he looked so much more comfortable with the new one in situ that it was time well spent.

All the residents who were able to had made their way to the dining room for tea, although there was no sign of the sort of high tea that some of them would remember. No delicate cucumber sandwiches and fresh cream pastries – all that was provided was a cup of tea and biscuits. At first Sarah had thought this was a bit mean, but she now realised that the main component of afternoon tea was the conversation.

Even most of the more frail residents could manage to hold a biscuit and only one or two needed help with the mug of tea and so they had time to chat. Maria was right, thought Sarah, as she spotted Enid Prosser perched like a small bird on one of the six chairs surrounding a large rectangular table. The other five occupants of that particular table were men and they were hanging on her every word!

Sarah resolved there and then that Enid, together with her

colourful memories, would not be the next sudden death and she would be bringing a bit of sunshine into the life of some of the gentlemen of the Parkland Nursing Home for a few more years yet – if Sarah had anything to do with it.

It was a hot afternoon and the windows were wide open but the sudden onset of summer was not liked by a few of the residents and Sarah helped the care assistants to get three ladies back to the cooler environments of their rooms.

Sarah went to the treatment room. She checked on clinical supplies and completed the pharmacy order, but it was an almighty effort to keep focused and with another three quarters of an hour before her meeting with Maria she looked around for something to occupy her body if not her mind.

Cleaning out the medicine cupboard was always therapeutic, and Sarah set about it with all the enthusiasm she could muster. After half an hour of checking expiry dates and putting medication no longer needed into the pharmacy returns box, she locked the cupboard door, washed her hands, and went in search of Maria.

Not able to see her, she gave a message to one of the other care assistants asking Maria to come to the office with her NVQ file as soon as possible. Sarah then boiled the kettle and was making two cups of coffee when the door opened and in walked Mr Cooper. He hadn't knocked of course – that wasn't his style and the sight of him started Sarah's thoughts spinning. What was he doing here? He rarely came to the nurses' office. Had Mr Doster told him about their earlier conversation and was he here to find out if she had been telling the truth?

She didn't have to guess for long.

'We've had no more visits from our detective friends, have we?' he asked, with a half-smile that to Sarah was more disconcerting than his usual snarl.

'No.' Sarah returned his smile and tried to make hers look a little more genuine. 'I don't expect we'll see any more of them. If what the papers say is correct, they've got more than their share of problems trying to find the killer. I only helped out briefly, and they have told me that they will not want to speak to me any more on that count.'

Sarah spoke the truth and so was able to sound totally convincing. Mr Cooper gave his version of a real smile.

'Well, that's fine then, and I'll leave you to get on with whatever you were doing,' he said. 'I expect you're looking forward to having your long weekend off.' With that he strutted out of the office and left Sarah with a truly terrible thought.

When Maria joined her ten minutes later she was still staring at her now almost cold cup of coffee, and the list of names on the desk alongside it. 'You look even more washed-out now than you did earlier. I saw Mr Cooper walking back upstairs a little while ago, has he been having a go at you?'

'On the contrary,' replied Sarah. 'For him he was half-decent, and apparently only wanted to be sure we hadn't had any more visits from the police. Have you ever known him to be aware of our duty rotas?' she asked Maria.

Maria looked puzzled as she answered, 'Only when we have a planned visit from the care standards people, and apart from that he wouldn't know if nurses or monkeys were running the show. Mr Doster on the other hand knows everyone's shift pattern down to the last minute, and will only authorise our wages on the basis of what is written down even if the hours we work are longer.'

'So how does Mr Cooper know that I have a long weekend coming up?'

'Does he?'

'Yes. He just asked me if I was looking forward to it.'

With fresh cups of coffee made and Maria's NVQ file open on the desk, Sarah filled Maria in with what she had done earlier.

'Why didn't you tell me what you were going to do so that I could have kept a lookout for you?' asked a stunned Maria.

'Well, number one, I didn't know you were here, and number two, I have never known Mr Doster return before five on a Wednesday – so I didn't think a look out was necessary. Thank God I did think of a story in case I was interrupted – but I honestly didn't think I would need to use it!'

'I can't believe what you're saying,' interrupted Maria. 'It can't be a coincidence that none of the notes for the names on our list are in that filing cabinet. They must have all been removed for a reason.'

'Then there's the issue of the entry Dr Shaw has made in the notes of Enid Prosser,' continued Sarah. 'I obviously didn't get the chance to read it properly, but it looked like a request from Dr

150

Shaw, made on behalf of Enid, regarding her wishes not to be admitted to hospital. There's no suggestion of her needing to be admitted – she's got dementia but she's physically quite fit. Has she had any visitors since she was admitted?'

'No. I remember being told that she hasn't been living in this area for some time and that her stepson lives abroad ... Bloody hell!' exclaimed Maria. 'I've suddenly realised the possible significance of Mr Cooper's interest in the nurses' duty rota. If you're off duty for four days it may be that on your return Enid Prosser will no longer be here. It would be possible for her to collapse on Friday and after a couple of days of treatment, but no hospitalisation, she could die well before you return to work next Tuesday. Oh bloody, bloody hell!'

'Calm down, Maria,' said Sarah, even though her own thoughts had already taken the route Maria was suggesting. 'I'll speak to DS Pryor tonight, and I'm trying to make up my mind at what point I speak to Care Standards and possibly my professional organisations. I don't want to make a fool of myself and there may well be perfectly simple explanations for everything we have been talking about. On the other hand, there is no way I am going to sit back and do nothing and have the premature death of a fantastic old lady on my conscience.'

Maria nodded in silent agreement and then asked Sarah if there was anything she could do to help.

'We're both working tomorrow so we can be extra vigilant,' suggested Sarah. 'But as for actually doing anything: that's a no with a capital 'N'.'

That was the last thing Sarah had said to Maria, but she knew that there was every chance that Maria, like herself, was having a sleepless night. Knowing sleep was impossible, Sarah got up to make herself a drink. Part of her frustration stemmed from the fact that she had not been able to speak to Matt. It sounded from the response she was getting from his phone that he was in an area where the signal was poor and she wasn't even sure she had reached his messaging service.

If she didn't hear from him by the end of her shift on Thursday, she would have to speak to someone else – there was no way she was going off on a four-day break without ensuring the safety of one of Tiger Bay's oldest daughters.

151

Chapter Thirteen

Martin checked his watch and realised he hadn't made the one-hour adjustment: it was still displaying UK time. Was it possible that it was now just 3 p.m. on Wednesday – and had it really only been first thing Monday morning when the Coopers Field body had been found?

The timespan seemed more like a couple of weeks than a couple of days and, when driving to Cardiff from home on Monday morning, Martin could not have dreamed that he and Matt would be in France by mid-week. Somehow he had even found time for a night out and to declare his undying love for Shelley – how he wished he were with her now instead of opening a can of worms in this quiet suburb of Nantes.

Matt paced up and down the hall and opened doors at random making ad hoc comments about the possible cost of some of the pieces of artwork.

'Look boss,' he said to Martin. 'There are lots of gaps – see there on the panels going up the stairs. It's obvious that there were originally paintings on all the panels, but now it's just the middle panels that are adorned. What does that tell us?'

'Could be anything,' replied Martin. 'However from the background we have received from Miss Forrester, it's likely that the missing paintings have been sold to raise funds – possibly to pay off gambling debts.'

'Just what I was thinking – and I'm also thinking it's taking far too long for Mme Sheldon to find the mistress of the house. I know it's a big place but she's been gone for almost ten minutes, shall we try and find them?' As if answering his own question, Matt walked through the door which led to a very large lounge, its wooden floors partially covered with Persian rugs. Here again the gaps were noticeable. There were two places where the floor had changed colour because until fairly recently the area had been covered, presumably with the missing woven masterpieces.

There was no one in the room and Martin called out loudly, 'Mme Sheldon,' and receiving no reply tried again. 'Mme Sheldon – is everything alright?'

Both men listened for a response, but the house was as quiet as the grave. Unwilling to wait any longer they began determinedly looking for the two women.

They entered a small study, lined from floor to ceiling with books, and were offered a choice of another two doors as possible exits. 'It's unusual for a room of this size to have three doors,' remarked Matt as he headed for the one nearest him, and was surprised to find nothing behind it but a flight of stairs. 'There's that magnificent sweeping staircase in the hall and then there's this hidden staircase – how intriguing.'

The door that Martin had opened led into what any self-respecting estate agent would describe as 'a classic French country kitchen'. The stucco walls were painted a butter-yellow, with a more mustard-coloured yellow on the ceiling. Some large exposed wooden posts, stained a dark brown, were positioned in the corners, and matched the criss-crossed beams of the ceiling. It was an impressive design, and along almost the whole of one wall was a stone-built structure housing bread ovens and a fireplace. Today was a warm summer day and the logs were just arranged along the hearth, but Martin could imagine coming home on a cold winter's evening to the sound of wood crackling and the smell of bread coming from those ovens.

A rustic farmhouse-style table occupied the centre of the kitchen, surrounded by ten rush-bottomed, ladder-back chairs made of wrought iron. In the middle of the table was a huge copper jug filled with lavender, and lots more copper utensils hung on hooks suspended from the ceiling.

Finding no one in the kitchen, Martin called out again and this time he thought he heard someone responding. 'Did you hear that?' he asked Matt. 'It sounded like Mme Sheldon to me, but I can't quite work out where the voice is coming from.'

'It's not inside the house,' replied Matt. 'I'm pretty sure it's coming from the garden, but I don't think we can get to the garden from here – what about that door there?'

As he spoke Matt made his way towards a door that was almost hidden by a large freestanding wooden cupboard. He opened the door, and beyond it was a short stone path which continued towards a much heavier external door. That did indeed lead to the garden.

It really was a beautiful afternoon, and the garden was at its very best, its emphasis being on small trees, flowering shrubs, and masses of herbs. Unlike the typical English garden, there was no real plan, and plants seemed to have decided for themselves where they wanted to settle. Martin liked the effect and wished that the business they had come to conduct could be more in keeping with the surroundings. They heard a voice – Mme Sheldon; but she wasn't speaking in response to the call Martin had made. In fact, she wasn't really speaking at all – she was shouting at Charlotte Lefevre.

As the two men approached, Mme Sheldon turned towards them and shrugged her shoulders. 'There's no budging her,' she said. 'Not only is she not moving, she's not speaking either. I've explained who you are but all she has done for the last ten minutes is sit on that seat and stare into space. I've never seen her like this; maybe I should ring M. Lefevre and ask him to come home. I don't relish doing that as I've only done it once before, when some men came here to get a couple of paintings.

'I was told they had gone to be cleaned, but that was months ago and there have been three more paintings removed since then. Anyway, M. Lefevre was not happy when I rang him at work, and I vowed I would never do it again – but look at her … what do you think?'

Martin looked at Charlotte and was about to sit down next to her when Matt's phone came to life and a series of bleeps and buzzes heralded the arrival of several messages.

'Sorry about this,' said Matt. 'Obviously coming out into the garden has given me a signal – I've had nothing since we got on the ferry.' As he spoke Matt scanned through the seventeen messages his phone indicated had been received and just as Martin was about to turn his attention back to Mme Lefevre he was once again stopped.

'Guv – you will want to see this!' exclaimed Matt and he stood beside Martin so that both of them could see one of the messages

Matt had received. The message was from Prof. Moore and contained an attachment that Matt had opened. The image on the phone screen had been created as a result of the work done by Professor Henrietta Van-Bruggen.

Martin looked from the phone to the woman on the bench and then back to the phone and he was left in no doubt that what Matt was showing him was a likeness of Charlotte's mother. He now knew beyond doubt that the body in Coopers Field was the murdered remains of Daphne Mansfield, and it was down to him to discover who had killed her and how.

Martin realised he had not responded to Mme Sheldon's question regarding whether or not she should contact M. Lefevre, and before doing so he took another look at the man's wife. If she needed her husband to be there then Martin would suggest he was sent for – but at the moment it was impossible to access her needs and Martin really wanted to initially speak with Charlotte alone. He sat on the bench beside her but not too close, although it didn't seem as if she had even noticed his presence.

'Mme Sheldon,' he asked the housekeeper politely, 'would it be possible for you to get us all something to drink? You will know best what Madame likes, and maybe her drink could contain some extra sugar, or even a drop of brandy, as she is obviously in a state of shock.'

Grateful to have something to occupy her, Mme Sheldon hurried off in the direction of the kitchen, and for several minutes the garden was peaceful, with only the occasional sound of birdcall.

Martin had no idea how much time they had before M. Lefevre was due to return home, and he couldn't risk putting his discussion with Charlotte on hold any longer. He hoped it would be a discussion and not a series of unanswered questions and he started out very gently.

'Mme Lefevre, I am DCI Phelps and my colleague here is DS Pryor. We are here because your aunt, Miss Elsie Forrester, reported her sister – your mother – missing a couple of weeks ago. We would like you to help us trace her whereabouts or tell us anything you can that may help with our enquiries.'

There was no response and Martin hadn't really expected one so he continued. 'We know that you and your husband went to

Cardiff to see your mother on July the fourteenth, and the following morning your aunt discovered she was missing. Miss Forrester tells us that she rang here and was told that your mother was going back to Maison de Retraite …'

Mme Sheldon had come back and she interrupted. 'I spoke to Miss Forrester on the phone,' she said, but before elaborating on the phone call she turned to Matt for help. 'If you can carry that table from over there I will put this tray down and give Madame her drink.'

Matt did as he was asked and Mme Sheldon sat down on the other side of Charlotte and managed to get her to take a sip of the drink she had prepared. The sip was obviously to Charlotte's taste, as she soon emptied the glass and looked to Mme Sheldon for a refill. Martin wondered what the housekeeper had put in the drink, but was grateful that it had produced the first hint of any response and hoped the second glass would loosen the tongue.

Martin spoke across Charlotte and asked Mme Sheldon if she could remember the gist of her telephone conversation with Miss Forrester. She said that initially Charlotte's aunt had been very angry – demanding to know what had happened to her sister.

'She rang not long after M. Lefevre had called in for the papers he needed and I told her all about that,' she continued. 'Then she demanded to know the exact whereabouts of Mme Mansfield. I told her I didn't appreciate being shouted at and that family feuds were none of my concern, but I did feel a bit sorry for her. I told her what M. Lefevre had told me. Madame and her mother were in the car and he was taking them to the nursing home.'

'But madame and her mother were not in the car!' rasped Mme Lefevre.

For some reason Martin was expecting the voice of Charlotte Lefevre, when it emerged, to be quiet and gentle, but this was the sound of pure venom. 'No madame … no mother … but then when did I last have a mother … or ever have a mother come to that. What mother brings a daughter into the world knowing that she's destined for years of pain and suffering – she deserved all she got.'

The one most shocked by this revelation was Mme Sheldon and she got to her feet and made a dash back into the house but not before Charlotte had relieved her of the third glass of the truth-revealing liquid and drank it with a single swallow.

Matt switched his phone to voice record and told Madame Lefevre he was doing this, but she was oblivious to him or anyone else. Martin prompted her. 'What do you mean when you say she deserved all she got?' he asked, but unfortunately Charlotte had returned to her world of silence.

Martin decided to put all his cards on the table and tell her what he believed had happened. 'We know of the serious financial situation that you and your husband are in and of the way you have extorted money from your mother over many years. From what we have gathered your husband has a serious gambling addiction and you needed to be in control of your mother's affairs to ensure his creditors were kept at bay.'

'Gambling addiction ... gambling addiction! – you can say the words so easily, but you have no idea what they mean ... what hell they describe ... what absolute purgatory.' Charlotte shouted the words that she had probably wanted to speak for years but Martin didn't want to listen to her woes he wanted to know what had happened to her mother.

'Tell me what happened on the morning you last visited your mother in Cardiff,' he persisted. 'We know what your aunt has told us but we would like to hear your version of events.'

'Well, she's got that wrong to begin with,' scoffed Charlotte. 'It wasn't the morning, it was early afternoon before we got there. We went to England first because my husband's brother, Claude, lives in style in Sussex and they are quite frankly filthy rich.'

'Frederick has tapped his brother lots of times for money and he has helped out – Claude's wife stepped in and said "no more", but we still had to try. How desperate is that?'

'Needless to say we were not made welcome, and we only stayed long enough for Frederick to help himself to whatever he could stuff into my handbag in the way of jewellery from his sister-in-law's dressing table. They know we took the stuff, but they aren't reporting it because we're family – but we have been told never to darken their doorstep again. Can you imagine how ashamed that makes me feel?'

Her shame was of no relevance to Martin, and he urged her back to what was relevant. 'What happened when you were with your mother?' he asked.

'Oh, the usual,' came the flippant reply. 'Frederick tried his

158

charm offensive in an attempt to get her to come back to France with us, but I could see it was no use. Her beloved sister had obviously persuaded her to stay in Cardiff and pay the bills for the house that by rights should be mine, and hopefully soon will be.'

Matt couldn't help butting in. 'Perhaps your mother wanted to stay with her sister rather than return to rot in the place for the living dead you had in mind for her.'

Charlotte glared at him. 'Shows how much you know. My husband had promised that my mother could come back to live with us, and who in their right mind would choose a backstreet in Cardiff in favour of all this.' She dramatically lifted her arms and pointed to the garden and the house.

'What made your mother change her mind and come back with you, if that's what she did?' asked Martin.

For a few minutes Martin thought his luck had run out and Charlotte had decided to return to silent mode, but then she shrugged her shoulders and continued.

'My mother didn't change her mind, and we all just sat around for hours. Eventually Frederick said he was going out for some air and left me with instructions to talk some sense into my mother. My aunt stuck her head around the door when she heard Frederick go out and asked if we wanted anything to eat. We said we didn't and when I heard her stair-lift thing taking her up to her bedroom I knew that was the last we would see of her that day.'

'My mother and I said nothing. We haven't had anything to say for years and when Frederick came back he took over where he had left off. The conversation got more and more heated and Frederick was more furious than I have ever seen him. He called my mother a spiteful bitch and she had the audacity to laugh. I think that's what did it – the laugh. He picked up her walking cane and pushed it towards her, trying to threaten her into changing her mind. That's all he was doing – but the metal end of the cane flew off and struck my mother on her temple and she instantly fell back onto her pillow. It was an accident – he didn't mean to hurt her and he certainly didn't mean to kill her – it was an accident!'

There, she had said it, and she knew there would be no going back – and in any case she was relieved to have shared her secret and sat with her head in her hands, no doubt expecting the world to feel sorry for her.

Martin had hoped for, but not expected, some sort of confession, but now he was on strange ground – not to mention foreign soil – and was not absolutely sure of his legal position. He covered himself by informing Charlotte of her rights in the way he would have done if they were in Cardiff, but in any event she waved his words aside and continued.

'There wasn't much blood – hardly anything really – and for a moment we were both unsure of what to do. There was no point in calling an ambulance, and we thought about calling the police – but who was going to believe it was an accident? You must understand, Inspector, there was no love lost between me and my mother, and so I wasn't sitting there devastated by her death. To be honest, my husband and I have not been very close for some time, and I suspect he has a mistress, but for a few hours after my mother died we worked together as we had when we were first married and came up with a plan.

'We knew if we left my mother's body in the house it would be no time before the police came looking for us – so we had to move it. Frederick thought we should remove everything from her, including her false teeth and her nightdress, and wrap her in a blanket before deciding where to leave the body.

'We then considered dressing her, but not in her own clothes, and I wrote out a list of clothes we would need to do that together with the sizes. The worst part was when Frederick went to purchase the clothes and left me in the room with my dead mother – can you imagine how horrible that was for me?'

Martin and Matt stared at Mme Lefevre in total disbelief. She really did expect them to feel sorry for her!

'He was gone for over an hour, and when he came back we checked everything only to discover he hadn't bought a bra. Apparently the shop assistant had helped him with all the purchases, but she was taking longer than he wanted and so told her not to bother with the last item.'

Charlotte was now leaning back on the bench and relating the events with no more emotion than if she had been talking about a trip to the races.

'Just after Frederick got back, we heard my aunt moving about upstairs so our plans to dress my mother in clothes that couldn't be traced to her changed, and Frederick just wrapped her up in the

160

blanket he had brought from the car and carried her out. I made sure the walking cane that was now in two pieces and my mother's leather clutch bag were not left behind – she wouldn't have gone back to France without those.

'It was tipping down with rain and we were both drenched and didn't really know where we were going, just somewhere off the main road. I have no reason as to why, but something took us to Bute Park and we drove along a road, one I didn't even know existed, and then Frederick veered off the road and across a field.'

'We got her body out of the car – well, at least, Frederick did, as I find lifting anything more than a glass quite an effort. I put the blanket we had used to carry her, together with her nightdress and her false teeth, in the M&S bag after Frederick had taken the new clothes out. The thought of touching her dead body and putting the clothes on her was making me feel sick but as it happened I was spared the trauma.'

Matt shook his head and found it hard to believe that the timid looking woman sitting beside Martin was capable of such inhuman behaviour to other people, even to her mother, but appeared at all points to expect sympathy for herself.

'Why was that?' prompted Martin.

'The headlights of a van beamed across the field and for a moment we thought we had been seen but the van didn't stop. It was enough though for us to decide to just leave the clothes in a pile at my mother's feet and just get the hell out of there. It really was quite exciting in a macabre sort of way.'

'Exciting? You call dumping your mother's dead body in a field and leaving her there naked to rot exciting?' Matt could barely contain his disgust, but Martin silenced him because there were other things the DCI wanted explained.

'We were fairly certain of the identity of the body we found in Coopers Field within hours of the discovery, but there were a few things that didn't make sense,' he said. 'We were led to believe that Mme Sheldon had seen your mother in the back of your car outside this house after she had been reported missing. We now know that Mme Sheldon didn't actually see Mrs Mansfield, but just believed your husband when he told her that you were both waiting for him to pick up the papers. So that's one thing we have clearly explained.

'The clothes were a bit of a mystery to us, but unfortunately for you the till receipt was still with the bundle you left and gave us such details as the owner of the card used to purchase them – one Frederick Lefevre.'

Charlotte responded to this. 'What an idiot. Using the only credit card that we have left, because it's supported by my mother's regular payments – using that instead of getting cash – he's not just a hopeless addict, he's an idiot!'

Martin ignored the short outburst and continued on to the question that had vexed him the most. 'The real stumbling block for us was when we were unable to match the DNA from the body with that of your mother. When Miss Forrester reported her sister missing we took a routine DNA sample using hair from the silver-handled hairbrush she left on her dressing table, but when it was examined in relation to the body there was no match.'

If Martin and Matt already considered Charlotte Lefevre to be strange they now thought she was an absolute raving lunatic.

She let out howls of unnatural laughter, and the first words they were able to decipher were 'and it's worth a small fortune,' and then 'So that's where we left it.' Martin suggested that she calm down and explain to them what she found so amusing.

'The thought of you lot trying to match my sister-in-law's DNA to that of my mother,' she gloated. 'Still don't get it, do you? One of the things my husband took from his brother's wife's dressing table was a solid silver hair brush, designed by the famous Parisian silversmith Antoine Perrin and manufactured by Christofle. It is worth a serious amount of money – and you lot thought it belonged to my mother!'

'Believe me, Inspector, if my mother had owned anything like that we would have relieved her of it years ago – along with all the other treasures we persuaded her she no longer needed. I must have left that brush on my mother's dressing table when I got out a pen to write the list for the clothes.'

Her laughter was now hysterical and Martin let her carry on. He was grateful to have the mystery of the DNA clarified, and with such a comprehensive confession, duly recorded by Matt. Martin made a call to one of the numbers he had programmed into his phone.

'Lieutenant Beaumont,' was the reply.

'This is DCI Martin Phelps from South Wales Police, we spoke yesterday,' Martin reminded him.

'Yes, I remember, and I take it from this call that you are in my country and things are going according to plan,' came the response.

'For the moment I have one woman who at the very least will be charged with perverting the cause of justice, but we are expecting her husband to return home at any time and I am not sure how he is going to react to the news that his wife has described in detail how he killed her mother! I could do with some back up.'

'Consider it sorted.'

Chapter Fourteen

Martin had barely finished thanking Lieutenant Beaumont when the sound of a powerful car, being driven at high speed, came into earshot and within a matter of seconds had come to a screaming halt at the front of the house. If only it was the backup he had been promised – but for the French 'boys in blue' to have arrived at that moment they would have had to be mind-readers, not to mention time travellers.

Remembering Mme Sheldon's comment about Lefevre's driving being too fast for her liking, there was little doubt in Martin's mind about who had just slammed the door of his car and presumably was just about to enter the house. Martin tried to consider all the possible ways in which Frederick Lefevre would respond when he realised that his wife had opened her heart, if indeed she had one, and with dire consequences for him.

DCI Phelps knew that Mme Sheldon was in the house and although the housekeeper had not heard Charlotte tell the detectives the whole story she would have heard enough to realise that her employers were in some way responsible for Mrs Mansfield's disappearance.

Would she consider it her business to confront Frederick Lefevre? Martin rated the woman as quite astute and felt fairly certain that she would not, but he was much less certain about how Charlotte Lefevre would react when she saw her husband.

The three figures waited in the garden, looking like something out of a French farce – but only in that the plot was incomprehensible, because the situation certainly wasn't funny.

After a couple of minutes Matt asked Martin if he wanted him to go inside and make sure that it was M. Lefevre who had arrived. In response Martin shook his head and suggested that the longer they waited for Lefevre to come outside the more chance there was that Lieutenant Beaumont and his team would have arrived and be around to help if things got difficult.

There was nothing, from what was known to them, to suggest that Frederick Lefevre was a violent man. Not even the description given by Charlotte about the way in which her mother died did that. She had painted a picture of an angry and desperate man, but not of a violent murderer.

Yes, his actions had undoubtedly caused the death of Daphne Mansfield, but any good lawyer would be able to prove that his plan had been to take her back to France – and that it was not in his best interests to kill her.

She was arguably less valuable to them dead than if she were alive, because while she was still living they were able to live on her income. There were probably assets that could be sold after her death, but given the level of gambling that appeared to be out of control, those assets would not last long. Martin could imagine a clever barrister telling the court that there was no way in which his client could have known the silver globe at the end of his mother-in-law's cane was loose. It was something she had used for years and had always appeared quite sturdy.

The barrister would tell the jury how devastated the couple were when they realised that such a gentle blow to Daphne's head had caused her death. Up to that point there would be a reasonable case for accidental death, but the prosecutors would have a field day when it came to motive. The Lefevre's only defence for what came later would be for their barrister to claim they had simply panicked.

Martin thought that if the couple had contacted the police immediately they may well have got away with a verdict of accidental death. Explaining the elaborate plotting and the bizarre actions that followed would be different and something out of a defence counsel's nightmare.

They would know from the recording Matt had made of Madame Lefevre's account, that her husband had been using the cane to threaten Mrs Mansfield. Martin wondered if the Crown Prosecution Service would consider that to be enough for them to be looking to apply a charge of manslaughter. Additionally the couple would be facing charges of conspiracy to pervert the cause of justice and then there was theft – not to mention the fraud and embezzlement that was already under scrutiny in France.

Martin would be asking Lieutenant Beaumont to 'look after' the couple, pending arrangements for them to be extradited to the UK for trial on whatever charge the CPS decided. It wasn't something he had ever done before but he was sure that between the two of them they could manage the situation appropriately.

'Mme Sheldon is coming out now,' observed Matt. 'But there's no sign of Frederick Lefevre.'

Walking towards the group, but deliberately blanking Madame Lefevre, who was now seemingly beneath her contempt, the housekeeper spoke only to Martin and Matt. 'M. Lefevre arrived home about five minutes ago and I told him you were in the garden with madame, but instead of coming to see you he chose to shut himself in the study. I don't think he's there now because I am sure I heard him walking about upstairs. He must have gone up the side stairs and in to a room that is used as a dressing room and walk-in wardrobe. If he had come back out of the study and up the main stairs I would have seen him.'

'Did you tell him the nature of our business?' asked Martin.

'I just said that two detectives from Cardiff were here to ask about the possible disappearance of his mother-in-law.'

'And what was his response?' questioned Matt.

'He asked if Charlotte was out here with you and I told him that she was. That was all that was said, and then he just shrugged his shoulders and went into the study, closing the door behind him.'

At that moment the phone rang from somewhere in the house and Mme Sheldon walked back to answer it.

As her footsteps retreated they all became aware of the sound of heavier footsteps walking towards them and they turned, in unison, to see the smiling face of M. Lefevre. Martin realised that until then he had only had a mental picture of what Frederick Lefevre looked like, none of the people who had spoken about him had ever described him. For some reason Martin's image had been that of an averagely built Frenchman, whose dark hair would be streaked with grey and white – but the real life figure was very different. M. Lefevre was well over six foot tall and would have weighed in several stones above Martin's fighting weight.

There was not an ounce of fat visible on him and he looked extremely fit. Martin could immediately see that he would have had no trouble lifting the body of Daphne Mansfield. His most striking feature was a shock of greying, auburn hair, and the countless number of freckles he had on his face and arms. Mme Sheldon had said he could be a charming man, and as he came forward with a smile and an outstretched hand Martin could easily imagine how some women would still find him attractive.

'Welcome to my home. I assume English is the language of the moment,' he said. 'Mme Sheldon tells me you are here regarding the possible disappearance of my wife's mother. How can I help?'

Martin ignored the outstretched hand and played for time with a protracted introduction of himself and DS Pryor, but he knew what had to be done and he proceeded to give the appropriate caution.

'Frederick Lefevre, I am arresting you in connection with the death of Mrs Daphne Mansfield. You do not have to say anything, unless you wish to do so, but it may harm your defence if you do not mention, when questioned, something which you later rely on in court. Anything you do say may be given in evidence. Do you understand?'

Lefevre looked away from the detectives and turned his gaze on his wife. Although Martin had more than a reasonable grasp of the French language, he had difficulty keeping up with the torrent of abuse that her husband now hurled in her direction. Martin was so busy concentrating on the translation that he missed the next, totally unexpected, movement.

Taking two steps backwards, Lefevre pulled a gun out of his pocket, and pointed it in the direction of the terrified-looking woman sitting on the bench. The potential use of a gun hadn't come into Martin's thinking. He knew of course that the French Police were routinely armed with semi-automatic pistols, and he had handled one at a firearms convention in Glasgow. And it now looked as if Frederick Lefevre was menacingly pointing such a weapon at his wife's heart …

The slim shape of the gun had made it easy for the Frenchman to conceal it in the pocket of his jacket, and for the moment all Martin could do was watch and wait for Lefevre's next move. Out of the corner of his eye Martin saw Matt inch forward and quickly ordered his sergeant to stay exactly where he was. 'No heroics, Matt! I mean it – no heroics.'

Matt stood perfectly still. He hadn't really had a plan anyway, just a feeling that he should do something.

With the gun still in the same position Lefevre supported Martin's words. 'That's good advice, DS Pryor – you should listen to the Chief Inspector's good advice …'

He seemed to have more to say, but he was cut short by the words of Mme Lefevre. She either didn't understand the precarious nature of her position or she simply didn't care because her voice was neither pleading nor nervous. It was the same rasping sound the detectives had heard earlier and she spat the sentences out in her husband's direction. Charlotte chose to deliver her words in English in spite of the fact that he had addressed her in his native tongue.

She was presumably responding to what he had said as she replied. 'I didn't drop you in it, you did that for yourself. If you had waited to hear the whole story you would know I made it clear that my mother's death was an accident – I should have said you had bashed her head in deliberately and got you locked up for life. So what are we going to do now? What's your big master plan this time?' she mocked.

Martin glanced towards Matt and saw that they were each watching in nervous disbelief and both thinking that if someone was pointing a gun at them they would probably be more respectful. With the same glance Martin just caught the appearance and almost simultaneous retreat of Mme Sheldon and he hoped she had not been noticed by M. Lefevre.

Martin needn't have worried because the couple were continuing their spiteful conversation, and he thought it was bizarre that, although Frederick was holding the gun, it was Charlotte who seemed to have the upper hand.

They seemed almost oblivious to the two detectives and continued raking over the miseries of their married life, with bitter accusations and recriminations bouncing between them, swapping from English to French depending on who was speaking.

For a moment Martin's attention was taken away from them as he thought he could hear the sound of an engine not too far away, but when he strained his ears he was disappointed because it was not getting any nearer. Now he couldn't hear it at all. Where was their back up? How long would it take Lieutenant Beaumont and the cavalry to arrive?

169

Martin didn't have a clue how far away the French officer had been when the offer of help had been made, and now he was worried that the sudden arrival of a police car would prompt Lefevre to use his weapon. Suddenly Martin could imagine the arrival of police officers with guns similar to the one pointed at Charlotte, and the possibility of a shoot-out.

Although Martin had these brief thoughts he had not missed one word or even an inflection that passed between the couple. When it came to character assassination Charlotte was proving to be something of an expert, though to be fair she had plenty of proven material on which to base her judgement of her husband. Gambling, embezzlement, and theft were amongst the vices she levied at him – but it was her accusations relating to his betrayal of her faithfulness, with his numerous love affairs, that turned the tables.

This time the howls of surreal laughter came from the man holding the gun, and he lost no time in telling his wife that his affairs had started less than a month after he had found himself married to a prude of the first order. When he had discovered that she could not even bear him the son he wanted, of course he had taken a mistress. Lefevre could see that these revelations were hurting Charlotte much more than her knowledge of any of the other crimes he had committed – and so, cruelly, he continued.

Under normal circumstances Martin would just have been embarrassed to hear some of the details that were being described but now he found himself hoping that the extramarital flings had been many and varied and that M. Lefevre was going to give them a blow-by-blow account. Not that he wanted to know the sordid details – he just wanted to kill time and hopefully avoid anyone else being killed.

The insults had now come around to the role that Mrs Mansfield had played in their lives, and it was clear that she had been seen by both of them as nothing more than a cheque-book. It seemed as if this was something on which the couple agreed but then Frederick Lefevre put the final nail in the coffin that was a fitting image of the couple's pseudo-marriage.

He told his wife how, every time he looked at her mother, he saw a physically crippled old woman who felt pain at just the touch of another human being and he could see Charlotte heading fast in that direction.

'At least your mother produced one child,' he said. 'One more than you could manage, and you always knew how much I wanted a son.'

It was then the final bombshell was delivered and he laughed as he spoke the words. 'But don't you worry your pretty little head on that score – I haven't just got the one son you denied me – I have two sons!'

At that moment, and simultaneously, both Martin and Frederick Lefevre saw three men pointing guns in their direction. There was an ear-piercing noise as a single bullet was fired.

Martin didn't need to check on Matt or Charlotte Lefevre to see if they were alright and he also knew that none of Lieutenant Beaumont's men had been responsible for the gunfire. He knew because he had watched, unable to move, as Lefevre had taken a single step backwards before inserting the barrel of the gun inside his mouth and pulling the trigger.

Unlike the images often seen on film screens, Lefevre's body did not contort or twitch but just dropped like a stone. Whatever had been blown through the back of his head had been spread over the hydrangea macrophylla, and it was ironic that the last thoughts of M. Lefevre were now covering the white and pinkish white blooms of a variety known as the 'blushing bride'.

For what seemed like an eternity, but was probably just seconds, no one moved, but then the two men who had arrived with Beaumont moved towards the body.

Martin looked at Charlotte, who was sitting with her head resting on her hands and staring at the place where her husband had been standing. He was about to suggest they go inside when Mme Sheldon stepped in. 'I will take madame to her room if that is permissible,' she said. 'There is nothing either of us can do here, and you gentlemen will have things to sort out. Madame will undoubtedly like some tea, and I'll make some strong coffee for the rest of us – it will be in the kitchen whenever you are ready.'

As Mme Sheldon took her mistress's arm and guided her towards the house, Martin marvelled at the composure of the housekeeper. Matt must have been doing the same. 'Now that's what I call being calm under pressure,' he remarked. 'Charlotte Lefevre is lucky to have her around.'

'Perhaps we are all lucky to have her around,' suggested Lieutenant Beaumont. 'It was she who alerted us to the fact that Frederick Lefevre was armed. Apparently she was bringing a telephone message out for Lefevre when she saw the gun, and she told us that she had got back to the house without anyone seeing her.'

'I saw her,' responded Martin. 'I hoped she would get in touch with the police, but as time went on I wasn't really sure what she had done.'

The men spent the next few minutes formally introducing themselves and then Matt wandered over to where his opposite numbers were looking at Lefevre's body. It was a strange feeling for Martin and Matt to stand back and watch others make the necessary arrangements with the various criminal investigation departments, but that was what they had to do.

'What exactly happened after you got Mme Sheldon's call?' asked Martin.

'I suggest we all go inside and make good use of the coffee she has made,' said Lieutenant Jules Beaumont. 'We both have information that needs to be shared.'

Moments later the five men sat around the kitchen table and Martin explained the events that had brought himself and Matt to France. As the two officers with Jules Beaumont understood very little English some translation was needed, and Martin and Jules, now on first name terms, shared the task.

It seemed somewhat unnatural that they were all sitting around sharing coffee in the home of a man who had, to use a common expression, just 'blown his brains out'. Martin explained about the body that had been found in Coopers Field and about how closely it matched the description of a missing person, namely Daphne Mansfield, Mme Lefevre's mother. He asked Jules what he would have thought if he discovered the DNA from the body did not match the DNA they knew had been taken from Daphne Mansfield's hair brush.

'I would have said the body could not possibly be Mme Mansfield,' he answered. 'So what made you pursue that line of enquiry?'

'It was the grit and determination of Miss Elsie Forrester – Daphne Mansfield's sister. She is over eighty years of age, and she recently travelled all the way to the Maison de Retraite to find out for herself how her sister was faring.' Martin went on to explain how on her return Miss Forrester had made arrangements to bring her sister back to Cardiff. He related how Elsie had been able to totally convince him that under no circumstances would Daphne have gone back to France of her own free will.

'Sorry,' said Jules. 'You've lost me. So where is this woman now? She can't be your body if her DNA is not a match!'

Martin smiled and related what Mme Lefevre had told him about the hairbrush.

'That's one for the books,' was Jules reply. 'It's a good job you have understanding senior officers. I can't see one of our lot letting me and one of my juniors go to England on the basis of something an old woman believed.'

Both Martin and Matt laughed at this as they envisaged the fit Superintendent Bryant would have had when he had read their retrospective request for travel. Hopefully they would be vindicated by the outcome of their journey.

'You were going to tell me what happened when you got the call from Mme Sheldon,' Martin reminded Jules.

'Yes, we were on our way here anyway as you know, but we stopped when we heard Lefevre was armed, figuring the sound of an approaching car could force his hand and possibly result in a bloodbath. So we walked from the nearest crossroads and came through the side entrance of the house – aided by Mme Sheldon.'

'I was sure I heard an approaching car at one point,' said Martin. 'At the time I was disappointed that it stopped, but now I appreciate your actions.'

'To be honest,' continued Jules. 'I would have been surprised if Lefevre had turned the gun on you. The action I anticipated was him shooting his wife and then turning the gun on himself, and I still think that would have happened if he hadn't spotted us and reacted instinctively.'

All the men nodded their heads – even the two who did not fully comprehend the conversation.

'Where do we go from here?' asked Martin. 'I guess the only thing we will want Mme Lefevre for is in relation to her conspiracy to pervert the cause of justice. If we were in the UK I would arrest her on that basis, but in light of all that has happened, and especially the suicide of her husband, there'd be no problem with her being granted bail pending a trial. But your system may well have a different way of dealing with this scenario.'

'I think we will do best if we treat this situation as two separate but related events,' suggested Jules. 'We will deal with the suicide of Frederick Lefevre, and when you get back to Cardiff you can set in motion the necessary arrangements to deal with Mme Lefevre. I don't think we will be locking her up, as I can't see her going anywhere, and hopefully the bailiffs will leave her enough to live on.'

'Yes,' replied Martin. 'If her husband had life insurance it may well be null and void depending on the small print relating to suicide, and I don't know how your French law works regarding a wife's responsibility for her husband's debts.'

'It's complicated in the extreme,' was the reply.

'Can't be as convoluted as our Proceeds of Crime Act 2002,' said Martin. 'If Mme Lefevre is implicated in the death of her mother, she may not be able to inherit any of her mother's assets even if they have been willed to her. There is also the issue of the two sons he mentioned. The woman is left in a real mess, isn't she?'

'I can't believe you're feeling even a modicum of sympathy for that woman,' exclaimed Matt. 'I still can't get over her saying that she found the dumping of her mother's body in Coopers Field quite exciting – I was horrified when she said that. If there is anyone that has my sympathy, it's Mme Sheldon. If the house has to be sold to pay off debts, or whatever, then she'll lose her home too.'

'Well, thankfully, those things are not for us to sort out – and on that subject, is there anything else we have to do before leaving?' asked Martin.

'Nothing at all,' was the reply from Lieutenant Beaumont. 'Do you plan making the journey back today, or getting an overnight stay and going back in the morning?'

Martin checked his watch – he had still not physically made the time adjustment and although it was only a question of adding an hour to the time his watch was showing he could not quite believe that it was only 4.35 p.m. French time. He checked with Matt.

Matt agreed the time and thinking along the same lines as his boss added. 'It seems unbelievable that it is only just over one and a half hours since we pulled up outside this house. So much has happened and I must admit there was a time when I wondered if we would be leaving feet first. No offence, Jules, but I was born in Wales and that's where I want to die – though not just yet.'

They all laughed and Martin looked up from searching the internet on his iPhone. 'There's a ferry tonight – in fact there are two. Both go from Cherbourg, but not to Poole – they go to Portsmouth. It means a different route home, but not much difference in the crossing time or the journey back to Cardiff from the terminal. Only problem is, will we make it to the ferry in time?'

'What are the departure times?' asked Matt.

'First one leaves at a quarter to eight and the next at a quarter past. It took us about three and a half hours to get here, so if it takes the same time to get back we should get to the ferry port around eight o'clock. So the first ferry is out of the question, and we'll only make the second one if the traffic allows. What do you think?'

'I'd like to give it a try,' replied Matt. 'We could crash out on the ferry, and then be in the UK before 10 p.m. and home in the early hours – it's worth a go, isn't it?'

Lieutenant Beaumont had been listening to the conversation and suggested they get moving, as the traffic around Nantes would soon be at a peak. 'I will make an official call through to the ferry company and ensure that the 20.15 crossing from Cherbourg to Portsmouth does not move from the port until DCI Phelps and DS Pryor are on board,' he added.

No one knew if this order would have any bearing on the departure time, but it would be worth a shot and they made their way to Martin's car.

'Please say goodbye and give our thanks to Mme Sheldon,' said Martin. 'We're very grateful for all the help you have given us, and especially for the spirit in which it has been given. If there is anything we can ever do for you ...'

The words had barely left Martin's mouth when Jules pounced on them. 'The next time Wales plays France in the Six Nations in the Millennium Stadium I will expect some tickets – preferably with some hospitality attached.'

This time it was Matt who responded, echoing the words previously spoken by Jules.

'Consider it sorted!'

Chapter Fifteen

Sarah dragged herself out of bed, wishing she had never got back in it after she had made herself that cup of tea earlier. She would have been better without sleep rather than suffering the effects of the dozing, dreaming, and tossing and turning she had endured for the past couple of hours. A brisk shower now and lots of coffee during the day would see her through, and then she had four days off work to look forward to.

Without a doubt she would normally be looking forward to her days off and she had agreed to visit one of her ex-workmates in Bristol on Saturday. If that went the way it usually did it would be a laugh a minute, and the sort of therapy Sarah felt she needed, but her heart wasn't in it at the moment and she could think of nothing else other than the possible fate of Mrs Enid Prosser.

She drew back the blue check curtains in her kitchen and saw the promise of a warm sunny day but not even this lifted her spirits. Please let me be wrong about all this she told herself – all these premature deaths – it's like something out of a crime novel, not anything to do with real life.

Sarah had left two messages using the number DS Pryor had given her, but he hadn't come back to her yet and she was reluctant to call again. He probably thought she had an overactive imagination and had decided there was not enough substance in her concerns to warrant police intervention. Unfortunately for Sarah he had asked her to take a look at something and now she couldn't get it out of her mind and the more she looked the more questions raised their heads – all requiring answers.

Regardless of whether or not the police thought an investigation was needed, Sarah had reached the point where she was not prepared to do nothing. She planned to get a proper look at Enid Prosser's medical record and read the note Dr Shaw had made regarding Enid not wanting to be admitted to hospital.

Sarah thought it would also be useful for her to check a couple more of the existing residents' notes just in case this was something he wrote in everyone's records. Sarah could not think of any possible reason why this should be and in fact she then remembered that Mavis Edwards had actually been admitted to hospital two days ago – so there was obviously nothing in that resident's record.

For the past two days Sarah had taken a different route to work because she hadn't wanted to pass the spot where the body had been found. Today she followed the steps she had taken on Monday morning, and tried to see the beauty of the surroundings rather than imagine the horror of what had been found there. The trees and flowers were truly magnificent, and normally walking through Bute Park before 7 a.m. would be a fairly solitary experience, but today there was something of a bustle.

Preparations were already underway for a day of celebrations, planned to mark the awarding of yet another Green Flag for the area. Who would have thought, when the body had been discovered in the miserable drizzle of Monday morning, that by the start of Thursday the place would have lost its ghost and would be displaying such glorious shapes and vibrant colours?

She wondered if Matt and his DCI had made any progress with discovering the identity of the woman, and if that had led to them finding out who had murdered her. What a job, she thought, it must make you suspicious of everyone – a bit like I am at the moment. Then she thought about the peculiarities of chain reactions and the what-ifs associated with them. What if she hadn't been on duty on Monday morning – what if she hadn't stopped to help with the woman who had found the body? Those two things had led to Sgt Evans, with his nose for trouble, visiting Parkland to take a statement from her – but then again, what if Mr and Mrs Morris had not been around when the police had visited?

Was it a question of ignorance really being bliss or was there some unknown phenomenon at work – and was it creating an opportunity for the forces of evil to be discovered?

It really was a one-thing-leads-to-another situation, and what worried Sarah at that moment was where it was leading her. All she knew was that she would not be finishing her shift today before she was absolutely certain that Enid Prosser was not at risk. If that meant rattling a few cages, then so be it. She had a professional duty of care to all the residents, and so what if it turned out that she had misread the whole situation – better for her to look a fool than for Enid to meet an untimely death.

As she reached the drive to the nursing home Sarah wished, once again, that Matt would answer her call, but of course she was unaware that at that moment he was not answering anyone's messages – he was sound asleep!

He had been dropped off by DCI Phelps at twenty past one in the morning, and it had taken hours before sleep arrived but now he was well and truly out of it and unlikely to stir any time soon.

Sr Grey was waiting for Sarah, and jokingly asked her what the body count had been on the way to work today. Sarah didn't respond to her colleague's dubious humour and instead asked a question of her own. 'How is Enid – Enid Prosser, is she alright?'

Eva looked puzzled. 'Enid Prosser?' she questioned. 'As far as I know she's fine, at least she was when I did a round earlier, but I didn't wake her. Why do you ask?'

'Oh, no reason really,' Sarah answered quickly. 'For some reason she was on my mind earlier.'

'She is on the mind of quite a few of our elderly gentlemen,' said Eva. 'You'll never guess what she had them all doing last night – playing charades! Enid got Patsy, one of our new care assistants, to bring that trunk from her room down to the residents' sitting room. There were wigs, masks, costume jewellery, and all sorts of dressing-up clothes in the trunk and they all had a whale of a time. It wasn't just the men who joined in, and it was way past most of the residents' normal bedtime before everything was packed away.

'With Patsy's help, even the residents who are chair-bound were decked up with hats or crowns, and there was no one who didn't join in. I took some photographs with my phone, take a look.'

She showed Sarah the images, and they both laughed fondly at the sight of some of the usually more sedate residents dressed up and obviously enjoying themselves. 'Every nursing home needs an Enid Prosser,' said Eva. 'I thought I would have the devil's own job getting them all settled last night, but the opposite was the case, and I can't remember when we last had such a quiet shift. It's strange though that you should ask about Enid this morning.'

Sarah wondered what Eva would think if she really knew the reason for the enquiry. 'Make the most of your days off,' said Eva. She had finished the handover and was making her way towards the front door. 'I'm here for the next three nights but then I'm off so I'll see you at the end of next week – have fun and don't do anything that I wouldn't do.'

As was customary, Sarah had walked with her colleague to the reception area, and had made sure that the front door was locked after the night staff had left.

She checked her phone, hoping to see a message or evidence of a missed call from DS Pryor, but there was nothing. Maria would not be starting her shift until 11 a.m. and Sarah had promised herself that she would not play the detective until her backup was on the premises. The thought of her and Maria in those roles amused her but sort of scared her at the same time.

By the time Sarah had checked some of the care plans and made her way to the dining room most of the residents were already eating breakfast. The feeling of bonhomie had prevailed and most of the conversation was about the enjoyment of the previous evening and Sarah looked around for the person responsible for this unusually pleasant atmosphere.

Her heart sank when she couldn't see Enid. Feeling anxious, she turned quickly and made her way to Mrs Prosser's room.

She needn't have worried, as Enid was on her hands and knees rummaging through the notorious trunk. She looked up when Sarah entered her room. There was no sign of any impending death surrounding this old lady and the only problem she had was soon voiced. 'Oh, I am pleased to see you. It's one thing for me to get on all fours but quite another thing for me to get back up!' She held out her hand for Sarah to give her the support she needed, and as Sarah took both her hands she noticed the twinkle in Enid's eyes.

'Did you hear about last night's entertainment?' Enid asked. 'I was just wondering how to follow it, but I think we've already used most of the props I have. What do you think?'

Sarah replied with a smile. 'What I'm actually thinking is that I hope I have even half your sparkle if and when I ever get to your

180

age. But there is one thing you could try if you are planning future evening performances. According to his notes, Eric Mills used to be a professional pianist, but we've never been able to get him near the piano. If anyone can persuade him to play it will be you.'

Enid was now walking with the aid of just one stick alongside Sarah, and she stopped. 'That's a brilliant suggestion, and it's possible that some of the others have hidden talents so that's my new reason for living, or as the French say, my raison d'être – didn't know I could speak French, did you?'

Sarah shook her head and smiled as she thought that nothing Enid told her would cause surprise, and her resolve to keep this amazing old lady safe hardened.

For the next couple of hours Sarah threw herself into the management of the nursing home and ensured that the care assistants were making best use of their time. She gave out medication as required and helped with bathing some of the bed-ridden residents and with the changing of dressings. Time normally flew by, but this morning it was going so very slowly and probably not helped by Sarah looking at her watch every five minutes.

Eventually the hands did creep towards eleven o'clock and Sarah gave a brief report to Maria and Carla, another care assistant, when they both appeared for their shift. Carla could not have been more different to Maria, and moaned constantly whenever Sarah suggested anything resembling what could be considered as hard work. Normally Sarah would have ignored Carla's grumbles, but today, probably because of lack of sleep, she found them extremely irritating.

'You are here to work, you know,' Sarah told Carla. 'If it's too much trouble for you to help make our residents' lives more comfortable, then perhaps you should think about a job that suits you better.'

Maria looked hard at Sarah, not because she disagreed with what had been said but because it was out of character for Sarah to dress down one member of staff in front of another. Carla, on the other hand, seemed not to be bothered. She shrugged her shoulders and slouched off, presumably to do as little as she could get away with.

'Are you alright?' asked Maria when she and Sarah were left alone in the office.

'Yes, I'm OK – just worried I guess. I was hoping to hear from DS Pryor but so far he has not been in touch. I barely got a wink of sleep last night and one way or the other I need to put my worries to rest. I can't ignore what I believe cannot possibly be just a series of coincidences and even if I lose my job I have to raise my concerns.'

'How do you intend doing that?' asked Maria. 'Please tell me you aren't going to confront Mr Cooper head on.'

'No, but I may try and find out what, if anything, Mr Doster knows.' Sarah picked up two medical folders from her desk. 'I was supposed to have taken these back to his office before I went off duty yesterday, but I deliberately forgot. They are the records of two current residents, chosen at random by Doster for the imaginary research I am conducting. I checked this morning and neither set of records contain a note from Dr Shaw about the residents' wishes regarding hospital admission. So as far as I can see, the only people whose notes contain an instruction of that type are the ones both you and I put on our lists.'

'Be careful, Sarah,' said Maria. 'If there is something funny going on, whoever's behind it is not going to thank you for your interference. Wouldn't it be better if you waited for the police?'

'I'm not going to do anything stupid, just return these notes and ask if there is some sort of protocol regarding hospital admission. I am well within my rights to be asking such a question, and there is no reason that such a question should be regarded as suspicious.'

'Under normal circumstances, no,' agreed Maria, 'but we are both almost certain that we are not looking at normal circumstances!'

'Look, Maria, I promise not to say anything if I sense trouble and I will have no problem dealing with Mr Doster, but Mr Cooper would be a different kettle of fish – and that's where you come in. His car isn't in the car park, so he's obviously not here this morning, but if he does arrive I would like to know about it. I'll make sure my phone is not on silent so that you can ring me straight away if you see his car pull up. That will give me plenty of time to make my excuses to Doster and get back here.'

Maria agreed, and Sarah made her way to the administrator's office clutching the two sets of notes that were going to be her reason for being there.

She knocked firmly on the office door but did not wait for a reply before walking in. Peter Doster seemed not to have heard her knock and visibly jumped as Sarah entered the room.

'Sorry,' said Sarah, 'I did knock. I only came to return these notes. I did promise to bring them back yesterday, but I got involved with trying to calm down an argument between two of our old ladies – you know how it is.'

Sarah knew that Peter Doster would not have a clue regarding the behaviour of the residents, and she doubted if he would even recognise any of their faces, just their names in his ledger. There were only four places in the home where Sarah had ever seen him, namely his office, Mr Cooper's office, the nurses' office, and the kitchen. He only knew there were residents in the rooms because of the income and expenditure they generated.

Sarah missed a heartbeat as she noticed that, apart from a couple of catalogues for office and catering equipment, the only other thing on his desk were Enid Prosser's notes.

She pretended not to see the folder and put the two sets of notes she had returned on top of Enid's. As casually as she could, she picked up one of the catalogues. 'How much would something like that cost?' she asked pointing to an item at random. 'It's something I've always wanted.'

Peter Doster looked in the direction she was pointing wondering why on earth Sr Thomas was enquiring about the price of something labelled as a 'High-tech Heidolph VV Micro Evaporator kitchen distiller'. It apparently had the capability of extracting intensely flavoured syrup from almost any type of food.

Realising the stupidity of the item she had pointed to Sarah laughed. 'Only joking, of course,' she said but she knew that her nerves were getting the better of her.

Doster made some effort to go along with Sarah's so-called-joke, but she had already observed that his colour today was as grey as it had been yesterday and now she also noticed that his hands were shaking.

'As I was saying yesterday,' Sarah ventured. 'I think we are all working you too hard, you really look as if you could do with a break. Any holidays planned?'

Once again, Peter responded to Sarah's words, and accepted what others would consider just a throwaway question as words of concern, things that were rarely directed at him. He seemed to relax a bit and Sarah took full advantage of the position.

'I was too late for breakfast this morning, and we've been short of staff so I haven't even had a coffee. Maria and Carla came on at eleven, so I'm OK for the moment, and they know where to find me if necessary. Shall I make us both a cup of coffee?' she asked. 'You look as if you could do with one.'

Peter was too taken aback to say anything and just nodded as Sarah walked over to where she had noticed his pint-size kettle and flask of milk standing on a half-size filing cabinet.

No one before had ever offered to make him coffee and, looking at Sarah in disbelief, he helped with the process. 'The coffee and mugs are in the bottom drawer,' he said. 'But I'm afraid there's no sugar.'

The tiny kettle took only a moment to boil, and Sarah just about managed to get two meagre mugs of coffee from the amount of water it held. Well, at least he applied the same cost-cutting rules to himself as he did to the rest of the home – with the exception of Mr Cooper of course.

By the time Sarah had carried the two mugs to the desk, Enid Prosser's notes had disappeared and two round coasters had been put in their place.

Sarah felt awkward and uncomfortable in his company and she tried hard not to show it, but she knew that he was experiencing the same feelings.

'This is nice,' she said looking around. 'It's a pity they stripped the old beams and ceiling architraves from the rest of the home when it was converted. You were lucky to get this office with some of the original features still intact.'

Even to her own ears, her chit-chat sounded ridiculous, but she continued. 'We should try to get together on an informal basis like this from time to time. After all, we both have the same vested interest in the successful management of Parkland.'

Not knowing what to say, Peter just nodded and so Sarah went on. 'For example, we could look at the admissions policy, I'm never certain how the next resident is selected – is it on a points based system or what?'

Sarah knew she was waffling as much now as she had been the last time she was in this room, but so what – if Peter Doster was seeing her as a bit of an idiot, so much the better.

In his best home administrator's voice he painstakingly explained that it was on a totally fair, first-come-first-served basis. 'When a person's name reaches the top of my list he or she is eligible for the first room that becomes available, it's as simple as that.'

'So no exceptions?' questioned Sarah with a smile.

'None whatsoever,' was the reply, and although the words were emphatic Sarah knew that they were lies. She knew that at least four of the people on the list she and Maria had drawn up had jumped the queue.

Hesitating for barely a moment Sarah then jumped in the deep end. 'That's good, and then what about our admission to hospital policy – I'm a bit confused about that.'

Her question had hit the spot and Peter Doster's colour deteriorated from an unhealthy, sallow grey to an almost transparent white.

'What do you mean?' he questioned, his voice sounding a bit shaky.

Sarah knew she needed to give him a bit of reassurance and she said earnestly 'Well, it's nothing to do with you, of course, but recently Mr Cooper informed me that Colin James' daughter had told him that Colin didn't want to be admitted to hospital under any circumstances.'

'So?' interrupted Peter. 'That's well within their rights.'

'Absolutely.' agreed Sarah.

'What's more,' continued Peter. 'We have a policy that is to be used when such a request is made.'

'We do?' questioned Sarah.

'Yes of course we do! Mr Cooper is the one who usually receives such a request and then he ensures that Dr Shaw makes a note of the request in the particular resident's records – always ensuring that the request is dated and signed.' He spoke a bit like a robot reciting words that had previously been programmed.

Sarah couldn't help herself and her next words just tumbled out. 'Do you know if Mr Cooper and the relatives make the decision for non-admission to hospital with or without the resident's knowledge?'

Even as she spoke the words Sarah knew she had gone too far.

The pallor of Peter Doster's face was becoming infused with a florid red and it was not a pretty sight.

Sarah had no idea what he was going to say next but his response was in any event cut short by the interruption of his telephone buzzer and again in robotic mode he instinctively picked it up. The person on the other end had obviously not given him time to speak and Sarah was left in no doubt that her saviour for the moment was none other than Mr Cooper!

'Yes,' stammered Peter Doster, responding to the first question that had been bellowed at him. 'Yes, I have them here but I think we should wait –'

His words were cut off, and Sarah had no difficulty in hearing the voice that boomed from the other end of the telephone line.

'You think? Well that's a new one, you think! I suggest you leave the thinking to those of us with sufficient grey matter to do a half-decent job.'

Sarah had never liked Peter Doster but at that moment she felt profoundly sorry for him. Cooper was a bully, and although Sarah was witnessing the effects of his bullying she felt unable to do anything and just continued to listen to the torrent of abuse he was handing out. 'You know what you have to fucking well do,' Cooper yelled. 'So don't think – just do it,'

With that he slammed his receiver down and Peter sat looking at the phone. He didn't replace the receiver his end and he didn't say anything. Sarah's first instinct was to ask him if he was alright and if there was anything she could do to help but something held her back. She tried to put herself in his position and decided that he was probably feeling acutely embarrassed and that her best course of action was to get out of the office and leave him alone.

How was all this going to end she wondered? What was it that Peter Doster was supposed to do? Obviously not something he was doing of his own free will – and what was that he had said about thinking they should wait?

Wait for what, or wait because of what? Anthony Cooper had made it very clear that he wasn't going to be waiting for anything and it seemed to Sarah that it was that fact that caused Mr Doster the most distress.

She had heard Cooper say that there were others who could do the thinking. Thinking about what? Who were they? Was it just

Doster and Cooper or were there others involved?

With these questions charging like demented devils through her brain, Sarah walked quickly back to her office and for some irrational reason wished she had a key with which to lock her door. For the umpteenth time that day she tried to persuade herself that she was being totally irrational. Her past experience of the two men she had heard arguing on the phone told her they could have been quarrelling over increases in the electric bill or the need to cut down on the cost of the weekly groceries.

Sarah could possibly have convinced herself on either count but for the look of absolute despair she had witnessed on Peter Doster's face.

She took her mobile phone out of her pocket and hit the number Matt had given her, praying it would not be the same answerphone response as before.

She thanked God as she heard Matt's voice.

'Hello, Sarah, this is Matt – how can I help?'

Chapter Sixteen

Matt had been on the phone for more than ten minutes, and when he closed the conversation Martin asked him if everything was alright. 'I don't really know,' was the honest reply. 'Sr Thomas assures me that neither she nor anyone else is in any danger, but she is worried, and I have promised to call in and speak to her on my way home.'

'So you still think there is something strange going on at Parkland, do you?' asked Martin.

'To be honest, guv, I haven't got a clue and the trouble in that place is that all the residents are old and any one of them could die at any time, but I don't rate Sr Thomas as anyone's fool – if she's worried, then so am I.'

Martin and Matt had spent the past few hours putting together the paperwork surrounding what they now knew to be the death of Mrs Daphne Mansfield. There were several things that needed to be done and when it came to winding up any investigation, getting them in the right order could sometimes seem impossible.

The CPS needed to be put completely in the picture before they could decide what crime had been committed and what the appropriate charges should be. In this case whether it was murder or manslaughter would make not one iota of difference to the perpetrator, Frederick Lefevre – he had decided on his own punishment.

This morning, with the help of his recently formed French alliance, Martin had learned a great deal about Lefevre's financial situation, and in particular about the sort of punishment that could have been dealt him by the criminal fraternity with whom he had become involved. He probably was better off dead!

Quite legitimately, the Lefevre home had been used as equity to cover his gambling debts and feed his insatiable habit, but the property was no longer an asset and the loans secured against it had spiralled out of all control. As Martin had seen for himself, anything of any value was systematically being used instead of money to satisfy the creditors.

From what he was hearing, Charlotte Lefevre was going to be left without a roof over her head – and her possessions would also be seized as most of her husband's financial wheeling and dealing had been done in their joint names. Martin was finding it difficult to see how she could avoid the serious charge of attempting to pervert the cause of justice but was sure that if the case got to court there would be a mountain of mitigation in her favour.

Martin did believe that the death of Daphne Mansfield had been an accident, and if her daughter had subsequently treated her mother with just a shred of human decency he would possibly be feeling sorry for her predicament. However, remembering how the poor woman had been dumped, naked and stripped of her identity, made him relieved that the method of dealing with one of the people involved with that act was not for him to decide,

The public had the right to know that the Coopers Field body had been identified along with the identity of the people who put her there. Together Martin and Matt put together all the facts that were needed for a comprehensive press statement to be released. The Press would have a field day with the Lefevre side of the story, and Martin could see some potential headlines: 'KILLER OF THE COOPERS FIELD BODY BLOWS HEAD OFF IN FRANCE' or 'GRUESOME END FOR THE COOPERS FIELD KILLER'.

Now that the crime had been solved, the media would quickly lose interest, but there was one thing in particular that Martin had to deal with before the news broke – breaking the news to Elsie Forrester.

Helen Cook-Watts had the day off, but as Matt had briefly met Elsie when he had gone to the house to collect the books and the drinking glass, Martin decided that they should go together.

'How do you think she'll take the news?' asked Matt as they pulled in near the curb outside her house.

'I think she'll be relieved to know the truth,' Martin said. 'I've had the feeling all along that immediately she heard about the body in Coopers Field she knew it was her sister Daphne.'

190

Elsie Forrester had seen the car pull up and even as Matt raised his arm to ring the bell, the door opened. 'I've been expecting you gentlemen,' she said. 'Don't stand there, please come in.'

Martin tried without success to read her body language but as soon as they had all sat down in the lounge she quickly put him in the picture. 'I was expecting you because Charlotte has been on the phone. She has told me everything that happened yesterday, and how Frederick committed suicide.'

Martin could have kicked himself for not realising the possibility of that phone call, but he had not envisaged Mme Lefevre being prepared to tell her aunt the full story. But had she told her the full story, or just the part about Frederick Lefevre shooting himself?

'What exactly did she say?' prompted Martin gently.

'She told me that when they were last here Frederick became very angry with Daphne because she was refusing to go back to France with them. He picked up my sister's walking cane and waved it around. According to Charlotte he had no intention of striking her mother, but the round silver globe flew off the end and hit her on the side of the head.'

She looked at Martin as if waiting for his views but he just nodded his head and so Elsie continued. 'I believe her, you know, Inspector. Frederick was a weak, stupid, and I now believe a very selfish man, but he was never violent. Charlotte still has the walking stick – did you know that? Even with the damage to it and with the knowledge that it had caused Daphne's death Frederick apparently thought it to be too valuable to just dump. Can you believe that?'

Martin could believe anything, and he made a mental note to ring Lieutenant Beaumont regarding the cane. He listened as Elsie went on. 'It's such a relief to know that my sister wasn't deliberately murdered, and that she died instantly without suffering. When I heard of the body that was found in Coopers Field I knew it was Daphne, but of course I bowed to your scientific knowledge when you said the DNA was not a match. Charlotte told me about the issue of the hairbrush and if my eyesight was better I would have been able to see for myself that the brush wasn't Daphne's.'

'I have imagined all sorts of terrible ways in which she could have got to Coopers Field, and I have even envisaged her being brutally beaten and left barely alive, tormented by foxes and other vermin. The truth, although tragic, is a relief compared with the black places my mind has taken me since I found her missing.'

Tears welled up in the old lady's eyes and she resolutely pushed them aside with the back of her hand. 'One thing leads to another, doesn't it? I can't help but think that if I hadn't been such a headstrong old fool Daphne would still be alive and safe in Maison de Retraite.' More tears filled her eyes, and this time there was no stopping them as they tumbled down the wrinkled cheeks.

Martin got to his feet, located a box of tissues, and placed a couple of sheets in Elsie's trembling hands. 'From what you previously told us about that place, it was little better than a nightmare, and your rescue enabled your sister to spend the last days of her life here with you. We don't have to go over this now unless you want to,' he said kindly. 'Our only real concern was to ensure you knew exactly what had happened before reading or hearing the media's interpretation of events.'

'I appreciate that, Chief Inspector,' said Elsie quietly, and then with the greatest of efforts she forced herself to sit upright and continued. 'I didn't ask Charlotte why they took her mother's body to Coopers Field, and perhaps I never will – it's time to lay her to rest and think about the future. What will happen to her?'

Assuming she was talking about her sister, Martin told her that the body would now be released and that arrangements for her burial or cremation could go ahead.

'No, Inspector, I know what will happen to Daphne. I meant what will happen to Charlotte? She and I have never been close, but she is still my sister's daughter and Daphne would not want me to turn my back on her now.'

Martin briefly explained the complexity of the criminal justice system and how he would no longer be directly involved with the process. 'It is likely she will be brought to the UK to face charges relating to the death of her mother but I can't tell you exactly what those charges will be – that's for others to decide.'

'There will be no requirement for her to be brought from France,' said Elsie, now showing the sort of Dunkirk spirit that had taken her on that epic journey to Maison Retraite. 'She will be living here. When I spoke to Mme Elise Sheldon, the housekeeper, this morning, she told me the creditors were already stripping the house and I have told both of them that for as long as they wish they can have a home here in Cardiff. Will that be a problem with the authorities?'

'I'm sure it will be nothing that can't be sorted,' replied Martin. Secretly he hoped that Miss Forrester was not making a mistake. His own, honest opinion of Charlotte was that she was an out-and-out bitch. He could only hope that with the influence of her aunt and Elise Sheldon, both strong-willed women, Charlotte might even turn into a half-decent human being.

There was a knock on the door and Matt got the signal of approval from Elsie before getting to his feet and answering it. At the door, struggling with two overflowing 'bags for life' in each hand, was a tall skinny youth who introduced himself as Darren from next door.

'It's OK,' said Darren as Matt offered to help. 'I can manage this lot, but don't close the door because my mother is getting the rest of the shopping from the car boot.'

A few minutes later Darren and his mother were emptying the six carrier bags into the fridge and the kitchen cupboards under Elsie's supervision. It was an ideal opportunity for the detectives to take their leave, and they did so, in the comforting knowledge that Elsie was not going to be left on her own.

On the way back to Goleudy, both men marvelled at Elsie Forrester's resilience and her seemingly forgiving nature.

'As you know,' said Matt 'I have four sisters and each of them has three daughters. I can't imagine a scenario whereby one of my nieces, after being complicit in the killing of one of my sisters, would be welcomed into my home. Maybe we become more accepting of things as we get older and learn to live with whatever life throws at us, because we know that life itself may not be around much longer … or maybe it's just that Elsie Forrester is an amazing old lady.'

'I'll go for the latter,' Martin said. 'All I really want to do now is get some lunch. The sight of all that food they were unpacking has made me hungry.'

As they walked into the staff dining room they were met by a sea of Welsh flags and red, white, and green garlands. The catering staff wore either Welsh rugby shirts or national costume, and as

Matt turned to Martin he echoed what they were both thinking. 'Has someone moved St David's Day? Tell me we're at the end of July and haven't slipped back to the first of March.'

All the tables were covered with paper Welsh flags and there were matching napkins, but best of all there was the Welsh food.

Whoever had arranged the menu had gone to a lot of trouble. There was something to suit everyone and Martin's eyes went straight to the Celtic crab and Cardigan Bay prawn risotto. 'What's all this about?' he asked Iris, whose hair was tucked into a Welsh bonnet.

'We plan on doing a "Cuisine of the Country" day once a month,' she replied. 'It makes life more interesting for us who do the cooking and serving, and hopefully for those of you who do the eating. It's got nothing to do with actual national days, it's just a rolling programme – and where better to start than Wales? Hope you like it!'

Matt had made a beeline for the cawl and Iris told him it had been made following a recipe that had been in her family for years. She said the secret was to trim any excess fat from the neck of lamb and to cook it with the potatoes, leeks, carrots, and any other seasonal vegetables available, but never to eat it on the same day. 'I cooked that yesterday and let it infuse overnight,' she told him. 'This morning I skimmed the fat off the surface and boiled everything together, seasoned it, and it's been simmering ever since. The meat has fallen off the bone and I think you'll enjoy it.'

Matt said he was sure he would, and then both men headed off to join Alex and Charlie who had been trying to attract their attention.

'Bet this even beats the French cuisine,' Charlie said. 'Alex had the cawl and he's finishing off his second slice of bara brith, so no prizes for guessing he's been won over by this initiative.'

'This is so good! You really must get the recipe from Iris,' said Alex to Charlie. 'She says the secret is soaking the dried fruit for as long as possible in very strong black tea – all I know is that it's delicious.'

'We heard all about your adventures in France,' said Charlie. 'So the man who murdered the woman that was found on Monday ended up shooting himself – is that right? What about you two, were you in serious danger of losing your lives?'

Charlie always bordered on the theatrical and all three men laughed in spite of the potential truth in her words.

'So come on,' insisted Alex. 'Explain the DNA mismatch or are you going to tell me that scientists all over the world have got it wrong.'

Martin told him about the hairbrush.

'As simple as that!' laughed Alex. 'Who would have thought that the hairbrush on someone's dressing table would belong to someone else? Who would have thought that?'

'Well, obviously none of us did,' replied Martin. 'We live and learn and fortunately it didn't stop us following things up, thanks mainly to a very determined and plucky old lady.'

'You should try this as a dessert,' said Charlie. 'It's Perl Las and pear salad and it is absolutely delicious.'

'Since when has a salad been a dessert?' asked Matt.

'Well, it's not exactly a dessert, more like something you could have instead of a cheeseboard – but you've got the pears as well, so it's a bit like a dessert.'

'Sounds a bit schizophrenic to me,' laughed Matt. 'What is Perl Las anyway?'

'It's a soft creamy blue cheese, and it's made by Caws Cenarth – they've won awards for their cheeses. Alex and I get it from our local deli and eat it with walnut bread, it's heavenly!'

'If I lived with you two for any length of time I would really be struggling with my weight! The pounds are already piling on since I gave up the rugby. I have no intention of dieting so I'll have to think of another form of exercise.'

'You need a good woman to give you the runaround,' suggested Charlie, as she reversed her wheelchair, swung it around, and headed for the door.

It surprised Matt that, when at the mention of a good woman, the image of Sarah Thomas came into his mind, but he soon convinced himself that it was because of the phone call he had received from her earlier. Nothing whatsoever to do with her being just the right height for his perfect woman, and he could see she had a brilliant figure even in that shapeless uniform. But he was most struck by her very dark green eyes, and it was with those eyes, as much as with her mouth, that she smiled …

Matt made up his mind. He would spend some time with her

later and after convincing her that all was well at Parkland Nursing Home he would ask her out – please don't let her be married with half a dozen kids!

When Sarah had switched off her phone after speaking for a good ten minutes to Matt she was feeling a lot calmer. Her shift didn't finish until 8.30 and so he had promised to call in at Parkland for a chat on his way home. What time did detectives finish work? She hadn't thought to ask him, but he'd told her that the Coopers Field mystery had been solved so maybe he was back in a nine-to-five routine.

It had been a long time since Sarah had even thought of the possibility of a man in her life, but she had to admit there had been an instant spark between her and Matt and she felt somewhat excited by it.

Did this mean she was finally over Hugh Keats? It was two years now since she had discovered that the paediatric cardiac surgeon she had practically lived with for a year hadn't been going home to his elderly mother every other weekend. Sarah realised now that she had probably been the last person in the hospital to find out that, in Essex, he had a wife and two sons waiting for him to finish his secondment to Cardiff.

Where was he now, she wondered? Maybe on secondment in Bristol, shacked up with another eager-to-please ward sister helping him while away the hours between his work and his family. Hugh Keats was a charmer and, without doubt, a bastard, and someday his wife would find out – or maybe she already knew that she was just helping him pass the time between his work and his lovers. Some women would put up with anything for the sake of a luxurious home and a husband who brought in the money to provide the matching lifestyle.

Sarah felt good that she was now able to think of him, and with the contempt that those thoughts deserved. At the end of the day it was her pride that had been most hurt and it was high time she moved on.

Matt had eased her worries with his logical explanations for some of the facts she and Maria had found puzzling, and Sarah vowed to put the whole topic to one side until she met with him later. But not without first checking on Enid Prosser.

The lady was not in her room, but within minutes of Sarah reaching the dining room she had located Enid, alive and well and sitting at the piano. It was once again tea and biscuits time, and the room was full. The conversation was equally full, of the antics of the previous evening. Enid could play the piano, but seemingly not very well, and after listening for a few minutes Sarah was almost certain that some of the wrong notes were being struck deliberately.

'Oh, I can't remember my notes,' Enid said. 'It's hopeless! I'm getting them all confused.'

There was no response from anyone to her apparent distress and she continued making the same mistakes in an effort to play, what sounded a bit like Brahms' *Lullaby* – but with so many hesitations and wrong notes it was difficult to tell.

Eventually her determination paid off, and Eric Mills got slowly to his feet and walked over to the piano. Sarah watched with amusement as she could see that, although Enid had spotted his approach, she had chosen not to greet him and had just continued with the murder of one of Brahms' best-known works.

'I think you are getting your sharps and flats confused, if you don't mind me saying,' said Eric at the end of a particularly painful but thankfully short movement.

'I don't mind you saying at all,' said Enid. 'I used to be able to play this piece with my eyes shut but now I just wish it were my ears that were closed.'

They both laughed. 'Do you play at all?' asked Enid.

'I used to,' came the reply, 'but not for some time.'

Not wanting to lose the moment, Enid slid off the piano stool and patted it as if to welcome her new friend on board. 'Well, you can't do any worse than me,' she laughed, and gave him a pleading look that was impossible for him to ignore.

Half-reluctantly, he sat down at the piano, pushed the stool back slightly, and for several minutes just sat there.

'Come on,' coaxed Enid. 'The piano is in good tune, it was just my playing that was an affront to the ears.'

Eric just rested his hands on the keys and then quietly practiced a few random scales and chords. Sarah could see that he was now in a world where only he and the piano existed and she, along with Enid and the other residents, listened in silence to the music that

Eric had once again found within himself. It was one of those life-stopping moments and, as Eric's confidence returned, so his playing moved from the relatively simple notes of Brahms' *Lullaby* to the complex arrangements of chords in the third movement of Beethoven's *Moonlight Sonata* – and then to an abrupt end.

Enid looked in horror at the tears that were streaming down Eric's face. 'Oh, please don't cry!' she begged. 'I wouldn't have asked you to play if I had realised it would have upset you so much.' She took hold of Eric's hands because she could see that they were shaking.

'Thank you,' he said quietly. 'Thank you so much.'

The silence that had been in the room now erupted into a continuous buzz as everyone tried to talk at once about the piano playing they had just heard, and the rest of Eric and Enid's conversation was known only to them.

One by one the residents left the dining room making for the television lounge or just to their rooms for a nap or to read. As they passed her Sarah listened to snippets of conversation and learned that Stanley Protheroe had once been a drummer in a band and that Susan Fellows had played the flute in the National Orchestra. Sarah couldn't imagine how Enid would get hold of a flute or a set of drums but she had a sudden image of her forming the Parkland Trio – at the very least.

Sarah had been thinking about her career, and had known when she left the NHS that being at Parkland, or any other nursing home, was only a stopgap, but she was still completely undecided about which direction to take. When there were moments like the one she had just witnessed she couldn't think of anywhere she would rather be, but most of the time she felt restless and vaguely dissatisfied.

Sarah's thoughts were interrupted by the arrival of Maria, who had come to tell her that a gentleman had arrived to see Mr Doster.

'Well, just show him to the administrator's office,' suggested Sarah. 'We don't usually get involved.'

'That's what I did,' replied Maria. 'He says Mr Doster's office is locked and Mr Cooper's car is not here so no one will be in his office.'

'Peter Doster is here somewhere,' said Sarah. 'I saw him earlier, and if he's gone walkabout he's not supposed to lock the office door, we've all got better things to do than chase around after him. Who is it that wants to see him?'

'He says his name is Brian Prosser and he is the grandson of our Enid – but he doesn't want to see her, just says he has an appointment with Mr Doster, arranged because Mr Cooper has been held up somewhere. Well that's what he said, anyway.'

Sarah took a sharp intake of breath. Wasn't this one of the set of events surrounding the premature deaths that she and Maria had looked at? In every case a meeting between Mr Cooper and the next of kin had happened a few days before each death.

'I have a key to the administrator's office,' said Sarah, unpinning a set of keys she had attached to her belt. 'Mr Prosser can wait there until Peter Doster decides to turn up and I decide what I'm going to do. Tell Mr Prosser I'm opening the office for him.'

Sarah moved quickly up the short flight of stairs and tried the door of Peter Doster's office. It was indeed locked and she used the key she had brought with her.

The sight that greeted her left Sarah with no doubt about what she was going to do next. She dialled Matt's number. 'I suggest you come here now,' she said. 'It's in relation to another premature death!'

Chapter Seventeen

Sarah had worked in major accident departments and had seen the results of attempted suicides by shooting, hanging, and overdoses, and on one occasion had witnessed the barely living body of a man who had set fire to himself.

But this was different.

This wasn't an attempted suicide – this was a successful suicide.

This was someone she knew.

This was in an office where just hours earlier she had been drinking coffee with the man who was now hanging there.

Peter Doster was no longer the whitish-grey colour he had been when she left him, or the liverish colour she had witnessed when he was angry.

Peter Doster's face was now displaying all those colours – superimposed on the underlying blue colour associated with asphyxia and oxygen deprivation.

His eyes bulged and his lips were bloated and Sarah was in no doubt whatsoever that he had been dead for several hours – possibly within minutes of putting the phone down after she had left his office earlier.

It certainly was another premature death, but not the one she had been expecting.

That was when she used her mobile phone, pressing the button for Matt's direct line number. She heard his initial response but before he had time to say anything else she blurted out her piece and put the phone back in her pocket.

She realised that she had not fully opened the door and was still standing half-in and half-out of the room staring at a sight she knew would be with her for many nights in the future. Sarah was suddenly aware of footsteps on the stairs behind her and guessing the approaching stranger to be Enid's grandson she closed the office door and stood in front of it.

'You can't go in there,' she said and was amazed to hear her voice sounding so calm and in control. 'There has been a terrible accident and I have just called the police.'

Brian Prosser's reaction was bizarre, and if someone had just told him the place was on fire he couldn't have turned on his heels any quicker.

The shock of what she had seen began to grip Sarah and she felt herself go weak at the knees and so deliberately sat down on the top step of the stairs. She hadn't been there more than a few minutes when Maria appeared and flew into a panic when she saw Sarah. 'Are you alright?' she shouted as she approached her. 'I saw that man Prosser almost running through the front door and guessed something had happened. Are you alright? What's happened? Why are you sitting on the floor?'

'I'm OK, Maria, at least I will be, just give me a moment and I'll tell you, but you must be prepared for a shock – I've certainly had one.'

Maria knelt down beside Sarah and rubbed her friend's hands, not knowing what else to do. After a few moments Maria started to get up. 'I'll get you a drink of water from Mr Doster's office,' she said. 'You seem to be getting a bit of colour back.'

Sarah grabbed hold of Maria's skirt to prevent her from getting up. 'No, Maria. No! You mustn't go in there, seriously, you mustn't go in there.'

Before Maria had time to ask Sarah why not, they both heard the sound of police sirens getting closer and closer and then stopping outside the main entrance.

'What's going on?' asked Maria, but Sarah did not reply and within a matter of seconds Matt appeared and then came to the top of the stairs in two strides.

'Are you hurt, Sarah?' he asked, and Sarah shook her head as she pointed towards the office door. 'It's horrific,' she said. 'It's our home administrator, Mr Doster. He's in there but he's dead – he's killed himself.'

Martin had been immediately behind Matt as they came up the stairs followed closely by Sgt Evans and PC Davies. There was nowhere for any of them to go except through the door ahead of them but on hearing Sarah's words it was Maria who had now freaked out.

'Oh my God!' she screamed. 'What's happened, Sarah? How do you know he's killed himself? Has he overdosed, or what?'

Having Maria's hysterics to deal with was perversely therapeutic for Sarah, and she linked arms with her colleague and led her down the stairs, not wanting her to witness the opening of the office door. Looking back up the stairs she could see that Matt, Sgt Evans, and the other man with them were already inside the office and the younger uniformed officer was standing outside.

Seeing her glance towards him, PC Davies introduced himself and explained that the men inside were DCI Phelps, DS Pryor, and Sgt Evans. Sarah of course knew two of them already, and had guessed that the third man was probably Matt's boss.

'I'm just going to take Maria to my office,' she told the constable. 'That's where we will be if anyone wants us for anything.'

As they walked along, Maria quickly regained her composure and apologised for her outburst. 'It's you who should have been hysterical,' she told Sarah. 'You were the one who actually found him. I didn't even see him.'

'You didn't,' agreed Sarah. 'But sometimes our imagination is more graphic than the actual sight of something, and yours probably ran wild.' Although Sarah said these words, she inwardly wondered how much more damage her imagination could have done to her mind than the horror she had actually witnessed.

'I don't really want to know, but I have to ask: how did he do it?' asked Maria.

'He hanged himself,' Sarah said simply and even as she did a fresh image of Peter Doster's face, cruelly distorted by the effects of strangulation, came clearly into her mind. She closed her eyes, but instead of going away the image sharpened and she wondered how long it would be before she was able prevent that happening.

In the administrator's office Martin was taking stock of the situation.

'Two suicides in two days,' he said, looking at Matt. 'Let's hope the expression 'everything comes in threes' doesn't apply this time. What's been going on here? I can't believe it's not connected in some way to the concerns that Sr Thomas has shared with you.'

'No, whatever caused him to do this is not something as simple as not balancing the books, but what?' asked Matt.

'Well,' said Martin, looking up at Peter Doster's lifeless body, 'he can rest assured that whatever it was we will now get to the bottom of it. We will be looking at everything that has ever happened in this nursing home, going back to the time it was built if necessary.'

Martin would have liked to remove the body from where it was hanging, but knew that it would have to wait until the SOC team and the duty pathologist arrived. It was unusual for the detectives to be on the scene first and Martin turned his attention to the paperwork on the desk.

There were eleven folders and Martin picked the top one up, confirming that, as he had thought, the folders were the medical records of some of the residents.

The one he now held in his hand was the file of a Mr Colin James. The name meant nothing to Martin, but he could see that the gentleman was recently deceased and there were a number of entries circled in red. The entries themselves seemed random, but one thing was possibly significant and it was the presence of a red pen at the side of the pile of records. Was this the last thing Peter Doster had done before he ended his life, and, if so, was this in effect his suicide note? There wasn't one to be seen.

Martin had been so engrossed that he had not heard the office door open, but now looked up to see Alex Griffiths and his team standing in the doorway.

'I hope you lot haven't messed up my crime scene, if that's what it is. Although from where I am standing it looks like a straightforward suicide by hanging.' Alex shook his head as he took in the full picture.

'He obviously used his belt and that long, not-too-thick leather type is perfect for the job. Poor sod, I couldn't even contemplate doing that to myself. Do we know why he did it? Be careful not to disturb that chair,' he told one of his team. 'I guess it's what he stood on to hook his belt over that beam, and it looks as if he then kicked the chair away.'

'Do we have any reason to suspect that it is anything other than suicide?' he asked Martin.

Martin replied. 'As you know, suicide should never be presumed, and we will have to find some evidence that Peter

Doster intended to take his own life and it will have to be beyond reasonable doubt. If we don't do that it is likely that all a coroner will do is record an open verdict.

'But first of all it's for us to decide – did he jump or was he pushed?'

As if on cue the door opened and in walked the very person to help them with that particular conundrum. It was Professor Moore, with his half-rimmed glasses perched on the end of his nose, his shirt sleeves rolled up to the elbow, and sporting a pair of ancient-looking open-toed sandals. He looked even more bedraggled than usual, and the only clue to his profession was the Gladstone bag he carried – although even that looked as if it belonged in a museum.

'When I got the message of an unexpected death in Parkland,' he said, 'I thought someone was trying to be funny. How would any death here be unexpected, it's what they're all waiting for, isn't it?'

Martin raised his eyebrows, and Matt hid a smirk at what was the nearest thing to humour the professor was ever likely to achieve. 'Who is this man? Is he the owner of the nursing home?' Prof. Moore stood to one side asking questions while he watched Alex and his team take countless photographs from every conceivable angle.

'He isn't the owner,' Matt said. 'I met the owner when I was last here and a nasty piece of work he is too. I never met this man, but as we are in the administrator's office it's a fair bet he's the home administrator … yes, in fact, Sr Thomas did say that, and she also said his name is Doster.'

'Who found him?' asked Alex.

'I haven't had time to talk to her yet,' stated Matt. 'It was Sr Thomas who phoned me, and I think it's likely she rang immediately after she had discovered the body.'

'So why did she ring you?' continued Alex. 'Why wasn't it a 999 call?'

Matt went on to explain that Sr Thomas was the person who had helped out when the woman, who found the body in Coopers Field, had become hysterical. 'Just as a matter of routine Sgt Evans came here to take a statement from her, and when one of the relatives of a recently deceased man behaved strangely I came back with John for a second look.'

205

'That's right,' said Sgt Evans. 'I came here first of all with PC Cook-Watts, and we anticipated a five-minute session, just to get a statement from Sr Thomas about her brief involvement on Monday morning. That would have been it, but the relative Matt just mentioned became really fazed by our presence and I just had a gut feeling that something was not quite right.'

Martin took up the thread. 'When John mentioned it to me I suggested a return visit with Matt. I didn't expect them to come up with anything but something told me not to just let it go – that gut feeling syndrome must be contagious.'

'To be honest,' continued Matt 'we didn't really come up with anything, but I think we planted some thoughts in the mind of Sr Thomas. It's obvious from a number of phone calls I have since had from her that she is concerned about what she now believes to be a number of unexpectedly premature deaths. When I got her call earlier I thought it was the death of one of the residents she was talking about – I certainly didn't expect this.'

Martin turned to Alex and the professor, and asked them if they had finished looking at things as they had been found and if it was possible to bring the body down to rest on the floor. There was agreement and two members of the SOC team handled the transition.

Martin continued. 'All I know about any possible malpractice is what Matt has just said, but in light of this probable suicide, I will now be looking into every aspect of the business. Will you please bear in mind when doing the PM, and collecting evidence from this room, the possibility that others may have been involved in this death. I don't honestly think so but it can't be ruled out.'

'I'll leave you to finish off here and take Matt with me to talk to Sr Thomas and the other nurse who was with her when we arrived.'

Matt led the way to the nurses' office and introduced Martin to Maria, but Sarah wasn't there. Maria explained. 'Sr Thomas won't be long, she just has to give out some tablets and sort out a PEG feed that has gone wrong. She told me to wait here in case you came down, and if you want I can make you a coffee.'

'Coffee would be great, Maria,' Martin answered. 'Tell me, were you with Sr Thomas when she found the body?'

'Oh God, no!' replied Maria. 'I didn't even know there was a body until Sarah told you that Mr Doster was dead and that he had killed himself. She told me later that she had found him hanging from one of the beams in his office, and then she was worried because she wasn't sure if she should speak about it – she only told me.'

'That's not a problem,' said Matt. 'So were you and Sarah going to see Mr Doster together, or did she go ahead of you, or what?'

'Neither of us had any plans to go to his office, but a Mr Prosser arrived and said he had an appointment. But when I went up to tell Mr Doster someone had come to see him, the office door was locked. All I can say now is I'm bloody glad it was locked, because if I had gone in and seen what Sarah found I would be demented.'

'What happened then?' asked Martin.

'Well, I went to find Sarah to tell her that someone wanted to see Mr Doster, and she said she had a key to his office so she would take Mr Prosser up and he could wait there. She went up ahead of him and I saw him follow her but the next thing I noticed was him heading for the front door at top speed. To say he looked anxious is the understatement of the year and I wondered what had happened, so I went looking for Sarah.'

'You must realise, Inspector,' she looked earnestly at Martin, 'Sarah and I have been getting a bit jumpy since we were together on Monday evening. That's when we both came up with an almost identical list of residents who had died. They had all gone downhill suddenly and, well, I'm not a proper nurse, but I wouldn't have expected any of them to go the way they did.'

Maria went into a confusing account of what she and Sarah had become concerned about, but Martin stopped her. 'I suggest we all drink our coffee and wait for Sr Thomas to get back. It's likely she will be saying the same sort of things that you are, so rather than go through things twice it will be better if you go through things together and starting at the beginning.'

A glimmer of a smile appeared on Maria's face. 'You don't need to be polite, Chief Inspector,' she said. 'I know I jump about all over the place, it's the same with my NVQ essays. Sarah helps me with those too.'

Martin had only taken two sips of his coffee when Sarah came back and smiled at Matt. 'Hope you didn't mind me ringing you instead of the emergency services?' she asked him. 'It was just that I didn't want the ambulance service or the police simply coming in and removing Mr Doster's body without a full investigation. I don't know if his suicide has anything to do with the things I have been looking at but I do know that the last time I spoke to him he was very defensive about our policy for non-admission to hospital – a policy I didn't even know existed.'

Matt reassured Sarah regarding her phone call and introduced her to Martin. 'DCI Phelps is already on record as saying he will now look at every aspect of the business here, and that will involve looking at all your recent concerns as well as scrutinising all the administrative and financial arrangements.'

Sarah turned to Martin. 'On that subject, do you think I should get hold of Mr Cooper, the owner, and tell him what has happened?'

'No,' replied Martin. 'I think you should avoid any discussions with Mr Cooper. We will make the call and explain the situation to him, as apart from anything else I would like first-hand knowledge of his reaction.'

'Oh, and what should we do about Peter Doster's family?' Sarah suddenly looked quite distressed. 'I'm ashamed to say that until this moment I hadn't even given them a thought. I've only met his wife once and she seemed like a shy but very nice woman, and there are children … God, I hadn't even given them a thought, how caring does that make me?'

Again it was Matt who reassured her. 'Finding the body the way you did must have been one hell of a shock, especially coming on top of a few days when you have been getting increasingly concerned for the welfare of some of the residents. As soon as we leave here we will be going to break the news to Mr Doster's family.'

Before he could say any more there was a knock on the door and a young man, dressed in white 'scrubs' with a nursing agency logo embroidered on the pocket, walked in, and Sarah rose to greet him.

'Thanks for coming so quickly, Craig. I asked for you because someone told me you're working for the agency, but it's not that long since you worked here so you will at least know the geography of the place.'

She turned to Martin. 'We aren't allowed to use agency nurses without Mr Doster's consent, and there has only been one other occasion when he agreed, but under the circumstances I needed cover so that's why Craig is here.'

'The agency was shocked to get your call,' said Craig. 'Tania, one of our recruitment consultants, told me she had asked you to check twice as she couldn't believe 'Do-me-a-deal Doster' was allowing an agency shift, or at least part of one. But I will need to be paid for …'

Sarah interrupted and asked Martin if she was allowed to tell Craig what had happened. To spare her the need to do so, Martin told Craig as much as he needed to know, and the man looked highly embarrassed because of what he had just called Mr Doster.

Sarah suggested that they move out of the office and into the relatives' room, so that Craig could have access to everything he needed. She offered to do a round of the residents with him but he said he would manage. 'I'm used to being dropped in at the deep end,' he assured her, 'and it's not as if you're leaving the premises.'

He went off to make himself known to the other staff and the residents, many of whom he remembered from when he worked on the staff at Parkland. There was a buzz of excitement throughout the home, mainly because of the arrival of the police and the large white van with the official South Wales Police logo and marked with the words 'Crime Investigation Unit'.

There were speculations about who the cream-coloured Lexus belonged to but no one guessed that the owner was both a distinguished professor and a brilliant pathologist – the best guess was it must be one of Cooper's cronies!

Martin, Matt, Sarah, and Maria settled themselves around the table in the relatives' room, and Martin asked Matt to remind them all of the events leading up to his first visit to Parkland. Matt did this and then continued with details of the actual visit.

He explained that Mr Morris, the man who had attracted Sgt Evans' attention, was the relative of a Mr Colin James who had died the previous evening. He said that it was during their discussions that Sarah had mentioned how surprised she had been by Colin's sudden and unexpected death.

209

'I questioned whether any death in the home could be classed as sudden or unexpected, given the age and medical profile of the residents,' said Matt. 'But she put me right on that.'

'Yes,' said Sarah. 'Although our residents are old there are a number of them who are fit and any underlying medical conditions they may have are not life-threatening. When Matt asked that question I particularly remembered Nancy Coleman, who had died when I was on holiday about six months ago. I was really surprised to find that not only had she died, but she was both dead and buried before I returned to work.'

Matt interjected. 'I asked Sarah to have a think about any other occasions when, with the benefit of hindsight, there were things that were perhaps not quite right.' He looked at Sarah. 'To be perfectly honest, I thought that was the last we would hear on the matter, but obviously Sarah had different ideas. As I recall, we were the interrupted by the crass arrival of Mr Cooper, and our meeting broke up soon after.'

'So, Sarah, you were left pondering on the question of whether or not some of the residents had met an untimely death and, if so, how had it been orchestrated and who was responsible,' summarised Martin.

'Well, I hadn't rationalised it that clearly at the time, but over the past few days yes, I suppose I have been thinking along those lines,' Sarah said. 'When I met with Maria on Monday evening I was quite amazed by some of our findings.'

'Tell me about that,' encouraged Martin. 'What did you and Maria discover?'

Martin listened with increasing interest as Sarah, with occasional input from Maria, explained how they had decided to think of residents whose death had been something of a surprise and had independently come up with lists of names that with one exception were identical.

'I had one more name than Sarah,' said Maria. 'But that was because Mavis Clegg was admitted when Sarah was on holiday, and died just one night after she arrived.'

'That does happen,' remarked Sarah. 'Maria said she was surprised by the woman's death and so we kept her name on our list.'

'Have you got that list handy?' asked Martin.

As Sarah took the list from her uniform pocket, the door opened and Alex filled its frame. 'Sorry to interrupt,' he began. 'Just to let you know that we've finished upstairs and we're about to move the body and some other bits and pieces back to Goleudy. Professor Moore says he's in Edinburgh tomorrow, so he wants to crack on with the PM as soon as possible. He believes there's nothing to indicate anything other than suicide, and he's usually right, but he'll give you a full report later.'

'That's fine,' said Martin. 'I'll see you later. Oh, by the way, before you go will you ask PC Davies to bring down those records that were on Mr Doster's desk – bag them if you need to, and bag that red pen – it may be evidence. It was certainly used to mark those notes, and we need to take a look at them.'

When Alex had gone, Matt explained who he was and what his role would be in determining a correct verdict regarding the cause of death of Peter Doster.

'What an interesting job he has,' remarked Sarah. 'Probably a bit gruesome at times, but very interesting.' She handed what was by now a rather crumpled piece of paper over to Martin. 'Here it is. This is the list of names Maria and I came up with, and the second list is the similarities between all the cases.'

'Remind me what they are?'

'Well, not one of these residents on that list was confined to bed. They were all able to walk about, some with the aid of a stick but the majority could make it to the shops or even the pub – like Colin James. So both Maria and I, especially with the benefit of hindsight, were surprised when they died.

'None of them had families that visited, although they all had relatives and we know that in a number of cases their next of kin had a meeting with Mr Cooper shortly before their death. The residents had not been visited by their relatives but we may find instructions in their notes regarding their non-admission to hospital. On at least one occasion I know for certain that the request was made without the knowledge of the resident to whom it referred, and I suspect it was the same with the others.'

'Sorry,' said Martin. 'I'm not really sure what you mean.'

'OK, well, under normal circumstances, if a resident is suddenly taken ill it would be just the same as if they were at home. We would send for the doctor and if the condition was treatable, for example pneumonia, they would most likely be admitted to hospital.' Sarah continued. 'Very occasionally we have a resident who expresses a wish not to be admitted under any circumstances, and to cover ourselves legally we ensure that those wishes are recorded in the medical records and are signed and dated by the doctor. The same would be the case if they refused any other sort of treatment or medical advice.'

'But it doesn't happen very often?' asked Martin.

'Only once since I've been here,' said Sarah 'and I've never known the relatives' wishes override those of the resident.'

Maria intervened. 'The other thing that struck me was that all these patients collapsed and died when Sarah was either on annual leave or had a long weekend, and that's the case with every one of them. When I think back, there were several times when I believe that if Sarah had been around she would have used her own judgement and sent for an ambulance anyway.'

Martin rose to his feet, but as he did so asked the two women if they could think of anyone who would benefit from the death of the residents they had identified. Neither Sarah nor Maria responded immediately but then Sarah spoke. 'I am probably speaking out of turn,' she said. 'I was due to go off for a long weekend just before Colin James died, but I had to work the Friday because of staff shortages. There was even the possibility that I would have to cancel my weekend.

'At about eight o'clock in the evening I was told that Mr Cooper was still in his office and wanted to see me. It's unusual for him to be here that late and when I went up it was obvious he had been entertaining, as there were empty glasses and bottles of whisky and he had definitely been drinking.'

'He told me that he had been speaking to Colin James's daughter and her husband – by the way, he's the man Sgt Evans saw in the corridor. I was told that after speaking to her father Mrs Morris wanted to be sure that everyone was aware of his wishes not to be admitted to hospital under any circumstances. She had apparently told Mr Cooper that she had concerns about her father's care and I'm afraid that at that point I lost my temper.'

'I had been speaking to Colin not long before I went to Mr Cooper's office and I know for certain that his daughter hadn't seen him for months – they weren't even here at Christmas.'

'As I left the office I noticed a very large bundle of £20 notes alongside the whisky bottles, and although I only gave them a passing thought at the time I wondered …'

Chapter Eighteen

Sarah had been able to give Martin the address of the Doster family, and she had also remembered that Peter's wife's name was Carol.

The family home was a period, mid-terraced property on Plasturton Avenue and like the nursing home it was within the Pontcanna area of Cardiff. As Martin parked on the road outside the house he could see that the building was in pristine condition, with immaculately groomed hedges and well-ordered flowered borders. The front door was painted a dark navy, almost black, and the brass fittings were without a single finger-mark. The outside of Peter Doster's house reminded Martin of the inside of the administrator's office – there was a place for everything and everything was in its place.

Matt rang the doorbell and from inside came a woman's voice. 'Use your key, Peter, I'm at a critical point with your omelette.'

It then dawned on the two detectives that if Peter was a nine to five man, now would be the time he would normally get home. There was nothing for it but to ring the bell again, and this time they could hear someone walking down the hall and the door opened.

Clearly expecting to see her husband on the doorstep, Mrs Doster stared enquiringly at the two men who faced her.

'Good evening,' said Martin showing his official ID. 'I'm DCI Phelps and this is DS Pryor. Are you Carol Doster?'

'Yes,' was the quiet response. 'Sorry, but I thought you were my husband, I can usually set my watch by him, but he's a few minutes late today.'

As she spoke, Martin could see she had already guessed that something had prevented Peter from coming home this evening, and she walked back down the hall and into the lounge just assuming that the detectives would follow her.

The inside of the house mirrored the outside. There was nothing out of place and everything about it had a purpose. The only thing that helped turn the house into a home was a large silver-framed photograph on one of the shelves. In spite of the way in which he had seen him earlier Martin recognised the man as Peter Doster and the woman was Carol, so presumably the two girls were their daughters. Judging by Carol's appearance it was a fairly recent photograph, so Martin guessed the girls' ages as somewhere between twelve and fifteen. How would they cope with the terrible news about their father?

Carol had sat down and motioned with her arms for Martin and Matt to sit down too.

'Is there anyone you would like us to get for you, because I can see you have guessed that we are here with some very bad news,' said Martin.

'The only person I would like you to get is Peter,' came the quiet reply. 'But I have no doubt that you have come here to tell me he is dead – am I right?'

'I'm afraid so,' said Martin. 'I am most dreadfully sorry.'

Martin waited for the news to sink in and expected Mrs Doster to break down but she held herself together and asked the questions Martin braced himself for. 'How did he die – was it a car accident? Where was it?'

'Not an accident,' replied Martin, rising from his chair and walking over to where Carol was sitting. He took both her hands and told her the dreadful truth. 'We have every reason to believe your husband took his own life. He was discovered hanging from a beam in his office, and much to everyone's regret it was too late for any help to be given.'

Mrs Doster startled Martin as she stood up, released her hands and physically pushed him away. 'You liar!' she shouted. 'You liar! Peter would never do a thing like that, you didn't know him. They say it takes courage to commit suicide, so let me tell you something, Inspector – courage was the one thing completely missing from Peter's make up.'

She sat back down and sobbed piteously and Martin suggested to Matt that he find the kitchen and put the kettle on. Matt did so and walked into a kitchen that had a dining table at one end and a pan on the range containing what was now a very flat, cold omelette.

The table was laid for just two people with cutlery, wine glasses, and napkins in place, and a small vase of flowers in the centre. Next to the flowers was a wine cooler and a bottle of rosé was chilling, waiting to be uncorked. Matt had no idea about the Dosters' normal evening meals, but this looked like one arranged for some sort of celebration.

After a few minutes he headed back to the lounge with a tray of mugs full of tea and some extra milk and sugar. In Matt's absence Martin had been told where to find a book of addresses and telephone numbers, and he handed it to Matt, asking him to ring Carol's sister.

'Apparently she lives in the next street, so could be here within a few minutes – and it may or may not be a good thing but the two girls are on a camping holiday with the Guides. They only went this morning and Carol was just telling me that this would have been about the first night she and Peter would have had alone since the girls were born.' As Martin spoke, Matt's mind went back to the kitchen.

He thought about the beautifully arranged dining table, and wondered what could have caused Peter Doster to do what he did – and today of all days.

Carol was relatively calm, much more than anyone could have expected, and she had been talking to Martin about her sister and the girls, but now Martin knew he had to take her somewhere she would not want to go – but he had no choice.

'I have to ask you some questions that you may find difficult, and if you like I can wait until your sister gets here – DS Pryor is phoning her now.'

'No,' was Carol's reply. 'I know when I see my sister we'll both be in bits, so let's get the questions over with.'

'Can you think of any reason why your husband would have committed suicide?' asked Martin, trying to make it sound like an everyday, routine question.

'It would have been nothing whatsoever to do with us,' she said in a whisper. 'We met at university and have had the happiest of marriages.' Tears welled up again in her eyes but she continued. 'I don't mean we were always happy, we had our share of ups and downs like most people, but there was only ever one thing on

217

which we totally disagreed.'

'For some reason, about five years ago, Peter gave up a perfectly good career and went to work for Anthony Cooper. They had known one another since their school days but I've never thought of them as friends, and they didn't even go to the same university. As I remember it Anthony dropped out after one or two years, and as far as I know Peter lost touch with him.'

'Anyway, he turned up again like a bad penny, and that's how I have always thought of him. I have constantly believed that he seemed to have some sort of hold over Peter. I did tackle Peter about it when he decided to take the administrator's job but he wouldn't tell me anything – but I know there was something.'

'He was never happy at Parkland, but Peter was always conscientious, some would say too conscientious, and he just got on with the job. Over the last two years things have been much worse, but in order to keep him as the home administrator, Anthony Cooper has been giving Peter ad hoc gifts of anything up to £1000. He has called them gifts, apparently to avoid tax, but contrary to what you would expect every time one was made Peter seemed to have a week or so of acute depression.'

'Would you be able to tell me when these gifts were made?' asked Martin.

'Easily,' replied Carol. 'Peter said he wouldn't touch the money, and wouldn't put it into our usual account, and instead he opened a university fund for the girls. It currently stands at around £10,000 and each entry is shown in the building society passbook. I can't tell you for certain why my husband chose to take his own life, Inspector, but it's got to be something to do with Anthony Cooper. I believe that in some way, and for whatever reason, the man has been bullying my husband – I suggest you look in that direction for Peter's demons.'

As Carol finished speaking, the doorbell rang, and Matt let in a woman, who sufficiently resembled Carol to be recognised as the sister they were waiting for. He told her briefly what had happened, and she let out a cry and ran to the living room to cradle her sister, whose sobbing was now out of control.

Martin pulled his car back into the car park of the nursing home, and as he and Matt got out another car pulled in behind them. It was a metallic silver Mercedes and Matt confirmed that it was Anthony Cooper behind the wheel.

'What the hell are you doing back here?' Cooper directed his question at Matt. 'I was told the police had been sent for, so what's it all about this time?'

'This is DCI Phelps,' said Matt, introducing Martin as formally and officiously as he could and with the desired effect.

'Bloody hell, the crime rate must be down if DCIs are being sent out to get witness statements – I take it that's what you are doing again?'

This time he directed his question at Martin who threw one back at him. 'If you don't mind, sir, I will ask the questions, and I would like to start by asking who was it that told you the police had been sent for?'

Somewhat thrown by the question, Cooper tried to bluff his way out of answering. 'Oh, Christ, I don't know, I just got a message, could have been anyone.'

'No problem, sir,' said Martin. 'I presume the message came to you via your mobile phone, so it will be easy enough to identify the caller.'

Martin held his hand out as if wanting Mr Cooper to hand over his phone and at the same moment Cooper's memory lapse evaporated. 'Of course, sorry about that, I remember now, it was Brian Prosser. We have his grandmother Enid as one of our residents, and he wanted to speak to me about her care, but I had been held up and so I asked Peter Doster, my administrator, to see him for me. Apparently when Mr Prosser got here he was told by one of my staff that there had been some sort of accident and that she was sending for the police. But why are we discussing this in the car park – shouldn't we go inside?'

'Certainly, sir,' agreed Martin and the three men headed for the main entrance. Under different circumstances the next event would have been amusing as on walking into the reception area the first thing that greeted them was agency nurse Craig, who was obviously on a recruitment drive. 'You should join the agency,' he was saying to one of the care assistants. 'You would get a much better hourly rate, and if Cooper started on the bullying tactics I witnessed when I worked here you could tell him to sod off!'

'What the bleeding hell do you think you're doing?' bawled Cooper. 'Don't tell me Doster has approved the use of agency

219

nurses – the man's taken leave of his senses. You may as well pack your bags,' he shouted at Craig. 'There's no way I am allowing Doster to sign your timesheet, and no way you're going to get paid out of my pocket.'

Craig looked startled but was mostly puzzled. Surely Mr Cooper must know that the person he rudely referred to as 'Doster' would not be doing anything – and certainly not signing his timesheet.

Martin took control and suggested to Mr Cooper that staffing issues could wait as there were things he needed to know and could they please use the relatives' room to talk in private.

As soon as they were in the relatives' room, Martin told Mr Cooper that Peter Doster was dead.

At first the home's owner said nothing, and this was followed by a considerable period of silence that Martin did not break because he wanted to hear Cooper's reaction to the news. Finally Anthony Cooper asked 'How did he die? – was it a heart attack? He was certainly heading for one.'

As well as listening to the words Martin was trying to judge what effect this news was having.

'We can't be certain, but we are fairly safe in assuming that it was an act of suicide, as he was found by Sr Thomas hanging from one of the beams in his office.'

'What in the name of hell is this going to do to the reputation of Parkland?' was his first reaction. It was followed by 'What a bloody nuisance – trust him to make a mess of everything. Suicide! I didn't think he had the balls, but maybe it was more like he didn't have the balls to live. What do you think, Inspector?'

Martin stared with open hostility at this man who had shown not one sign of concern or compassion for someone he had known for most of his life. 'In my experience,' Martin said bluntly, 'suicide is a very complex situation, and no two cases are ever alike. I cannot possibly imagine what level of torment a person must reach in order to perform such an act, and my sympathies at the moment are with his family. We had just returned from breaking the news to Carol Doster when we saw you in the car park, and she was clearly devastated.'

'Oh, yes, her,' said Cooper. 'I suppose I will have to go and offer my condolences.'

Matt interrupted. 'I wouldn't bother if I were you, because you certainly wouldn't be welcome.'

Mr Cooper shrugged his shoulders and Martin asked him if he could think of any reason why Peter Doster had taken his own life.

'How do you expect me to know?' was his predictable reply. 'I had enough trouble thinking of reasons for some of the idiotic things he did at the best of times, but this takes the biscuit. Christ! I've just thought of something: I hope they don't shut us down. Where's Sr Thomas? She should be notifying Care Standards and whoever else needs to be told. That's her job, not mine.'

For one moment Martin thought Matt was going to put himself in danger of a GBH charge. Instead he treated Anthony Cooper to a tirade of verbal abuse the level of which he had probably not used since his last game of rugby.

'I don't have to take that!' was Cooper's response. 'Did you hear that, Inspector? Your sergeant has no right to speak to me like that and I will be making a formal complaint to the superintendent. I know him personally.'

'Sorry, sir,' said Martin. 'I was busy looking at these folders I asked PC Davies to bring here for me. Did I miss something?'

Martin's obvious ploy in defence of his sergeant had the desired effect, and Cooper started to rant and rave about the lack of respect the police gave to law-abiding citizens. Ignoring the outburst, Martin started setting out the eleven sets of notes on the table in front of him and this action produced an immediate reaction from Mr Cooper and a simultaneous but very different reaction from Matt.

'Where the hell did you get those from?' demanded Cooper. 'You have no right to be looking at medical records, it's only allowed on a need-to-know basis.'

'Look at those names!' said Matt excitedly. 'The top three are a match to Sarah's list but no, look – there's more than three that match. This can't be a coincidence, can it?'

'You know me, Matt,' said Martin. 'I don't really subscribe to the theory of coincidence. Let's get this lot back to Goleudy and see what we can make of it all. There's nothing else we can do here anyway.'

'Wait a minute,' said Mr Cooper but he wasn't shouting now. He was looking decidedly pale and was very unsure of his position.

221

Nevertheless he persisted. 'You can't just take medical records without the proper authority.'

'I think you'll find,' smirked Matt, 'that we *are* the proper authority.'

Mr Cooper tried another tack and in a voice that was full of reason and cooperation he asked Martin why there was a need for the records to be removed. 'What possible connection has this got to poor Peter's suicide?' he asked.

Martin looked Cooper straight in the eye and replied, 'At this moment in time I think that these records may well be his suicide note, and hopefully they will ensure that he didn't die for nothing.'

Matt said he was going to see what was happening with Sarah and Maria, and he left Martin after agreeing to meet him in the car park in ten minutes. Anthony Cooper was a shadow of his former self, and he followed Martin just like a forlorn puppy as the detective made his way back to the administrator's office to speak to PC Davies.

They both stopped at the foot of the short flight of stairs and Martin said curtly. 'Sorry, sir, but you won't be allowed up there until we have finished our investigation, and nothing must be taken from the office until I say so.'

'But there are things I need, like the names and addresses of people I need to contact. Doster kept all that sort of thing. There are the relevant authorities that I have a statutory duty to notify, and you can't stop me doing what the law says I must.'

'Well, on no account will you be allowed into that room. PC Davies will be there for the foreseeable future, so I suggest that you use the phone from your office to this office and he will help as he sees fit. Thank you, Mr Cooper, you may go about your business for the moment.'

Enraged at being dismissed in the way he normally did the dismissing, Anthony Cooper turned on his heels and marched from one end of the nursing home to the other and then slammed the door of his office. During this relatively short route march the façade of compliance had disappeared from his face, and it now displayed a purple rage, but also something unfamiliar to him – abject fear!

He turned the key in his door, locking himself in, and sitting at his over-sized desk he phoned a number he didn't need anyone to find for him because he knew it so well.

The voice that answered was also well-known to him and he skipped the usual pleasantries. 'Fucking well get yourself here – and I mean now! Doster's topped himself and there are police swarming all over the place, taking medical records and all sorts. I'm bloody well not taking the rap for this – it was your fucking idea, not mine.'

Chapter Nineteen

It was gone seven o'clock in the evening and the two detectives were drinking coffee in Martin's office. 'Can you believe it's only Thursday?' asked Matt, rubbing his eyes. 'What a week. What's the plan now?'

Before Martin had a chance to reply his phone rang and Mrs Williams gave him the message that the professor had finished the PM and had gone home. He had asked her to let DCI Phelps know that the PM findings were consistent with suicide and no one else was involved with the death. Professor Moore had also asked her to say that his Edinburgh trip had been called off so he would be around tomorrow if the DCI wanted a word.

'Good,' said Martin, as he put the phone down. 'I was going to need a medical person to help with the interpretation of these residents' case notes, and if the Prof is going to be around tomorrow he will fit the bill nicely.

'I'm trying to get my head around what we're looking at here, and the worst-case scenario is that these possibly premature deaths could be murder. It's going to be a case of looking into every nook and cranny, and in particular looking at who had motive, means, and opportunity.'

'I'm going to get some of Alex's team to empty the administrator's office and bring every piece of paper that exists to Incident Room One, and we can make a start on going through the lot after a good night's sleep.'

Those were the best words Matt had heard all day, and he rose to his feet. 'As I mentioned on the way back, Sarah and Maria have now gone off duty and I have asked them both to come here for formal interviews tomorrow at ten o'clock. Sarah was planning to go away but, as she said, things have overtaken those plans and she's changed them.

'She's been in contact with the Care and Social Services

Inspectorate Wales, that's the official regulatory body for Care Homes that provide nursing care. So far she has told them about Mr Doster's death and that the police are conducting an investigation into possibly premature deaths at Parkland.' Then Matt laughed. 'I can't do the impression like Sarah,' he said. 'Apparently the woman she spoke to at the CSSIW went into a panic, saying she had done the last inspection and that everything was in order then.'

Before leaving the building Matt went to his own office to pick up a present he had left there earlier. It was his niece Ellie's birthday tomorrow, and he planned to drop the gift and card off on his way home. Already in the office was DS Janice Dilworth, and she was putting items into a cardboard box on her desk. It looked as if she was packing up her belongings, but at least she wasn't in tears, and Matt felt able to comment. 'Moving out?' he asked.

'Oh, hi,' she responded. 'I thought everyone had gone home. Yes, I put in for a transfer a few weeks ago and was told earlier this week that it had been turned down. That's when you saw me having a "feeling sorry for myself moment", I'm sorry if I embarrassed you.'

'Not at all,' was Matt's reply. 'I was just torn between going after you to see if you were alright and minding my own business. So what's happened, has someone up there changed their mind about your transfer?'

'I don't think they would have done,' replied Janice. 'I had applied to go to Essex, that's where I did my degree and that's where I met Anne and, well, we became more than just good friends. Problem is, Anne is a DCI and had been married to the Chief Super – but they had never been happy and were divorced even before I arrived on the scene.

'Anyway to cut a long story short, after my transfer was turned down one of their detective sergeants requested a move to Cardiff, and so basically we are doing a straight swap, starting Monday.'

Matt had enjoyed working with Janice, but after this revelation of her sexual preference he didn't know whether to kiss her, shake her hand, or just run. He chose the first, gave her a big hug, and kissed her cheek. 'Look after yourself,' he told her and then 'I don't suppose you know who we are getting in exchange for you, do you?'

Janice laughed and her whole face was full of mischief as she said. 'I don't know the lady personally, but you'll need to watch out, Matt, as rumour has it she's something of a man-eater.'

Matt picked up his parcels, and with a final wave towards Janice he made his way to the car park. He would drop the gifts off at his sister's house on his way home, and there was a fair chance that she would take pity on her bachelor brother and offer him a meal. They both lived in the Pontprennau area of Cardiff, with just a matter of ten minutes' drive separating their houses. If Beth wasn't up for cooking, Matt would double back to Waitrose and get one of Delia or Heston's ready meals.

On his way to Beth's house, Matt found himself hoping that Janice was not making a big mistake. Working with someone with whom you are personally involved was, in his view, never a good idea, and when it was something other than a straightforward heterosexual relationship it would surely be fraught with difficulties. It would be just like him and Martin being a couple! The thought made him laugh aloud, and he was still laughing when he was invited into Beth's kitchen just in time to share their later-than-usual evening meal.

Leaving his office Martin reflected briefly on the happenings at Parkland and then his thoughts returned to Shelley. Her rich auburn hair and dark blue eyes were never far from his mind, and he had tried to phone her earlier but her phone had gone straight to the messaging service. He had left a message but she hadn't responded and he felt a bit dejected as he started up his car and headed out of the city.

It was a stunning summer's evening and people were strolling around making the most of the good weather that had been a long time coming. As he took the road towards the coast, Martin thought more and more about Shelley and admitted to himself that he was head over heels in love with her. So what was he going to do about it?

Turning the final corner towards home and seeing the familiar much loved row of terraced cottages his heart missed a beat.

Shelley's car was parked on his drive – so she had got his message.

Feeling a bit like a silly schoolboy, Martin stopped the car before he got to the drive and walked quietly up the path. He let himself in as silently as if he were a burglar and then for a few moments just stood and watched Shelley as she stood at his kitchen-sink.

'This is a sight I want to come home to everyday,' he said quietly and with a lump in his throat.

Shelley shrieked. 'Crikey! Martin, you scared me to death.'

'You look very much alive to me,' he responded. 'Very much alive, and you look far too beautiful to be washing dishes.' Martin picked up a towel and tried to dry Shelley's hands, but she tossed the towel aside and threw her arms around his neck, covering them both with soapsuds. They laughed and kissed, and as the kissing grew more intense they moved from the kitchen towards the bedroom.

Half-heartedly Shelley mentioned the food she had prepared, but Martin had already turned off the oven, and it was two hours later before he turned it back on and they even thought about eating.

'What about making this a permanent arrangement?' asked Martin as snuggled on the sofa they shared a large bowl of the ham and broccoli pasta bake Shelley had made. 'I would have suggested it sooner,' he teased, 'but I had to check out your culinary skills first, and judging by this they are almost as good as your other attributes.'

'Cheek!' said Shelley, but then she was quiet.

'You haven't answered my question,' Martin said. 'Do you need some time to consider? I just thought you felt the same way as me and I really want to be with you on more than a part-time basis.'

Shelley kissed Martin on the end of his nose. 'I love you,' she said simply. 'I have wanted this for much longer than you have, but I can't just desert my father. He relies on me now that Mum's no longer around.'

For best part of an hour they thought about possible arrangements to accommodate the three of them, but nothing was quite right and, as Shelley admitted, it was something they needed to do with her father's input.

'Let's not think about this now,' said Shelley. 'Let's not think about the washing up either – let's just go back to bed!'

'You brazen hussy!' laughed Martin, as he chased her up the stairs.

Back at the Parkland Nursing Home Alex had decided to oversee the transfer of all the documents from the Administrators Office to Incident Room One at Goleudy, and he arrived just in time to hear PC Davies arguing with two men. Neither of the men was known to Alex and he asked PC Davies who they were and if there was a problem.

Not waiting for PC Davies to reply, Mr Cooper interjected. 'It's more a question of who are you rather than who are we,' he said, loudly and curtly. 'For your information, my name is Anthony Cooper and I am the owner of this establishment. This,' he said placing his hand in front of the other man, 'is Dr Shaw, and he is our residents' nominated general practitioner. We have every right to be here, but can the same be said for you, I wonder?'

'No need for you to wonder, sir,' said Alex in his most polite but officious manner. 'My name is Alex Griffiths and I head up the Scene of Crime Investigation Team for this area. We are investigating the possibility of a crime or crimes, and so legally I am well within my rights to be here.'

'Rubbish!' Dr Shaw spoke for the first time. 'Suicide isn't a crime – hasn't been considered so since the Suicide Act of 1961. Perhaps you haven't caught up with it yet,' he said rudely.

'Oh, I think I have,' answered Alex calmly. 'I can quote you the subsequent amendments if you like – but who said anything about the crime in question being suicide?'

'What else would it be?' the doctor demanded.

'That's not for me to say, sir. DCI Phelps is leading the investigation, and he will be the one to decide the nature of the crime. I am just here to ensure that everything he needs in order to reach that decision is made available to him. To that end I will be taking all the documents and paperwork from this office to Goleudy, the police headquarters in Cardiff Bay. I want to get the job finished before I go home tonight, so if you don't mind I will just get on with it.'

'That's the problem,' said PC Davies. 'It was when I told these gentlemen that you were coming to take the files and things that they started arguing with me.'

'I still say you have no right to take medical records. They could be needed if any one of the residents is taken ill during the night, and without access to the records a resident's life could be put at risk. You would be responsible, and you can be sure that I would have no problem in pointing the finger. Do you get that?'

Alex was losing his patience, but he had to admit that the doctor had a point and thankfully he had thought of a solution. He asked PC Davies for a pen and a piece of paper, and after writing down a name and a telephone number he handed the paper to the doctor.

'If the nurse on night duty needs to send for a doctor for one of the residents, she can dial that number straight after doing so. I can personally guarantee that the notes she requests will be here before the doctor arrives so no one will be put at risk.'

PC Davies had already boxed the things that were needed, and handed the first box to Alex who hurried off to load it in to his car. Realising they were not going to achieve anything by further arguments with the officers, Mr Cooper and Dr Shaw walked off and were heard arguing and swearing as they went in the direction of Cooper's office.

After he had taken what he believed to be the last box, Alex returned to check the room and to speak to PC Davies.

'I don't think there's any need for you to stay here,' said Alex. 'We can lock the door and take the key, and even if those two feel the need to come back here there's nothing left for them to interfere with. Why don't you call it a day and I'll give you a lift back?'

By the time Martin arrived at Incident Room One the following morning Matt was already there and had worked his way through three of the case files from the sets found on Peter Doster's desk.

'Morning,' he said as Martin walked towards him. 'First thing to say is that the red pen we found on Mr Doster's desk is the one that has been used to write on these notes, and the pen has his fingerprints on it so it was used by him. Not that there was ever any serious doubt about that but I knew you would want it confirmed.'

'Of course,' replied Martin. 'I have long since learnt not to take anything for granted.' He picked up the three files that Matt had already scrutinised and asked him what conclusions he had reached.

'No conclusions,' replied Matt. 'If you look at that whiteboard there, I've made eleven columns headed with the name of each of the residents whose case notes we have. To the left of the columns I am writing down the things that are marked in red in each of the records, and trying to compare things.'

Martin laughed. 'Watch it, Matt, you're in danger of becoming a columns man like me – but as the saying goes, imitation is the most sincere form of flattery. What can I say – I like your style!'

Taking a closer look, Martin saw that there were four things written on the left-hand side of the board. The first was no surprise, as in all the notes examined so far Peter Doster had circled in red, 'This resident does not wish to be admitted to hospital under any circumstances'

The next thing in common to the three sets of notes was the sudden increase in medication, and on the three resident's prescription sheets the red pen identified the dates that a variety of different drugs had been prescribed. Matt mentioned the fact that in the three cases the prescription drugs had been ordered by Dr Shaw, but they both agreed there was no real significance in that, as he was the designated GP for the home and would be the usual signatory for all the residents.

The next thing Matt had as a common thread was, perversely, a different name in each of the records. Martin asked him to explain what that was all about.

'I started at the top of the pile,' said Matt. 'The first case notes I looked at belonged to Colin James. In his notes alongside a date that is four days before his death is the name William Morris, circled in red ink. The next set of notes belonged to a lady called Connie Marshall, and in this case just three days before her death the name Edward Partridge appears and has been circled by Mr Doster. The last that I have looked at so far are the notes of a gentleman by the name of Terence Watts, and there is a similar pattern. In his notes, and again it's three days before he died, the name Caroline Wilson has been written, and again it's circled in red.'

'I have no idea who Caroline Wilson is, or Edward Partridge, but of course we both know the name William Morris. He's the gentleman who first attracted our attention, and we know he's married to Colin James' daughter. I'm surmising that the other names are either the next of kin of these deceased residents or are related to them in some way.'

Martin nodded, and looked at Matt's final line for comparison. This one needed no explanation. In all the notes the copies of the death certificates had been carefully stapled to the front cover, and each one gave the cause of death as pneumonia. Each one was signed by Dr Shaw. It now came as no surprise to find both these entries circled with the red pen of Peter Doster.

Martin picked up the fourth record and called out to Matt to tick the items off in his columns if they appeared – and they did! Mavis Clegg was the one Martin studied and, yes, the request for non-admission to hospital was there, as was the sudden increase in medication prescribed by Dr Shaw. There was a name on her notes, written five days before her death, but this time there was no first name, just a Mr Watson. Finally the cause of death was the same as the others and the death certificate signed by Dr Shaw.

The two men went through five more case records in exactly the same way and came up with exactly the same results.

'The other thing,' said Matt 'is that up to this point these people are the same ones that Sarah and Maria came up with when they were randomly thinking back to residents who they had not expected to die when they did.'

'Yes but we've got three more, why would that be?' Without waiting for a reply Martin answered his own question. 'Wait a minute; didn't you say that Sarah went back over the past six months and the next ones in this pile pre-date that.'

'How far do we need to go back then?' questioned Matt.

'The answer to that is just as long as it takes, and we might need to look at every single record, but I don't really think that will be necessary. I think that in some way Mr Doster was involved with whatever has been going on here, and he either got cold feet or was unable to cope with his conscience. I wouldn't be surprised if the notes he had on his desk are what he wanted us to see and in order to ensure that we didn't miss anything he meticulously went through each one and highlighted the relevant entries.'

'Do you think these people died as a result of the sudden increase in their medication?' asked Matt.

'It looks as if the medication was a factor, but I need expert medical opinion to verify that. For all I know, the drugs prescribed could be perfectly justified, or may be just simple vitamin supplements; I'm no expert,' said Martin.

'But what possible motive could Dr Shaw have for expediting the death of these residents?' asked Matt.

'Well, we all know about the cases where the doctor has decided to play God, but there is usually an underlying reason and, sadly, that reason has frequently got something to do with money. What I need you to do, Matt, is to find out who the people are whose names appear on the notes, and we need to interview them all as a matter of urgency.'

'Yes I was just thinking that,' replied Matt. 'We may have a quick route to that information, as I've just been buzzed to say that Sarah and Maria have arrived for their interviews.'

The mention of interviews reminded Martin that at three o'clock he was required to be one of the panel members interviewing Helen Cook-Watts on her possible transfer to CID. As far as he was concerned it was a formality, and he could see no reason why Helen shouldn't be considered suitable for a career in CID – but she wasn't the only candidate and due process had to be adhered to. He hoped it wouldn't take too long.

'Don't take them to the interview rooms,' suggested Martin. 'Bring them straight up here. They've been most helpful, and I'm sure they want to get to the bottom of this, probably even more than we do. Get us all some coffee on your way back, please.'

As Matt had anticipated, Sarah and Maria were able to identify the names on the notes as either relatives or the next of kin of the deceased, but in all cases it was only because they remembered seeing the names on the nursing notes and not because those people were caring, frequent visitors.

When asked about the additional three residents' names, they confessed to not being able to remember much about them. All three were residents who had not been much trouble to look after and none of them had required nursing care. If Sarah and Maria had gone back further than six months it was likely that the three names would have been included in their list.

Martin showed Sarah the case notes of Colin James and asked her if it was usual for certain entries to be circled in red. Sarah said that the last time she had seen Colin's notes they hadn't been defaced in that way. 'Who did it?' she asked.

Martin told her that a red pen had been found on Peter Doster's desk and he believed that Mr Doster had circled the same items in all eleven sets of notes to draw attention to those particular entries. He showed Sarah the entries, and her interest immediately focused on the prescriptions chart. She took in every detail of the drugs that had been prescribed in the days prior to death and without making any comments on the one chart she asked Martin if she could look at the other ten prescription sheets.

Matt took the prescription sheets out of the other notes and handed them to Sarah just as Professor Moore walked in. 'I've just been informed that you would like my expert opinion on something, but if this is not a good time you can catch me later. I was supposed to be in Scotland so there's nothing in my diary.'

Martin introduced the professor to Sarah and Maria and explained their involvement. The professor obviously knew about the suicide at Parkland, as he had done the PM, but this was the first he had heard about an investigation into possibly premature deaths of residents. His professional interest was immediately aroused and he sat down next to Sarah and for the next hour they both poured over the type, frequency, and dosage of the medication prescribed in each case.

While they were doing that, Maria helped Matt to identify the names circled in all eleven notes, and within half an hour CID staff, accompanied by uniformed officers, were on a mission to bring in seven of the eleven names for questioning. Those seven people had local addresses, but the remaining four names lived further away – three in England and one in Scotland.

Martin made contact with his opposite numbers in the relevant areas and was assured that the people identified would be brought in for questioning and the outcome made known to him.

It was looking increasingly as if the demise of all eleven residents was deliberately orchestrated, and if so he was looking at eleven counts of murder – or possibly more!

Dr Shaw had prescribed a concoction of drugs, but had they had a lethal effect, and what possible motive could the doctor have for killing off these particular patients? Martin was sure that Cooper was involved, and now believed that Doster had been an unwilling partner in crime.

Money had to be at the bottom of this, and Martin rang Charlie to help with accessing personal financial information in relation to Cooper, Shaw, and Doster, as well as the eleven names taken from the notes. She was in her element, and looking over her shoulder just twenty minutes into the task Martin could see she was already compiling a pretty damning spreadsheet. Dates relating to the transfer of large sums of money fitted the dates of deaths.

Matt went to the interview rooms, where one of the identified relatives was already telling Sgt Evans that he would say nothing until he had spoken to his solicitor. In an adjacent room was a woman, and although she had been told of her rights she was much more forthcoming. 'I didn't want to have anything to do with it,' she protested. 'My son-in-law said people were always popping off in these nursing homes so no one would be any the wiser. The doctor told him it would be a blessing, and the life insurance money was certainly a blessing to us. We would have had it eventually anyway but who knows, we could have been waiting years.'

After reminding her that she was being interviewed under caution, Matt left her and went back to tell Martin what she had said.

Martin had just finished speaking to Charlie and Professor Moore, and with the information Matt had brought he had enough to proceed.

'OK,' he said to Matt. 'Let's do it!'

Chapter Twenty

Just over an hour later, Martin and Matt were back in Incident Room One, and Dr George Donald Shaw and Mr Anthony Ian Cooper were in adjacent interview rooms – both waiting for their lawyers.

It had been a frenzied hour culminating in the arrest of both men in connection with the deaths of a number of residents over a period of months. Martin had not used specific names when making the arrests, and would be waiting for the results of the interviews and seeking advice from the CPS before formalising any charges.

They had made their first stop at Parkland Nursing Home, and had found Mr Cooper in his office shredding bank statements and a variety of other documents. It took some persuading to get him to stop and the air was blue when Matt explained that shredding was a waste of time, as copies of everything could be obtained electronically or even pieced back together.

When faced with the choice of being handcuffed or walking out of the home to apparently help the police with their enquiries, he chose the latter. However this did not stop every window in the home being full of faces as staff and residents witnessed Mr Cooper having his head protected by the police officer as he was guided into the back of the police car.

Their next stop, with a second squad car not far behind, was at the palatial home of Dr Shaw in Llandaff. There were a number of beautiful homes in the area but the Shaws' residence was exceptional. It was detached, set in at least half an acre of landscaped gardens, and had been recently extended. Neither Martin nor Matt had ever met Dr Shaw and as they pulled up outside the house, just to lighten their mood, they had a bet on his age and description. Matt guessed at a short, portly man nearing the end of his professional life, and Martin settled for a middle-aged man who wore rimless glasses.

They were none the wiser when in response to their ring the door was opened by a rather gorgeous blonde who, unless she was already seriously into facelifts, was on the good side of forty – his wife or his daughter maybe?

'Good morning,' said Martin. 'I am DCI Phelps and this is DS Pryor. We are hoping to speak to Dr George Shaw, please.'

'I'm afraid it's just me at home, as I rarely see my husband during the hours of daylight, Inspector,' was the reply, in a Scandinavian accent. 'His PA at the clinic is much more likely to be able to help you than I am, so I suggest you try there.'

She gave them the address and watched them walk back to their car but Martin had looked back and noticed a shadowy figure in one of the rooms at the front of the house and retraced his footsteps to the front door.

'On second thoughts,' he said to Mrs Shaw, 'a quick word with you could just be all we need.' Without waiting to be asked in, Martin took two steps into the hall and opened the door leading to the room where he had seen movement.

'Georgie – it wasn't me! I didn't let them in!'

The doctor's wife continued to protest as they all entered the room to find Dr Shaw closing the lid of a suitcase that was alongside five other cases, already packed.

'Going somewhere, sir?' asked Martin of the elderly gentleman with rimless glasses – one point for him and one for Matt.

Minutes later the doctor was being offered the same mode of transport as Mr Cooper, but this time there were no witnesses at the window, just a slightly tearful blonde left on the doorstep.

On their return Incident Room One was a hive of activity with all the excitement that goes with the knowledge that a case is being cracked and every effort was going into discovering the details that would be essential in order to obtain a conviction.

Sarah and Maria had left but Prof. Moore was still poring over the prescription sheets now helped by the last two monthly copies of MIMS (Monthly Index of Medical Specialities – the profession's guide to pharmaceuticals). He was up to date, and in fact a world leader in his own field of medicine, but with new drugs arriving on the scene every week it was impossible to keep abreast especially when not directly involved with prescribing. The

MIMS, sent to all GP practices free of charge, was also available to other healthcare professionals, and the prof. had a regular copy delivered. He could never remember not having access to this essential prescribing reference, it had certainly been around for more than fifty years and was updated every month. The online version was on one of the computer screens in front of him and he was finding it easier to cross-reference the interaction between different drugs with the aid of the programme it offered.

'He's been on the phone to pharmacists and toxicologists and various other "ists" ever since you left, and I've never seen him so animated – he's almost excited,' smiled Charlie. 'I think he may be after your job – this has certainly brought out the detective in him.'

Martin walked over to the professor who looked up and smiled – yes, actually smiled – at him, but his voice mirrored the contempt he was feeling for a fellow doctor.

'We may well conclude that the man is an evil bastard,' he stated, 'but he is a clever one, and without the bizarre series of events that brought us to this point it could have been years before these crimes were discovered, if ever.'

'He has used quite ordinary, run-of-the-mill drugs, but he has combined them with serious consequences and they have reacted one with the other in textbook fashion. Even a fit man like you, Chief Inspector, would have been made seriously ill, and quite quickly, by these deadly combinations.'

'Wouldn't the nurses administering these drugs know about the possible adverse effect of certain drugs when used together?' asked Martin.

'It's more than likely that someone like Sr Thomas, especially if she saw a deterioration in the resident's condition, would have questioned the drug regime, but that's another point where our doctor has been devious. Sister was always on a series of days off when the medication was prescribed, and the dosage times for each of the different drugs meant that a different nurse gave a different drug at various times of the day.'

'No, Chief Inspector, I wouldn't blame the nurses for not knowing of the possible consequences of this combination of medicines, since reading this latest copy of the MIMS I can't believe how many new drugs are released on a monthly basis. It's almost impossible for the average practitioner to keep up.'

The professor paused for effect before announcing, 'Then we have the grand finale!'

The room was quiet and Professor Moore had everyone's attention.

'Each of these residents had deteriorated to the point of the nurses phoning Dr Shaw, something I have picked up from the nursing Kardex. In all cases he made a visit, regardless of the hour of the day or night and on the pretence of alleviating pain and suffering he administered diamorphine hydrochloride. In all cases the resident had died before he left the home, having first commiserated with the nurses and signed the death certificate. The cause of death in all cases is given as pneumonia with complications commensurate with the age and general condition of the resident.

'No post-mortems would have been required, as each of the residents had been seen and treated by a doctor immediately prior to their death. It scares me to think how relatively easy it has been for him to cover his tracks. He didn't give a one-off overdose of diamorphine to kill, as was the case with Harold Shipman – that I'm sure would have been picked up with the routine checks that are made on the usage and storage of all controlled drugs.'

'What he did was inflict yet another potent drug on top of the ones already causing harm, and with lethal effect. What kind of message is this going to send out to residents and their families in nursing homes throughout the country? I take it the motive was money but where did the money come from? Did he persuade the residents to make him their main beneficiary? Surely that would have caused an uproar from indignant relatives? So what did he do?'

Charlie had left Matt with all the details of her investigations into bank accounts and investment portfolios. Martin asked him to go through the findings and he did so, first of all focusing on the eleven names that had been identified in the records.

'All the names are those of either the actual next of kin of a resident or someone very close to that person. In every case the sum of five thousand pounds has been withdrawn in cash from the accounts of our named individuals, usually days before, but anything up to a month prior to, a particular resident's death.'

'So far we have looked at eleven sets of £5000 amounts, and

within days of the money being withdrawn the exact same amount is paid by Mr Doster into the Parkland Nursing Home account. However, it doesn't stay there very long, and two amounts are electronically transferred to the personal accounts of Dr Shaw and Mr Cooper.'

'I couldn't initially make any sense of the split because it wasn't always the same. It was Charlie who found that on the same day a cash deposit was made into Mr Doster's girls' university fund. I still don't understand the split but it looks as if Doster was allowed to take between seven hundred and a thousand pounds in cash, and the rest was sent in equal amounts to Shaw and Cooper.'

Professor Moore erupted. 'You mean the bastard actually committed murder at least eleven times, and for a total less than he earns in a month!'

Matt stopped him. 'No, not just for that amount, that's not where it stops,' continued Matt. 'The big pay-out comes weeks and in some cases months later when the various insurance companies pay out on the resident's life insurance. The last claim, that is the one in relation to the death of Colin James, has been lodged but not yet paid out, but the Co-operative Insurance Company told me it will be issuing a cheque for £75,000!

'In relation to the ten other names the insurance claims have been around the £50,000 mark and each time half of the amount awarded to the family is paid into the nursing home account, and then as before electronically transferred between Shaw and Cooper. On these occasions Doster doesn't come into the equation – other than it is he who does the transfers.'

'I'm beginning to feel really sorry for that man,' said Martin. 'The other two must have had some strong hold over him to secure his silence for a pittance in relation to what they were getting.'

'Yes, guv, but it doesn't even end there!' said Matt.

Martin looked at Professor Moore, who held his head in his hands and appeared to have taken on board all the sins of his profession. Martin hoped that later his elderly colleague would be able to balance the good of the majority in favour of the evil of one bad apple.

Matt went on to explain that most of the next of kin also inherited the estates of their relatives, and that in two cases alone the estates had been worth almost half a million pounds. No wonder the relatives had been prepared to accept a solution to the problem of the possible longevity of their particular resident.

'Four months after the death of Nancy Coleman we see another deposit from her daughter's husband into the Parkland deposit account. It's for £52,000 and it ties in with the release of money from her estate. The man who owns the account it was transferred from is in one of our interview rooms and I think he realises we have discovered what has been going on. I have advised him it would be better if he helped us, and I don't think it will take much persuasion for him to tell us the exact series of events.'

'I suspect the same will be the case with most of the others,' suggested Martin. 'There is no way I am condoning their complicity in all of this, but they are not hardened criminals, neither are they the instigators of these crimes. Some may even have thought they were relieving their relatives of pain and suffering if the doctor fed them that line. My guess is that most of them will be quite relieved to put an end to their involvement with the likes of Shaw and Cooper. However, there will be a number of conspiracy charges, and none of these people are blameless.'

'It's going to be one hell of a job for us,' continued Martin, as he cleaned the whiteboard and began listing all the names of the people who would have to be interviewed. 'The obvious ones are Shaw, Cooper, and the eleven names from the medical records, but those eleven will most certainly lead to others who were complicit. On top of that we will need statements from the nurses at Parkland and they will be advised to seek representation from their professional organisations, so that will take time and it will be months or even years before this case gets to court.'

A PC interrupted to say that a rather posh-looking solicitor had arrived, and was apparently representing both Dr Shaw and Mr Cooper. He had briefly spoken to both men and was now demanding that Dr Shaw should be interviewed first.

'In that case tell him that DS Pryor and I will be interviewing Mr Cooper in five minutes' time.'

The PC grinned, and would enjoy passing on the message.

An hour of 'no comment' from Mr Cooper, and more of the same with Dr Shaw, was exactly what Martin had expected, but he had more than enough evidence for their continued detention and he was happy to leave them to stew while he attended to more

242

pleasant duties.

At ten minutes to three he made his way upstairs to the office of Superintendent Bryant and sat with him at the table prepared for the interviews. It was the same office and the same table where he had sat when being interviewed for a post as a detective sergeant, and he felt strangely nervous on behalf of the two candidates they were expecting. One other person was already seated. It was Kate from Personnel, and was there to ensure a correct and fair process was adhered to.

Martin knew Kate as she had represented Personnel on a number of previous interviews, and he knew she would not interfere unless she had to – unlike some of her colleagues.

She suggested that the interviews start as both candidates were available and she brought in a fresh-faced young man who looked as if he could still be in the sixth form. It transpired that Paul Clarke was a university graduate who wanted to join CID, but didn't want to go through the route of the Police Force Graduate Direct Entry Programme. Martin asked him why not and was pleasantly surprised by his reply.

'I see the need for a lot of hands-on experience in this role,' he said. 'I can get the theory from books and the web, and I intend doing that too, but it's only by working alongside people like yourself that I will get a real understanding of detection.'

The superintendent asked a number of questions, but spent most of the time answering them himself, much to the frustration of Kate and Martin. However they both knew he would behave in exactly the same way with both candidates and so his style of interviewing was not questioned. The final question that was to be put to both candidates was the usual. 'Where do you see yourself in ten years' time?'

Paul's answer was a bit vague, and he confessed to not having thought that far ahead, but then hoped he may have redeemed himself by suggesting the possibility of internal promotion or a transfer to the Metropolitan Police Force.

After he had left the room the super made his first and only comment. 'Why do these young graduates always assume that the Met. has more to offer than we do?'

'I could work with him,' said Martin. 'He wouldn't be a bundle of laughs, but I guess we aren't interviewing for the next Tommy

Cooper!'

'Let's get Helen Cook-Watts in now, shall we?' suggested Kate. 'We can have our discussions after they have both been interviewed.'

Helen looked more nervous than Martin had ever seen her, and he sympathised. It was always more difficult being interviewed by people you know. Remembering the response from the first candidate regarding graduate entrants, Martin began the interview. 'You'll be aware that we try to move people into the position you are applying for from a number of different backgrounds. What do you think are the benefits to a team of having graduate entry at this level compared with a straight transfer from our uniform section?'

'Whoops!' thought Helen. 'Here am I sat opposite two men, one of whom I know has come up through the ranks and the other for all I know could be a graduate entry. I'll just have to get a grip and say it as I see it.'

What she actually said was, 'I can see the merits in both ways of becoming a detective constable, but that's not the full story – the whole thing is about the team, not the individual. If a team is made up of all graduate entrants it will lack the experience that can only be gained from grassroots police work. On the other hand it's easy to focus on just one way of looking at things and the academic input of a graduate could provide a different approach. So in my view the best team would be formed from as many different backgrounds as possible, and it will be for the team leader to make the most of everyone's attributes and potential.'

After about half an hour Martin asked the agreed final question and Helen smiled as she said, 'Sitting where you are, sir!'

After a welcome cup of coffee and a respectable length of discussion time Martin made his way to his office and spent the next fifteen minutes on the phone to the CPS. He explained the happenings in Parkland and the factual evidence that had been discovered and sought official confirmation on the charges he had considered. This was duly given and he went in search of Matt to give him the news.

Both men then headed for the interview rooms, and Mr Cooper was charged with conspiracy to murder by virtue of section 1(1) of the Criminal Law Act 1977.

There was no immediate reaction, but then Cooper began

making random accusations about how Dr Shaw had persuaded him to get involved. His solicitor already knew his client had said too much, and tried to stop him talking, but Cooper was on a roll.

'It was all his idea,' said Cooper referring to Dr Shaw. 'Funny thing is, we were at a funeral last October and he suggested a fool-proof way of getting rich and solving my waiting list problems at the same time.'

At this point the solicitor did intervene and on the basis of his advice Cooper said nothing more.

A few minutes later the solicitor, Martin, and Matt were in the next interview room, and it was Dr Shaw who was charged, and this time not just with conspiracy to murder but with actual murder – and on eleven counts. The elderly GP stared straight ahead through his rimless glasses and showed no outward signs of emotion – it was the solicitor who was looking the most agitated and couldn't believe his ears.

Matt called the duty sergeant and waited until both men had been taken to the custody cells, before joining Martin who had gone back to Incident Room One. It was now almost six o'clock, and Martin asked him if he would like to be the one to take the news of the arrests and charges to Sr Thomas. 'I suspect she will be waiting at home for your call, and I'm sure you'll be able to think of some way of rewarding her for the enormous help she has been to us this week,' he teased Matt. 'Apart from that, after the week from hell we have had, neither of us should have a weekend alone – I don't intend to, that's for sure.'

'I couldn't agree more,' replied Matt. 'I was planning on ringing her as soon as I left here, but now that I have your blessing I will do it straight away.'

He grinned as he took his mobile out of his pocket and was about to dial her number when Martin stopped him.

'There is just one thing before you do that,' he said, and as he did so the room was suddenly filled with every CID and uniformed officer who was left in the building at this time on a Friday night.

At Martin's request, Shelley had joined them, and although Professor Moore had been invited he had offered his apologies as he was in no mood for celebrations.

'Make way!' said Iris as she pushed through the gathering throng with a trolley laden with sandwiches, cakes and drinks.

She handed plates around and it wasn't long before everyone was enjoying the spontaneous party.

Matt looked puzzled. 'It's been a good week in terms of results, but you don't usually treat us this well.'

'Well if I don't then maybe it's time I did,' responded Martin, and he asked for quiet as he publicly thanked everyone for their amazing efforts. He brought them all up to date regarding events at the Parkland Nursing Home and the arrests that had been made.

'You have all been terrific,' he said. 'If it hadn't been for Sgt Evans' twitchy nose we would never have begun the investigation at Parkland, and who knows how many more residents would have been killed? And I think it will bring some comfort to Elsie Forrester to know that the finding of her sister's body in Coopers Field has led to us to being able to help other vulnerable people sleep safely in their beds.'

There was general agreement and lots of glasses raised to that thought.

'Finally,' said Martin. 'Let me tell you the other reason for our little celebration. She doesn't know the result herself yet, but I do, and I ask you now to all raise your glasses to a new member of the CID team. Welcome on board, Detective Constable Helen Cook-Watts!'

Author Inspiration

It's fitting that for a murder mystery I've chosen to point to a field named after an unknown man. No one really knows who Mr Cooper was, and although his name is attached to this piece of land in surveys dating back to the late sixteenth century, there is no official record that he ever owned it.

Coopers Field, situated in the southernmost part of Bute Park and within easy walking distance of the city centre, is today mainly used as an events area and hosts popular attractions such as 'Sparks in the Park', an annual Bonfire Night firework display that raises money for local charities.

Bute Park is freely available to the people of Cardiff and to all the city's visitors, and provides an amazing area of green parkland at the heart of the vibrant capital city of Wales. It is bordered on one side by the River Taff and along one of the other sides by the walls of Cardiff Castle. Sophia Gardens and Pontcanna Fields complete the outer perimeter of the Park. In all there are 56 hectares full of historic interest as well as beautiful horticultural and environmental features.

The park was once part of the grounds of Cardiff Castle, and gets its name from the third Marquess of Bute whose family were the landowners. It was the fifth Marquess who gifted the land and Cardiff Castle to the people of Wales in 1947, and the legacy continues to be managed by Cardiff Council.

The area was originally designed by the nineteenth-century gardener and horticulturist Andrew Pettigrew, and to add to his work an interesting mix of rare and ornamental trees has been planted since 1947. The park is now home to over two thousand trees.

As well as trees, the park provides a refuge for a variety of wildlife, and observant visitors will not just see the squirrels and the more common birds, but also tree creepers, otters, herons, and woodpeckers, to name just a few.

There is a wealth of historic interest dating back to Roman and medieval times ,but if it's just a picnic you want then it will be easy to find a quiet spot even at the busiest times. If you may want to take the easy option and not even make the sandwiches the Summerhouse or the Secret Garden Café are brilliant alternatives.

A quick and easy way to learn all about the park's history, trees, flowers and wildlife is to visit the Bute Park Education Centre. There is usually a range of craft activities on offer and the staff will suggest trails and provide maps that will ensure you miss nothing and see the best of what the park has to offer.

Wonny Lea